**'You?' she observed as she finally opened heavy eyelids, her gaze still half dazed with dreams of him.**

'Me,' Jack replied, as if even he was surprised.

'You should be with your guests, not hob-nobbing with a nonentity like me,' she said with a drowsy smile.

A frown twitched his dark brows together and instead of going away, as she told herself she wanted him to, he sat himself beside her so she couldn't get up without an undignified struggle.

'I won't have you categorise yourself a non-entity, since we never entertain any of those at Ashburton, my dear Miss Pendle.'

'Don't mock me,' she ordered him crossly.

'Not you, but I do deplore your quest to constantly belittle yourself, Jess.'

Forcing her mind to sharpen, when it wanted so badly to soften, she met his eyes steadily. 'And I shall never join the chase and allow others to belittle me instead, Your Grace.'

'What chase would that be?' he asked silkily, and moved so close to her that her breath came short. 'It's the closed season for most country sports, Miss Pendle.'

'Other than spinster-baiting and duke-hunting, Your Grace?'

**Elizabeth Beacon** lives in the beautiful English West Country, and is finally putting her insatiable curiosity about the past to good use. Over the years Elizabeth has worked in her family's horticultural business, become a mature student, qualified as an English teacher, worked as a secretary and, briefly, tried to be a civil servant. She is now happily ensconced behind her computer, when not trying to exhaust her bouncy rescue dog with as many walks as the Inexhaustible Lurcher can finagle. Elizabeth can't bring herself to call researching the wonderfully diverse, scandalous Regency period and creating charismatic heroes and feisty heroines *work*, and she is waiting for someone to find out how much fun she is having and tell her to stop it.

**Previous novels by the same author:**

AN INNOCENT COURTESAN
HOUSEMAID HEIRESS
A LESS THAN PERFECT LADY
REBELLIOUS RAKE, INNOCENT GOVERNESS
THE RAKE OF HOLLOWHURST CASTLE
ONE FINAL SEASON
   (part of *Courtship & Candlelight*)
A MOST UNLADYLIKE ADVENTURE

# THE DUCHESS HUNT

## Elizabeth Beacon

MILLS
BOON

First published in Great Britain 2012
by Mills & Boon, an imprint of Harlequin (UK) Limited.
Large Print edition 2012
Harlequin (UK) Limited, Eton House, 18-24 Paradise Road,
Richmond, Surrey TW9 1SR

© Elizabeth Beacon 2012

ISBN: 978 0 263 22530 3

Harlequin (UK) policy is to use papers that are natural,
renewable and recyclable products and made from wood grown in
sustainable forests. The logging and manufacturing process conform
to the legal environmental regulations of the country of origin.

Printed and bound in Great Britain
by CPI Antony Rowe, Chippenham, Wiltshire

# THE DUCHESS HUNT

# Chapter One

'And you're quite sure the Duke of Dettingham kidnapped or killed that delicious Mr Seaborne we all swooned over when we came out, Eugenia dear?' a young matron asked on a nervous titter at one of the last great balls of the London Season.

'The gentlemen are taking bets on how he's got away with it for so long, Lottie,' her over-excited informant told her as if it was gospel truth. 'Nothing was entered in the betting books, of course, since the Duke must challenge any man who declared him guilty of such a dreadful crime and he's a crack shot. He certainly wouldn't balk at putting a bullet in any gentleman brave enough to expose him when he's disposed of his heir in such a villainous fashion.'

'Although the Duke is rather delicious as well,' Lottie said wistfully. 'That air he has of not caring a snap of his fingers what any of us think quite makes my heart flutter and when he actually looks at me… Ooh, even now meeting those compelling green eyes of his makes my knees knock together and then I can't think of a single sensible word to say.'

'I don't approve of conscienceless rakes,' Eugenia told her friend stiffly.

'Once upon a time you would have given your best pearl necklet if it persuaded him to even dance with you, and sold your soul for anything more.'

'Which means I know what a heartless care-for-nobody he truly is,' Lottie's disgruntled confidante informed her as if that settled the matter.

'And how you wish he'd once played the rake with you,' Lottie argued.

'Only to find myself murdered in my bed once he grew bored with me? I rather think not,' Eugenia said coldly and went to find more receptive ears to pour her poison into.

Jessica Pendle had never found it more difficult to sit quietly and pretend she was deaf and daft as well as lame.

'Jessica!'

She could almost feel her mother willing her not to stand up and publically denounce that malicious cat for circulating such silly, damaging stories about Jack Seaborne, Duke of Dettingham.

Jack and his cousin Richard would not harm each other even if their very lives depended on it and anyone who knew them at all well would happily swear to the fact, but she knew a single lady, even one of her advanced years, could never defend an unrelated gentleman without making bad worse.

'Mama?' she murmured absently.

'Pretend you didn't hear them,' Lady Pendle urged softly.

'It doesn't even make sense,' Jessica muttered distractedly. 'Jack's already the duke, so why would he need to kill anyone to secure his position, let alone his cousin? Do they think Jack will now hunt down every male Seaborne in the country on some lunatic rampage to exterminate all competition?'

'You don't suppose such inveterate gossips consider the implausibility of the stories they make up then spread as if they were truth, do you, my love? It all sounds like the plot of a very bad sensation novel thought up by some bored creature without anything to do and too much time to do it in, but how much good do you think it would do Jack if we both swept into battle on his behalf?'

'None at all,' Jessica admitted. 'But that woman made such ruthless efforts to trap Jack into marriage when we first came out that I wonder he didn't go about in a suit of armour. If he was prepared to murder anyone, it would have been her.'

'A woman scorned can be very dangerous indeed, but we will discuss this at home when nobody else can hear but Papa, if he happens to be in one of his listening moods. For now we must pretend we have heard nothing untoward,' her mother advised.

'But Jack is an honourable man. Even when he's looking down his lordly nose in a way I can't help but find so infuriating that sometimes I long to smack him, I still know that much. I could never believe him capable of such villainy,' Jess continued with a bewildered shake of her head.

'You make yourself such an easy mark for his teasing by flaring up at him on the slightest provocation, my love,' her mother said mildly and Jessica wondered why her family and his never seemed to find Jack's regal-duke act infuriating.

'There's no need for him to play the autocrat whenever he isn't being such a disgraceful rake nobody will even whisper in my hearing what he's really been up to since he came down from Oxford even now,' she muttered grumpily then caught an amused glint in her mama's eyes and looked at her enquiringly.

'Sometimes you sound just like Jack's grandmother, my dear,' her mother declared with a smile that would have made Jessica suspicious, if she wasn't so busy being horrified.

'I don't, do I?' she asked, wincing at the very idea of resembling that dreadful old aristocrat in any way. 'I'll never snap at him again,' she added fervently and wondered exactly why her mama looked so pleased.

Before she could consider the idea further

there was a flurry of excited interest around the entrance to the ballroom created by some important arrival then a delighted susurration of whispering. She realised why when the Duke of Dettingham himself strolled into the ballroom as easily as if he was taking a stroll about his own garden, then bowed to his hostess with roguishly exaggerated grace and a wicked smile. That middle-aged matron acted the blushing damsel of twenty years ago rather than the formidable society hostess she was now and simpered girlishly when he kissed her hand like some old-time chevalier.

Jessica frowned as she watched Jack insinuate himself into what had been a hostile environment with his usual careless aplomb. He ought to look as if he'd dressed by guess in the dark, considering his almost-fitting coat and carelessly elegant cravat, she decided critically. Instead he was dark and dangerous, and so careless of the fashion he carried off as if he'd heard of it and decided to try it in his own unique fashion that he was the model all the would-be dashing young men scrambled to emulate. In her opinion they would never succeed, but even she realised he had the casual elegance so many others strove for in vain.

Meanwhile the Duke of Dettingham surveyed the assembled company as if he was mildly amused by the antics of a pack of well-dressed monkeys on the strut then spotted friends in the crowd and forged his way towards them. No risk of losing sight of him, even if he hadn't been so tall that he was head and shoulders above most of his peers, Jessica decided with some exasperation. Wherever he went there was a flurry of greetings and he went about his ducal progress as if he had no idea most of the guests had only just stopped whispering tall stories about him and his missing heir.

Of course he belonged to an aristocratic and powerful breed and had started out with a good many unfair advantages, but the current Duke of Dettingham was taller, long limbed and more leanly muscled and formidably intelligent than even the Seaborne clan expected of their titular head. He was probably a bit too much the leader of the pack for some of them, too, considering most Seabornes were as determined to go their own way as their piratical forebears had been, but she doubted a single one of them would put out a scurrilous story about Jack and Rich to clip his wings a little and keep him busy with his own affairs instead of theirs.

Dismissing his current notoriety, since he was clearly as indifferent to it as a rock, Jessica concentrated on dealing firmly with her own senses and the feral beat of excitement his presence awoke deep inside her without any effort on his part. Her body had an infuriating habit of getting into a silly flutter at the very sight of Jack in his full arrogant glory and it would never do to let even a hint of that show. There were other good-looking and active gentlemen of Jack's ilk with rank and power at their fingertips and she told herself he wasn't that special, but a deeply buried and highly excitable Jess whispered they didn't possess the air of such casual power that Jack had no need to flex to prove himself, or that infernal natural charisma he would still possess even if he'd become a boot boy at sixteen instead of a duke.

She had been a sad tomboy and had wanted to join his and Richard's wild rides and rough sports when he was sixteen, but they usually managed to evade her. Jessica recalled her twelve-year-old self doggedly searching up hill and down dale when they left with the dawn and came in at dusk to avoid her and might have blushed, if she wasn't too old to flush when her cool composure was threatened by a careless aristocrat nowadays.

'Richard was always terrified something would happen to Jack and he would be obliged to take on the dukedom,' she muttered under her breath and heard her mother's shocked gasp that she should even think about such things now.

'Kindly remember where you are before you start discussing a very good friend's premature demise, Jessica.'

'That wasn't what I meant at all, and nobody is paying the slightest attention to me. They are all far too busy being intrigued or scandalised by Jack to listen to anything a plain nonentity like me has to say about him and his.'

'You always set yourself too low,' her mother scolded and Jessica heard the note of concern in her mother's voice and tried to pretend interest in the company while Jack sauntered about the room as if he owned it.

She even managed to carry on a laboured conversation with a sober young gentleman of political ambition in search of a well-connected wife. Jessica knew she was well born and related to many of the *ton* in some degree or other, but wondered why this plodding young man thought she could be that wife. At three and twenty she was nearly on the shelf—the eighth child of parents who had provided livings and dowries for the other seven already and were therefore not rich, powerful or careful enough to make good in-laws—possessed of only moderate looks and a damaged left ankle. Still, she supposed she had the modest fortune left her by a great-aunt, in the belief Jessica would stay single and need it; her father was a viscount and her godmother was the Duke of Dettingham's beloved aunt by marriage. Luckily Jessica didn't like Mr Sledgeham enough to admire him for finding that a desirable connection, despite Jack's current notoriety.

'So what do you say, Miss Pendle?' the wretched

man asked all of a sudden and she tried not to look at him blankly.

'Thank you, but, no,' she managed civilly but firmly and it seemed a good enough answer as he only looked mildly disappointed.

'Then can I fetch *you* some refreshment, Lady Pendle?' Mr Sledgeham politely enquired of Lady Pendle and Jessica breathed a sigh of relief.

'No, but thank you for the offer and your company, Mr Sledgeham,' her mother said with such brisk kindness that he accepted it as his dismissal and took himself off.

Jessica hardly had time to repress a shudder at the very idea of enduring a lifetime with such a prosy bore before Jack Seaborne loomed over her in person and she promptly forgot Mr Sledgeham altogether. Her heart thumped uncomfortably at Jack's proximity and she ordered it to behave itself. Of course he would come and be civil to them if he was on his best behaviour tonight, she reassured herself. Lady Pendle was a long-time friend of his Aunt Melissa and Jessica was that lady's goddaughter, so he could hardly stroll past them as if they were mere nodding acquaintances, even if that was all they really were now-adays.

Jack presented her with a glass of lemonade without even asking if she wanted it, as if he'd armed himself with it in case she was overcome with artless enthusiasm at the very sight of him. Then he insinuated himself on to the *chaise* between herself and her mama with a faintly amused air of omnipotence.

'Your Grace,' she managed with a stiff nod and an indistinct murmur that might be a thank-you for the lemonade, if he had an obliging imagination.

'Miss Pendle,' he said blandly with an annoyingly elegant seated bow. 'I trust you are enjoying robust health and spirits?' he asked, as if was addressing some ageing spinster at least twenty years older than her three and twenty.

'I am very well, thank you,' she replied repressively.

He had always delighted in provoking her, then sitting back to watch her struggle with her stormy emotions in public. It was annoying and ungentlemanly of him and she silently told him so with a furious glare disguised as a weakly smile. He grinned and stretched his long legs out in front of him as if he hadn't a care in the world. Jessica reluctantly admired his *élan* even as she felt the flex and steel of sleek, masculine muscles next to her and wished him a great deal further off. With his black-as-midnight, slightly overlong, curling hair catching all sorts of devilish lights in the candles' glow and the starkly male beauty of his sensual mouth added to that hint of a smile in his gold-rayed green eyes, he might look like the answer to a maiden's prayer, but she couldn't dream the dreams other well-born society ladies indulged in.

Somehow she fooled herself he was a run-of-the-mill gentleman who had stopped for a polite conversation to stop herself colouring up like every other idiot he smiled at in that way. Jack Seaborne wouldn't want her if she was presented to him naked on a platter with an apple in her mouth, like the wild boar's head at Christmas. The very idea of him prostrating himself at her imperfect feet made her smile so wryly to herself that she met his enquiring gaze with a fading memory of it on her lips.

'That's good,' he said blandly and she cast him an even more suspicious glance, 'because I came to issue an informal invitation to a house party my darling aunt has got it into her head to organise at Ashburton this summer. We dearly hope Miss Pendle and her lovely mama, along with her rather-less-lovely sire, will join us in Herefordshire for a fortnight, as soon as this fiasco is finally over and done for another year,' he said lightly, then looked almost serious as he met Jessica's eyes with something that might have been a plea in his own, if she wasn't who she was and he were not the most eligible duke in the land. 'You'll be as welcome as the flowers in spring; you always talk to me as a human being and not merely a duke. Won't you agree to come and make the whole business a little more bearable for us all?' he coaxed shamelessly.

'If I'm sure of only one thing in life, your Grace,' Jessica said as lightly as she could manage when the sincerity in his eyes made her want to grant him anything he wished, 'it's that you're perfectly capable of looking after yourself.'

'Not this time, Princess. I suspect my dragon grandmother has put out an edict that I must be wed post haste, now I'm racing towards thirty and nigh in my dotage,' he said, a touch of bitterness in his deep voice that made Jessica look a little more carefully at him than she'd dared to until now and note the lines of strain and tiredness about his firm mouth and the faint shadows under his eyes that spoke of a deeper weariness than anything merely physical. 'Won't you join us at Ashburton for a few weeks and add a little spice to a leaden occasion, Princess Jessica?' he went on. 'You will be such a relief from the sweet little débutantes my aunt is threatening to inflict on us. I'll soon be choking on too much undiluted sugar,' he appealed almost earnestly.

Not sure whether to be flattered or insulted, she told herself he'd spoilt his plea by using the nickname he inflicted on her when his aunt gave her the ground-floor Queen's Room at Ashburton after her accident to save her climbing the stairs.

'I have asked you not to call me that so often

I shall soon start saying it in my sleep,' she told him acerbically.

'Say you'll come to Ashburton for a few weeks this summer and I'll try very hard not to do it any more, Miss Pendle,' he urged.

'And you promise you won't hold me up to ridicule?'

'I would never do anything so unfriendly,' he said as if he found the idea impossible to even contemplate, despite all the teasing she'd endured in the old days. 'You will be an honoured guest and anyone who dares consider you otherwise will soon discover their error and a pressing engagement elsewhere.'

His words should have warmed her, so why did she suddenly want to cry? Because it wasn't every day a lady was asked to a house party as a sort of female jester, she supposed. 'I doubt very much Papa will agree to leave Winberry Hall and the hay harvest once he is back in Northamptonshire again at long last,' she managed to say coolly enough.

'He would tear himself away if that were all that was keeping him home, my dear, but don't forget his latest grandchild is about to come into the world and your father is a far more doting father and grandfather than he would have everyone believe,' her mother put in ruefully.

'Surely we cannot be from home at such a time either, Mama? This will be Rowena's first child and she is sure to need us even more,' Jessica protested.

'Rowena has many weeks to go and is robust as ever, despite that air of fragility her husband is clearly taken in by even though he's been married to her for more than a year now,' her mother argued. 'Both he and your father are worry warts, but I've no intention of sitting about clucking like a mother hen solely to make them feel better. A relaxing fortnight at Ashburton before I immerse myself in my grandmotherly duties once more sounds wonderful to me, so thank you for asking us to be your sadly pampered guests there once more, your Grace,' Lady Pendle said with an air of finality.

It seemed that Lord and Lady Pendle and their last unmarried daughter would be present in Herefordshire this summer to watch his Grace the Duke of Dettingham pick out his duchess, whether that daughter wanted to be there or not.

'I'll be very grateful for some leaven to add to so much dough, then,' Jack said with a lopsided grin that could charm a gorgon.

Jessica found herself unworthily hoping one of the young ladies invited to be looked over like fillies before a sale would turn him down flat when he asked them to marry him, but supposed that was too much to expect. Jack Seaborne was a temptation any sensible woman he wasn't planning to marry ought to avoid like pure sin, but even Jessica couldn't ignore a direct appeal for support. Yet why was he meekly going along with his grandmother's scheme to marry him off like this? His air of disillusioned cynicism usually kept all but the most maniacally determined husband hunters at bay and he had carefully avoided unsophisticated young ladies, however lovely, until now. So why had he decided to marry, after all the effort he'd put in to avoiding that state? Sighing at the unfathomable nature of Jack Seaborne's thoughts and motives, Jessica decided she'd find out quite soon enough.

'Perhaps I could stay at home, just in case Rowena needs me,' she said in a last-ditch attempt to escape.

'Why would she when she has a devoted husband ready, willing and able to look after her far more closely than you ever could now she is wed? At least we need you, Princess, so if you insist on being useful to somebody it might as well be us Seabornes,' he said and this time she could sense the steel under the velvet of his deep voice, as if he truly did need her to be there this summer while he picked out a bride for some peculiar reason all his own and was determined she would be close by.

'You don't need me and I would be out of place at such a gathering,' she insisted, her internal warning bells clanging.

'Not so,' he insisted tersely and she felt apprehension shiver down her spine as she met the challenge in his green-gold eyes.

'I'm not an uncritical little débutante,' she warned.

'Were you ever one of those, Princess?' he

asked with a smile that threatened to undermine her defences.

'And I'm even less wide-eyed and naïve now than I was then.'

'I think we all know that.'

'Then you must also know I'm not the sort of person you want at Ashburton if you're intent on persuading one of the guests to become your duchess,' she said recklessly and knew the instant it was out of her mouth that it was a dare too far.

His green-gold eyes darkened until they resembled obsidian and his mouth hardened into the look of arrogant superiority that had always raised her hackles. His unspoken contempt for her plain speaking was intimidating, as if she'd lost his good opinion so effectively it wasn't even worth him explaining why. Her hand shook and her breath hitched as she bit back the apology threatening to tumble from her lips.

'Perhaps you're exactly the sort of female I need to goad me into finding your exact opposite, Miss Pendle,' he said after a pause that somehow made it worse.

He was offended and furious, but at least she'd

hidden her instinctive horror at the idea of him taking a lovely and obliging female to wife. This was exactly the sort of scene she'd warned herself against at sixteen, but could it be she hadn't buried the romantic idiot she'd been then deeply enough? If she was about to watch some innocent succumb to his quick wits, spectacular looks and powerful masculine aura, then grown-up Jessica Pendle had better steel herself until she was as far from her immature self as Herefordshire was from Hispaniola.

'I'm already all that your duchess will not be,' she stated flatly, 'so why bother?'

'And I shudder to think how dangerous you could be, Princess, if you ever let yourself off the role of martyr for long enough to find out,' he replied enigmatically.

'True,' Lady Pendle interrupted with a sage nod that made Jessica flash her mother a furious look instead of him.

'At times like this, I should be able to rely on my mother for support,' she told her with as much dignity as she could manage.

'You will always have that, my love,' Lady

Pendle replied, 'but it's high time you tried out your own wings.'

'Even if they're broken?' she was shocked into protesting a little too revealingly.

'Nonsense, you always did refine too much on that damaged ankle of yours,' Jack told her impatiently.

'And you have rarely been more wrong, your Grace,' she informed him sourly.

'Not as wrong as you are if you let a few featherheaded fools make you see yourself as less than you are. You're as idiotic as they are if you have,' he said bluntly.

'Am I indeed?' she asked regally.

After enduring years of hot rooms, laboured conversation and pitying looks, with the occasional glimpse of his Grace the Duke of Dettingham in flight from a pack of eager young ladies to enliven her evenings, she was very familiar with her limitations. She refused to accept his opinion of her status from a man who only had to hint he wanted to marry to be chased by every eligible female in the British Isles.

'Yes,' he said, as if in no doubt about his omnipotence and her stupidity.

'At least I don't think it's my prerogative to dictate the lives of others.'

'Such heat, Miss Pendle—could it be that my faults are more important to you than you're prepared to admit?' he asked slyly.

'No, and you've got so many it would take me a lifetime to list them all,' she informed him, fixing a bland smile to her lips to disguise her ire from spectators.

'And how well you would get on with my grandmother, if only she was able to attend this little affair Aunt Melissa is organising so diligently on my behalf,' he said.

Recalling how much she disliked the dictatorial and often downright rude Dowager Duchess of Dettingham, Jessica would have laughed at the thought of them agreeing upon any topic under the sun, if his words didn't echo her mother's earlier ones and make her feel like crying instead.

'Then there's someone else in this world who refuses to take you at face value,' she defended herself haughtily.

'And such a handsome face it is as well, my boy,' Lady Pendle intervened with a repressive look for her daughter that spoke of what she might say when they were alone. 'Tell your Aunt Melissa that of course we shall come and, if I can drag Pendle away from his acres and our dear Rowena, he will lend you his support as well.'

'Thank you, my lady, I am truly grateful,' he said and Jessica felt an unladylike urge to kick him on his nearest perfect and lordly ankle, just to watch him limp away for once, instead of feeling so ungraceful in her own departure, which her mother signalled at last by rising to her feet and accepting Jack's arm when he declared it his opportunity to escape as well.

'I shall look forward to welcoming you to Ashburton once again then, Princess,' he murmured by way of farewell as he handed them into their town carriage with the effortless ease that somehow made Jessica even more furious.

'You won't notice I exist among so many beautiful and accomplished young ladies,' she replied ungraciously.

'Oh, I always notice you, Princess,' he said as if he should be congratulated.

Then he stood back with an insufferably superior smile on his handsome face as the footman slammed the door. Waving a careless farewell, Jack sauntered off into the night without so much as a walking cane to protect himself with, probably whistling carelessly as if to actually invite any waiting footpad to make the attempt to rob him as he went, Jessica decided crossly.

'If you always kept your word as diligently as you did just now, your father and I would soon be forced to disown you,' her mother told her acidly.

'What do you mean? I always live up to my promises,' Jessica protested, stung by the genuine anger in her mother's voice.

'You swore you would be civil to Jack not half an hour ago and you have just treated him to a display of childish temper I can only categorise as shrill and disagreeable.'

'I wonder why I feel this compulsion to go to bed without supper?' Jessica asked as lightly as she could. Part of her knew her mother was right; she had let the odd feeling that Jack marrying

might rock her own world to its foundations overtake good manners. 'I will try to keep a curb
on my tongue from now on,' she promised and
hoped she could hold to it for the two weeks of
Jack's house party.

Jack Seaborne was probably too much of a gentleman to hold her ill temper against her and she
didn't matter enough for him to bother holding a
grudge. He wasn't the sort of man who nursed a
slight anyway and after this visit they would not
meet other than by chance or at the odd dutiful
occasion. She had seven brothers and sisters and
he had five first cousins—four if you excluded
Rich—and a legion of more distant connections,
so there would be christenings and engagement
balls in common with the Duke and Duchess of
Dettingham, but Miss Pendle, the maiden aunt,
could fade into the background until the great
left the good to their celebrations.

Of course she pitied whichever deluded girl let
herself be blinded by the allure of the handsome
Duke of Dettingham to the true Jack Seaborne
underneath. He had a tyrannical will and an un-
bending determination to run the lives of those

around him for their own good. No doubt he would make the poor child a very uncomfortable husband, but watching him court his bride would not be an ordeal, more another duty to get through before she could retire to the country and breed pigs, or maybe finance canals and steam engines and make a name for herself as an eccentric lady of means.

'What more could a mother ask than your promise to try to be civil for a whole two weeks?' Lady Pendle mused ironically and Jessica shifted uncomfortably on the well-upholstered cushions as she reviewed her behaviour over the last hour or so. 'And you are not to play the old maid at Ashburton when the family will expect you to enjoy yourself as usual. I know the place is lovely at any time of year, but I have always found it especially so during high summer,' her mother offered, as if the natural and contrived beauty of the setting ought to console Jessica for renouncing the right to be rude to her host whenever the fancy took her.

'I always enjoy visiting Aunt Melissa and the children,' Jessica said.

'Indeed, it will be almost like old times,' Lady Pendle went on happily.

'Almost,' Jessica murmured, recalling those days when she had adored Jack so devotedly she had wanted to follow him about like a yipping puppy.

Then she had never doubted they would be friends for ever and maybe even more and had put him in place of the hero when she'd dreamt of fairytale marriages and happy ever afters, before she'd raced off into the chaos of a summer storm one day on her father's favourite hunter and lamed them both for ever. Best not to recall past follies, she told herself and concluded she and Jack would have been the worst-matched pair in the turbulent history of the Seabornes. A summer visit to Ashburton would make a pleasant interlude before she found her true purpose in life, but it would prove no more significant than tonight's ball or any other social occasion she had attended and then forgotten of late.

# Chapter Two

When she saw Jack strolling in the Park the next day, Jessica suddenly realised why she felt so uneasy about this projected house party of his. She caught sight of him long before he spotted the Pendle barouche and idly wondered at her ability to pick the Duke of Dettingham out from the crowd. He looked so alone, despite the chattering crowds and cheerful hails of his cronies. She marvelled at how many eager, beckoning looks the society beauties sent him in the hope of catching his notoriously discerning eye, despite the scurrilous stories they went on whispering about him behind their fans and their débutante sisters simply sat and simpered in the prescribed fashion.

It occurred to her that he looked solitary, although he could hardly be more at ease with himself, because she expected Richard to be nearby whenever she encountered Jack even now. The cousins had been inseparable as boys and so often together as young men she had come to think of them as brothers in arms. Jess suddenly realised why Jack intended to marry and gave a shocked gasp that she had to turn into a sneeze to disguise. He hoped his scapegrace heir would come home once he realised Jack was wed and there was little risk of him inheriting the family strawberry leaves. A worse reason for marriage evaded her and she wanted to scream denial over the chatter of the assembled throng.

'Idiot,' she muttered under her breath, as her gaze dwelt broodingly on the manly form ambling towards them as if her dark thoughts had drawn him to them as inevitably as north drew a compass needle.

'Dettingham,' her father greeted him genially.

'Your Grace,' her mother said as she held out a hand in public greeting to the latest butt of scandal to confound the tabbies.

'Jack,' Jessica managed flatly and in calling

him by his given name overstepped the mark once again in her attempt not to bluntly ask him what on earth he thought he was doing by thinking up such a cold-blooded method of flushing out his errant cousin.

'Really, Jessica, I know I asked you to be civil to him, but that's going much too far in public,' Lady Pendle scolded distractedly while she discreetly aimed an admonishing kick at her husband's ankle to remind him not to grin at the pair of them as if he could imagine nothing better than his daughter and the Duke of Dettingham being overfamiliar with each other.

'And did you promise to obey your mama in such a testing quest, Princess?' Jack asked with that almost-open smile that always threatened to do strange things to her insides if she let it.

'If I did, then I'm fated to make a liar of myself almost as quickly as you have, your Grace,' she told him with a reproachful look for the determined use of that hated nickname once again.

He bowed with such mocking elegance she had to bite back a chuckle. The last thing she wanted at the moment was a truce between them, considering she had a very large bone to pick with him the moment they were alone.

'I apologise for my lapse, Miss Pendle, but your best regal look always has a weakening effect on my already ragged manners,' he told her a little too meekly.

'If I went about making that sort of excuse for my follies, I would be banned from every drawing room in Mayfair,' she informed him sternly.

'Then I must try it whenever possible from now on, since I can imagine no fate more perfect than being forbidden the sticklers' company, preferably for ever.'

Jessica's father laughed out loud and drew the interested attention of all those straining to hear every word that fell from Jack's lips. 'Might put that one into effect myself, my boy,' Lord Pendle confided, seeming oblivious of all the sharp looks and eager speculation around him on the subject of their conversation.

'You won't if you wish to share *any* of the rooms in your London home with your wife during the next year or so,' she heard her mother murmur for what she thought was her husband's ears only.

From Jack's carefully blank expression he had caught that muttered threat as well and Jessica marvelled at the cat-like sharpness of his senses even as she reminded herself to keep a still tongue between her teeth in his company.

'Should you like to take a drive with me, Pr— Miss Pendle?' he asked with such an air of bland innocence that Jessica gave him a sharp look. 'Well, you can't say I'm not trying,' he told her with a cheerful shrug and a smile that had her rising to her feet in response before she'd even thought how he used that look to charm the birds out of the trees when she wasn't around to waste it on.

'In what, pray?' she asked as she plumped back down again against the comfortable squabs of the family barouche.

'My imaginary curricle?' he said with raised eyebrows and a boyish grin she truly did find ir-resistible this time.

'Oh, well, that's all right then,' she said and

looked down at him with laughter in her eyes and a smile tugging at her lips.

'Is it, Princess?' he asked with an oddly twisted smile and a look in his eyes as if he'd just witnessed something so unexpected it had almost robbed him of words.

'I thought we had dealt with that misname,' she managed to scold, even as she fought an urge to languish at him like all the other susceptible misses.

'Sorry,' he said as if shrugging off something irrelevant and getting back to the task in hand, 'it just slipped out; I obviously need more practice preventing myself from saying it. So will you come for a drive and allow me to put some in before we're immured at Ashburton together for two whole weeks, Miss Pendle? I truly have the means to take you for one over yonder and am not yet suffering delusions,' he said, waving a hand at the gleaming curricle halted under the trees.

The whole rig was attracting a great deal of gentlemanly envy for the spirit and quality of the perfectly matched team the tiger and his groom were fussing over. Jessica wondered who had attracted Jack's notice so successfully that he'd stepped down from such a splendid equipage in the first place, but managed not to dwell on a mental picture of the magnificent sloe-eyed siren rumour had it was his very secret lover as well a grand lady of the *ton*. His amorous adventures were clearly no business of hers, but his ridiculous scheme to flush Richard out of hiding felt so acutely wrong that she shivered despite the building heat of a sultry June afternoon and wished she was a special enough person in his life to stand even a chance of persuading him not to go through with it.

Jack snapped his fingers imperiously and the curricle appeared at his side as if the milling crowd did not exist. She speculated crossly on the nature of power and the powerful and found herself sitting beside Jack on the narrow bench seat without ever agreeing to drive with him in the first place so far as she could recall.

'Thank you, Brandt,' she said once she had almost shaken off the nerve-tingling effect of sitting by his master long enough to remember the name of Jack's head groom.

'It's always a pleasure to help a true lady into one of our carriages, Miss Pendle,' the middle-aged man said, as if he didn't think much of the females who usually graced the ducal curricle, and Jess bit back a chuckle at hearing his grace the Duke of Dettingham being scolded about the company he kept by his groom.

'Indeed it is,' Jack muttered blandly, then informed Brandt he could walk home as a reward for his impudence.

'Aye, your Grace,' the man said equably and took off at a brisk pace as if he relished the task.

They set off and Jessica tried not to look surprised and a little bit scandalised when Jack left the Park in order to set down his tiger not far from his house in Grosvenor Square, although she couldn't help but be amused at the swagger in the diminutive tiger's step as he doffed his cap to her with elaborate courtesy and cocked Jack a knowing glance before strolling off towards the Dettingham House mews.

'Where on earth did you find him?' Jess asked

as she waited for the greys to admit Jack was indeed their master and fully in control before he gave them the office to move off.

'The stews, but he's going to be the best jockey I ever had if only he'll learn to listen to those who know more about the art than he thinks he does.'

'So you punished his intransigence by making him your tiger? Your servants must tremble in their boots when you lose your temper with one of them, your Grace,' she teased, but secretly thought his leniency admirable, especially in contrast to the appalling way some powerful householders treated their servants.

'I don't have to lose my temper, Miss Pendle; all it takes is one of my ducal frowns and they all run about doing my bidding as if I were a king in his palace.'

'How things must have changed at Ashburton,' she said with a mock sigh. 'I shall look forward to witnessing it.'

'You'll do so in vain,' he said with a rueful smile that made her recall how likeable she might find him if she dared let herself. 'They're all con-

vinced they know how to run the place far better than I do.'

'They're probably right,' Jessica pointed out
helpfully. 'I doubt you had lessons on how to
order a china cupboard or keep a linen cupboard
supplied inflicted on you as a boy.'

'Something for which I am truly thankful,' he
said and turned his team out into the traffic.

'Where are we going?' Jess asked, clutching
her best bonnet, then tying the ribbons a little
tighter as he set the restless team to as fast a pace
as was safe in the London traffic.

'Somewhere they can have a half-decent run
and we can breathe in clean air for once,' he told
her rather distractedly as he skirted a wagon and
restrained his high-spirited team as they took of-
fence at a lady's parasol in a virulent shade of
green that would have made Jess do the same if
she had to stare at it for long.

'Won't there be gossip?' she protested half-
heartedly.

'Isn't there always gossip?' he said cynically.

'About you, yes,' she agreed, but not very often
about lame and respectable Miss Pendle. A rebel

voice within whispered it was about time she gave them a little fodder for their ever-more-ridiculous tales, so she might as well sit back and enjoy it.

'I doubt even the tabbies will believe Lord and Lady Pendle allowed me to abduct their ewe lamb in front of their eyes, so you can relax, Princess. I promise to get you home in one piece with your name relatively unsullied before anyone even notices you're gone.'

'Since this is my last foray into society, I suppose it doesn't matter what they say about me any more,' Jess replied half to herself.

'What do you mean by that?'

'I should have thought it perfectly plain.'

'Not to me.'

'I am on the shelf, your Grace—not that I was ever truly off it—and I have no intention of taking part in any more social Seasons as I don't particularly like London at this time of year. It always seems absurd to me that we all up sticks and move to town, when the countryside is at its most lovely and busy with new life, so we may spend that precious time of year being overheated and bored in a city that can't help but be malodorous in the wrong weather—which seems to be most varieties of an English spring and summer so far as I can tell.'

'Maybe,' he said, 'but you're far too young to be at your last prayers. Not that you ever made the slightest push at being a successful débutante when you were younger and I can't help but wonder why.'

'Isn't that perfectly obvious as well?' she asked exasperatedly.

'Again, not to me, which means that either I'm being particularly stupid, or you're wrong. How to walk the fine line between arguing with a lady when she says black is white and I know it to be otherwise, I wonder?' he mused as if his interpretation of events must be right, just because it always was, presumably.

'You could try silence.'

'Is that how you do it, Jessica? Use that quiet, sceptical manner of yours to frighten off all the sprigs of nobility who don't comply with your high standards?'

So now he thought her a snob, incapable of

finding any man fit to be her ideal pattern-card of a husband?

'What a very high opinion of me you do have,' she tried to joke.

'It can't be any lower than the one you appear to have of yourself,' he said impatiently and finally gave his team more rein as the traffic thinned at last.

'I am a realist,' she stated bluntly.

'If that were the case, you would be Lady Something or the Countess of Somewhere by now,' he scolded as if her single status actually mattered to him.

'And Lord Something or the Earl of Somewhere would simply overlook the fact they'd saddled themselves with a lame wife, I suppose?' she asked caustically.

'Yes, the only person who refuses to do just that is you, Jessica Pendle, and I'm weary of the whole tableau of the brave beauty, meekly accepting that her role in life is to make others feel pleased they are more fortunate than she is. It's almost an insult to those of us who value you as you are, rather than as you think you should be.'

'I'm lame, that's how I *know* myself to be,' she sparked back and tears she told herself were of temper threatened to undo her under his sceptical gaze.

'You limp a little, that's all,' he argued. 'It could have been so much worse, considering you spent a day and a night out in the pouring rain lying injured. You could have died, or been seriously crippled for life,' he said, the passion in his voice making his now-calm team jib again.

'I have never denied it was my own fault,' she offered a little too meekly for her own taste.

'Yes, it was, in so far as you took a horse you were forbidden to ride and dashed off on him into weather you should have known would terrify the poor beast. You had a quick temper and a wayward heart in those days, but none of us thought you set out to do yourself and that unfortunate animal injury. We would have been fools if we had, considering how well we all knew your fiery temper and tomboyish ways. No doubt you thought such an impulsive and ill-considered exploit would prove to the world you were every bit as good as any of your brothers at the time.

Us Seabornes and your own doting family were only relieved you were alive, so why can't you accept it as a minor miracle you survived relatively unscathed as we all did at the time?'

'I had no idea you even knew I had gone,' she said faintly.

'I always notice your absences, Princess,' he said with exaggerated patience, as if preventing himself from physically taking hold of her and shaking her until some sense had been driven in by force. 'In those days it was mainly because I was on pins to know what mischief you were in whenever you were gone, but that time we searched all night, then half the next day for you. I'll never forget how it felt to look in vain for a child lost in the darkness. Rich and I tramped the hills round Winberry Hall so fanatically I could probably guide a party round them, day or night, without pausing to get my bearings even now.'

'I didn't know any of that. When I recovered from the fever I got from being so wet and cold you and your cousins were all long gone, so I thought you must have already left Winberry Hall by the time I was found to be missing.'

'Not us, and just as well since your father was in such despair when you were not to be found that night and your brothers not much better, that if my Uncle Henry hadn't organised a systematic search of the area, we might not have found you until it was too late to help you.'

'Then why wasn't I told?' she asked faintly.

'The doctor said you were not to be reminded of your ordeal and would need all the peace and quiet you could get to recover when the fever broke and you were out of danger at last. So we took ourselves off, certain you would soon be your usual irrepressible self after giving us such an almighty scare, but you never really recovered your old spark, did you, Princess?'

For once she didn't argue with that nickname, too busy re-aligning events in her head to bother about small details. 'No,' she admitted at last.

'Why not?' he asked as if he was truly interested in her answer. 'You were the most intrepid female Rich and I ever came across and then you became a paper saint.'

How to explain that it was plain to her by then that none of her dawning hopes for the future could ever be, now she was imperfect and he was not? Impossible when he would think her still in love with him or some such nonsensical notion, she decided, and cast about for an excuse for losing interest in the things she'd once loved so much, like riding for hours about the Northamptonshire countryside, running like the wind and climbing every tree on her father's estate, then most of his neighbours' as well.

'As a way of preserving my dignity, I suppose,' she said finally with a shrug.

'It was a retreat—no, worse than that, a refusal to give battle in the first place,' he condemned sternly.

'How can you sit there and lecture me on cowardice when you have no idea what you're talking about?' she accused. 'You never suffered a moment of doubt that your limbs would hold you up for as long as you asked them to. How could you understand what it feels like to face a crowded ballroom, knowing you will have to limp across the dance floor to reach the chaperon's benches, where everyone knows you will stay all evening because you cannot dance? You never had to face the giggles and whispers of diamonds of the first water as they discuss you as if you're either not there or must be deaf since you're not perfect like they are. Some gentlemen even asked my mother if I would like tea or lemonade as if I couldn't decide for myself.'

'You seem to me to get on perfectly well with most of them. Rich and I could never get near you for a circle of assorted young ladies and spotty youths with fiercely protective expressions in their eyes when you made your come-out.'

'So I can't be quite as martyred and self-pitying as you say, can I?'

'I never said you haven't got a great many friends, just that you are very careful never to acquire lovers.'

'Something my true well-wishers must be thankful for,' Jessica said primly.

'You know perfectly well what I mean. There wasn't a single would-be lover or husband among those very young gentlemen. Not even one grown-up male with a mind and desire all his own, my dear Princess. You know, real, mature and rampant gentlemen who might take friendship for something more if you ever let them, so you've kept them sternly at a distance, haven't you?'

'No sensible female encourages the rakes,' she said scornfully, although she knew he was quite right.

'One fully aware of her own beauty and wit and who is prepared to take them and life on and win would, Princess, although a spoilt young woman who is too arrogant to play the game at all if she isn't guaranteed to win would probably not dare do so.'

'What an original take on my life you do have, your Grace,' she said icily.

'And how very much you would like to box my ears,' he said with a whimsical grin, as if he'd prefer her to revert to the wild Jess of old and do just that.

'Tempting, but not even you make me angry enough to risk being overturned, then having cause to limp on both feet ever after,' she teased, because it was that or rage, then probably weep all over him since no words came close to being able to express her fury at being held up for his lofty scrutiny and found wanting.

'Oh, Princess, what are we going to do with you?' he asked with a weary shake of his handsome head.

'Take me home and stop calling me that,' she said just as wearily.

It seemed for a long time as if they'd reached deadlock. Jack had taken a wide sweep round the road at a handy village green to turn his light carriage back towards London without feeling the need for any spectacular feats of driving to prove his skill. Jessica already knew he could do most things he set his mind to superbly and hoped she wasn't going to be his latest project, something mildly challenging to divert him from the more serious business of finding a wife.

'What an obedient duke I am,' he ventured after a few miles of wary silence.

'No, you're a devious, deceptive and dangerous one and I'm not in the least bit fooled by you, so don't try your tricks on me,' she told him grumpily.

'At least I'm open to life and haven't had my emotions preserved in aspic,' he argued scornfully.

'You're certainly open to making the biggest mistake of your life this summer,' she muttered under her breath at the arrogance of the man, thinking he could accuse her of being emotionless when he was contemplating taking a wife mainly to reassure his cousin he could finally come home, since the succession was about to be secured on to more direct heirs.

'How lovely for you,' she said insincerely out loud, but began to wonder anew about that cat-like hearing of his as he sent her a very peculiar look indeed.

'Promise me that you will at least try, Princess,' he admonished with a sigh after several more minutes of faintly hostile silence on both sides.

'Try to do what?'

'Join us erring and striving human beings for a change and come down out of your ivory tower for the summer. You might be surprised at what you find if you decided to embrace life instead of running away from it.'

'And you might get your ears boxed after all,' she snapped bitterly, for wasn't this pot calling kettle black with a vengeance?

'Promise?' he said relentlessly and she made the mistake of briefly meeting his eyes and seeing genuine concern in the gold-rayed green depths of them before he turned his attention back to the road once again.

'Only if you finally stop calling me Princess,' she conceded and might have kicked herself for conceding that much if it would have done any good.

'You would miss it if I did,' he said with a wry smile as if he had suddenly realised how absurd they must look as they quarrelled most of the way round the almost countryside, then back into London again.

'Like I'd miss chickenpox,' she said darkly.

'I take it all back, Jess, don't ever change,' he said with an easy grin and a laugh and she cursed herself for a fool when it felt more exhilarating than half an hour of flirtation with one of his rival rakes.

'Don't worry, I won't. So far as I can see there's very little hope you ever will either.'

'And why should I change?'

'Because marriage ought to do that to a man,' she horrified herself by coming right out and saying.

'Did I mention marriage?' he asked, his voice so silkily dangerous she couldn't fight off a visible shiver.

'Never to me and don't worry, I have no delusions in that direction,' she snapped defensively.

'I never thought you had, my dear,' he said so remotely that it felt as if they were only a pair of strangers who didn't particularly like each other.

'Which is just as well, considering you would have hated it if I had designs on your ducal coronet,' she recklessly added.

'Who knows?' he said vaguely, as if Jessica Pendle and her wayward ideas were a million miles from the focus of his thoughts, whatever that might be.

'I do,' she persisted disastrously, mainly because she couldn't let silence fall again now the words were actually out.

'You're right,' he admitted after a tense silence during which she had to actually bite her tongue not to make things worse by defending herself even more strongly and denying once more she had the least desire to attract him on any level. 'In a weak moment I gave in to my grandmother's edict and seriously considered marriage. It was obviously a moment too long, since I am now host to a gaggle of eligible young ladies and their assorted relatives and friends and will have a house party full of guests to consider when I return home.'

'Hence your invitation to the Pendles, so we can water down the obviousness of a pack of eager young ladies invited by your aunt before you had time to express your second thoughts?' she made herself say lightly, as if being considered an antidote to other more marriageable females didn't hurt her in the least.

'No, hence my invitation to the place I probably love most in the world to a family I consider part of my own. You are every bit as lovely as any of the ladies invited by my aunt and ought to know it by now, without having to be reassured at every turn that I will never see you as second-best to any of them,' he said drily.

'I am not lovely,' she objected as indignantly as if he'd accused her of being plain as rice pudding.

'Like it or not, you are so, my dear,' he said with such a knowing smile she felt the edge had been quite taken off the compliment.

'Just because you declare it, therefore it must be so, your Grace?'

'If that's what it takes to convince you I'm right. Now kindly take that about-to-be-martyred look off your face and behave like the proper young lady society knows you to be, Princess. It might be best if you pretend we just enjoyed a sedate tour round the leafier parts of Mayfair rather than a dashing tour of the outer villages perhaps.'

'Yes, much better—and you're still wrong,' she sniped as the dusty streets became familiar and she felt him slip back into cynical Duke of Dettingham persona and out of her reach once again.

'I'm not, you know,' he murmured as he passed over her reticule and fan when the Pendles' head footman had finished helping her down from the relatively high carriage seat.

'Not what?' she replied distractedly, for trying to descend gracefully from even a normal carriage was always a challenge and today she had wanted to land in a heap at his horses' feet even less than usual.

'Wrong, of course.' He reminded her of his assertion she was lovely with a look of such molten heat in his gaze that she almost believed him for a moment, until she reminded herself he was an accomplished flirt and very good at making susceptible females believe they were uniquely special to him.

'Hah! Try telling that to your other female guests when next we meet. They would have you declared insane or throw me in the moat.'

'I don't have a moat,' he argued as she stood back on the pavement and waited to bid him an acceptably polite farewell.

'They would dig one especially for me.'

'Should I consider that a challenge, I wonder?' he said with a teasing smile that threatened to leave her in a collapsed heap of compliance in the street.

'No!' she said a little too shrilly and stepped back as if just looking at him might burn her.

'Pity,' he said with a taunting grin she recalled seeing all too often when she was a child and he and Rich were about to escape her yet again. 'I always liked a challenge and so few other females grant me the delight of proving them wrong as often as you do, Princess.'

'Then count me in as just another female,' she advised with as much of a flounce as she could manage and turned to quit the scene if he refused to play the gentleman and leave her in peace.

'You could never be one of the crowd to me, Princess,' he assured her outrageously as he finally obliged her and drove off with a careless salute of his driving whip and a flurry of dust from his chariot wheels.

'Infuriating, arrogant, idiot,' she gritted between her teeth as she stood on the pavement, watching slavishly until he was completely out of sight.

'I beg your pardon, Miss Jessica?' the butler

said blandly, clearly having heard every word, but preserving the fiction that good servants were made of wood and set going every morning by a clock winder.

'Tea, I think, Wellow,' she said brightly. 'I stand in need of it after that.'

'What lady would not,' Wellow allowed himself to answer as he followed her into the hall.

Two weeks later Jessica decided that not even tea would cure this disastrous situation. Her father and mother had cried off at the last minute and she was about to reach Ashburton New Place to face the ducal summons alone. The carriage slowed to take the entrance to Jack's mansion and she fought a cowardly impulse to order her father's coachman to return to Winberry Hall instead.

Despite their oddly unforgettable encounters back in London, Jack would treat her with his usual absent-minded courtesy, then forget her, she reassured herself uneasily. All she had to do was limp about his glorious stately pile looking serene and untroubled for the next two weeks while he took his pick of the finest belles of the *ton*, then she could go home and get on with her life. Resigning herself to a fortnight of pretence, Jessica leant forwards for her first glimpse of Ashburton's famous deer park as the coach finally swung through the imposing gates and there could be no turning back.

'Her ladyship said I was to remind you to be polite to the duke,' her mother's ancient and formidable dresser informed her sternly as the coach slowed again.

'I'm not such a fool as to show his Grace up in a bad light while he's entertaining guests, Martha.'

'Your mother wouldn't want you hurt, Miss Jessica,' Martha said earnestly.

Then why had Lady Pendle been so insistent Jessica accept this invitation without her support? She must know the beauties invited for this fortnight would have their claws honed ready for the scramble to grab Jack's strawberry leaves.

'You can depend upon it, all is well, my love, despite all this panic from Rowena's husband,' her mama had told Jessica when a note was delivered by an exhausted groom as she and Jessica were finally packed and ready to leave. 'Rowena is as healthy as a horse, despite Sir Linstock fussing over her as if she might break, but she never would attend to her sums and has very likely got the date of her last courses wrong. I said she looked large for just over seven months last time we visited, did I not? Linstock and your papa will be quite useless until we're certain your sister is out of danger, so I must go and help the poor girl endure her confinement without having to worry about them as well as herself and the babe.'

Lady Pendle paused and considered the general idiocy of gentlemen when confronted with childbirth, gave a heavy sigh and shook her head. 'You must take Martha with you and Lady Henry will chaperon you at Ashburton, my love. Your godmother will be sorely in need of your help with so many giddy young misses in the house,' her mother said.

Lady Pendle clearly thought Lady Henry Seaborne faced an unenviable task keeping so many deadly rivals from scratching each other's eyes out in their scramble to become Jack's duchess. So how could Jess refuse to come here in Martha's sternly respectable company when her godmother had always given her loving support to her goddaughter whenever she needed it?

'His Grace and I are little more than nodding acquaintances nowadays, Martha, and I am only here to assist my godmother,' Jessica said now. 'Clearly I shall be far too busy to lounge about on sofas looking elegant, so you will not be required to dress me up like some aged *ingénue*. I suggest you regard this visit as something of a holiday and enjoy the comforts of Ashburton while you are here.'

'That I shall not, Miss Jessica. Lady Henry and your mama would never allow you to be less elegantly dressed than the rest of the company, even if the rest of us was prepared to let you make a spectacle of yourself,' Martha told her as if the very idea was preposterous.

'I am three and twenty and quite on the shelf, not some hopeful little miss of seventeen or eighteen,' Jessica countered lightly, but hoped there was enough steel in her voice to make it clear she considered that to be that.

She recalled what it was like to be that young

and artless and shuddered. At seventeen she had still dreamt young girls' dreams, even if she had put an embargo on any fancies about Jack. She had been cured of them quickly enough after overhearing a handsome and impecunious lieutenant who had sworn to her only the night before that she was the light and purpose of his life confide in his brother, the village curate, how her small fortune from her great-aunt would buy him preference and a commission. She could still hear every one of his cruel words now…

'Without her money, I should never look at such a dull little cripple, I can assure you, brother mine. If not for my need being so much greater than yours, she would make you a neat wife, Hubert. At least Miss Hop-Along will never be chased by the local squires or ogled by the sons of the gentry. Not that she wouldn't be easily caught if they chose to chase her, for she ain't able to run away, is she?' Julius Swaybon had said with a braying laugh that she had failed to notice was loud and unamused until that very moment.

Reverend Swaybon had been a much nicer gentleman than his brother and protested such a dismissive attitude to a girl the man was seeking to marry.

'Don't be more stupid than you can help,' his more worldly-wise brother told him scornfully. 'She wouldn't be looking my way if she had any prospect of a better catch. The wench must know she's flawed; she'll accept me and be thankful, or remain a drain on her family for the rest of her life.'

'I thought you said she had her own money,' Reverend Swaybon defended her stalwartly and if she'd had it in her to fall in love out of gratitude, she knew which brother she would have chosen, she reflected now.

She hadn't loved Julius Swaybon either, but she had been flattered by his extravagant praise and outrageous flirtation. Then she'd heard him speak of her as if she was a well-bred horse with a flaw that would bring her within his purchasing power and seen him for the straw man he truly was. It only confirmed her instinctive reaction to Jack when she was sixteen and eager for love, life and passion, but caution warned it would be a disaster for a girl like her to love him. He was seven years more cynical, experienced and dangerous now and an inner voice whispered he was also more fascinating, but she ignored it.

'Lady Henry has her ways of getting things done,' Martha said as they left the shade of the venerable oak trees and Ashburton Place came into clear view at last.

At least the magnificent mansion distracted her from wondering exactly what her godmother wanted to achieve this time and Jessica tried to dismiss that cryptic comment as if she hadn't even heard it. Even the Seabornes, who loved every stick and stone of the place, acknowledged Ashburton was a beautiful rabbit warren. The towers and domes of the mighty roof were punctuated with banqueting houses and fanciful pinnacles so fashionable in Tudor England, but at least the main house was brightened by arrays of bay windows in the highest fashion of the times. With subsequent additions in the same brick or sandstone, Ashburton was a vast yet welcoming ducal seat.

# Chapter Three

Imagining how fast the hearts of the young ladies arriving here must beat at the mere thought of becoming mistress of all this, Jessica could no longer forget why this gathering had been organised. If there was a girl of wit and character among the assembled beauties she supposed she would have to be glad, but most of the beauties of the *ton* would sell their souls for a catch like Jack, so she doubted such a girl would fight her way to the front of the eager crowd even if she wanted to. She shuddered at the very thought of the next few weeks and once more fervently wished herself back at Winberry Hall.

'Wretched man,' she muttered darkly.

'What's that?' Martha barked gruffly, as she always did when she hadn't quite caught what someone said and was pretending to herself and everyone else she wasn't growing a little deaf.

'None of your business,' Jessica replied pertly and waited for the steps to be let down with rather less relief than she should feel after being cooped up for so long with a woman who'd known her for her entire twenty-three years of life.

'Rag manners will get you nowhere in life, my girl,' Martha snapped caustically as only an old and valued family servant could and the footman who was peering cautiously in at them promptly backed away, before steeling himself to his duty and placing his stalwart hand for Jessica to steady herself with.

'You should know,' Jessica told her mother's old nurse as she stepped on to Seaborne soil and waited for it to steady under her disobliging feet.

'I don't know what you mean, Miss Pendle,' Martha replied with stately dignity.

'Of course you don't,' Jessica replied with a half-affectionate, half-exasperated smile and shook out her rumpled skirts as best she could as she went through the exercises her father's head groom had made up for her when she was first injured in order to soothe the protesting muscles in her damaged foot.

Even if she had to stand here until everyone else had forgotten her, she would not stumble up the short flight of steps looming in front of her and lose her hard-won dignity. The very thought of Jack Seaborne's face when he heard she had taken to tumbling about like a drunkard made her already-tense muscles tighten into knots, so she forced herself to forget him and relaxed until she felt the probability of collapsing at the wretched man's elegantly top-booted feet recede at long last.

'Oh, here you are at last, my love,' Lady Henry Seaborne exclaimed as she rushed down the steps to greet her. 'I'm so pleased you came, Jessica my love, even if we must do without your darling mama, but with this wonderful news of your latest nephew's precipitate arrival, even I can't begrudge Master Tremayne his doting grandmama's attention. Oh, did you not know your sister had been safely brought to bed of a healthy boy?' Lady Henry asked.

'No, Mama had to hurry off to Dassington

Manor as we were getting ready to set out. Papa insisted I kept the carriage and came on alone and was getting ready to drive to Dassington in his curricle. How happy Rowena and Sir Linstock must be, and how very clever of darling Row not to give herself time to be nervous about it all,' Jessica said, vastly relieved her sister was safe.

'Your father and mother were so anxious for you to get the news that Sir Linstock's groom must have taken a shortcut in his haste and missed you along the way. I was so afraid neither of you would come that I have been on tenterhooks, dreading every letter would say you could not join us either.'

'I could not let you down at such a time and Rowena would have been the first person to say I must come. I expect she is glad I have since most of our tribe of relatives have probably joined Sir Linstock at Dassington to fuss over her.'

'I am quite sure your sister would choose you over all of them if she could, for you two are marvellously close,' Lady Henry remarked.

'True, but Sir Linstock will make sure she is not overwhelmed by well-wishers in my absence,'

Jessica said lightly; indeed, she was glad her sister enjoyed such a loving and passionate marriage, even if sometimes she felt more like an old maid than ever in their company.

'I know how hard it must have been for you to continue your journey, so come here and be hugged and confound dignity and form,' Lady Henry ordered then engulfed Jessica in a warm, scented and loving embrace.

'Of course I came, Godmama dear. You're my favourite almost-relative and I don't see you half often enough.'

'For that you may have to be hugged again, Princess Jessica.'

'How I wish Jack had not decided to call me that after my accident, when you insisted I had the Queen's Room! I didn't realise until long after that you did so in order that I need not face the stairs after the interminable resetting and manipulation of my foot.'

'I'm surprised my darling daughter didn't tell you at the time, considering how jealous she was of you being allowed to sleep in a room I wouldn't even let her set foot in for fear of the damage she might do.'

'You must be such a dragon that she didn't dare disobey you,' Jessica teased.

'More likely she wanted the pony Jack promised her for her birthday so badly that she didn't dare go against his orders that you were to have that room and no argument. She knew he wouldn't hand over so much as a horseshoe if she didn't keep a still tongue in her head.'

Jessica had been sure Jack disliked her back then and wasn't altogether certain what to make of that information right now. Impatient of herself for thinking about him far too much, she was about to ask after Lady Henry's children when the prickle of unease she always felt in his presence of late warned her Jack had come out to meet her.

At the top of that suddenly endless flight of steps he stood at ease, superbly muscled under the loose, to-hell-with-fashion clothing he insisted on wearing in the country. He looked so much more mature than he'd been last time she visited him in his lair and in the bare two weeks since she had seen him last he seemed to have become even more potent and formidable, so much so that a craven part of her wanted to scramble back in the carriage and order it to race for home.

It didn't matter what she thought, she reminded herself. He was hosting this party to find himself a wife and most females seemed to like overlong sable hair and loosely tailored coats, at least on him, and the débutantes pursued him in packs whenever he set foot in town. At least he followed the fashion set by Mr Brummell in maintaining scrupulous cleanliness at all times, she conceded reluctantly, her critical gaze centred on his frowning countenance as she shivered with foreboding. A new sense of unease ran through her in fierce competition with the old now that she knew how it felt to have his acute gold-and-green eyes flare with interest on hers.

Warmth ran over her in a mortifying flush at the memory of heat shuddering through her the day he took her for a drive and she made herself avoid thinking of it so he couldn't read her wayward thoughts now. Confound the man, but why did he affect her so potently without trying?

Even if she wasn't a plain spinster, he had every beauty for miles around sighing over his manly charms and legendary vigour and casting shameless lures in his direction.

'Oh, there you are, dearest,' her godmother remarked as she felt her goddaughter stiffen and turned round to look for a cause. 'Hughes said you had gone to inspect the bullpens at Home Farm with Givage,' she said with a warm smile for her nephew Jessica would never dare replicate even if she wanted to.

'We saw a travelling carriage pull through the South Gate. How could I not be present to greet Miss Pendle when she is our honoured guest, Aunt Mel? Surely you brought me up better than that?' he teased. 'I take it Lord and Lady Pendle rushed off to meet their latest grandson and left you to honour the family obligations, Miss Pendle?'

'Indeed, and it seems to me as if everyone knew how my sister and her babe fared long before I did, your Grace,' Jessica informed him stiffly and wished she could be as natural with him as she was with gentlemen who didn't make her heart beat at the speed of a runaway horse and her knees wobble anew.

'The messenger arrived this morning,' he told her as if soothing one of those runaway horses. 'We hoped your mama might be able to follow you here, but she says she must stay at Dassington lest poor Rowena be driven half-mad by her doting husband and assorted well-wishers,' he added, descending the steps with such fluid ease Jessica frowned, then lifted a hand to rub it away before it betrayed her.

'Good day to you…Martha, is it not?' he greeted with a respectful nod that made her maid blush with delight and look at least ten years younger. 'Had we known you were looking after Miss Pendle's well-being, my aunt would have fretted a lot less.'

'Thank you, your Grace, you are very kind and we all knew Miss Jessica would be safe as houses once we were under your roof,' Martha replied with a curtsy fit for a king.

'And here's Miss Jessica all present and correct,' he added redundantly as he stepped down to her level at last. 'Welcome, Cousin.'

'We bear no relationship to each other whatsoever, your Grace,' she objected, getting a sharp look from Martha and a disappointed sigh from Melissa, but no discernible reaction from the man himself.

'How unforgivably forward I was in danger of being, Miss Pendle,' he countered.

'And think how flattering that would have been for me, your Grace,' she said, ironically feeling that blush threaten again as his gaze became sardonic.

'I dare say the flattery would have been all mine,' he said so smoothly that an observer might think he was being charming.

'It certainly would,' she defended herself.

His gaze seemed to grow sharper and she did her best to breathe defiance at the idea she was an easy target for his charm. Reminding herself the Pendles had been robber barons when the Seabornes were still little more than pirates, she tried her best to fight off her own wicked, deep-down notion that there was little point hanging on to those defences when she was marked for a life of spinsterly solitude. She did her best to ignore the very notion of letting herself ever be so undefended in his presence and instead imagined his wild rover ancestors squaring up to the ruthless overlord who had been her grandparent at many removes.

From what she knew of them, it would have been such a hard-fought contest their retainers would have had to pitch their tents and settle in for the night before their leaders conceded neither could win and shook hands on their mutual villainy. Suddenly the thought of swordsmen and spearmen on one side and trident and cutlass-wielding sailors on the other, falling asleep propped against their weapons and their rascally fellows, as their principals snarled defiance at each other, seemed so irresistibly funny she giggled, then did her best to pretend she hadn't.

'Spring fever,' she explained as he raised a questioning eyebrow.

'It's come on a little late this year then, has it not?'

'Maybe the sign of a golden summer,' she offered a battered olive branch.

'And how very welcome that would be,' he said

politely, but somehow she felt as if she had disappointed him.

'Speaking of welcomes, this is a very poor one indeed,' her godmother exclaimed. 'We are keeping you out here in all this wind, my dear, and it looks to me as if the heavens might open at any moment, whatever nonsense you two are talking about it being summer. Come now, Hughes...' she turned to order the resident butler, who was hovering at the top of the steps '...have Miss Jessica's luggage brought inside then conduct her maid to the Queen's Room so she may supervise the unpacking. We shall take tea in the Blue Parlour as soon as Miss Pendle has put off her travelling cloak and bonnet.'

'My aunt is undoubtedly right,' the Duke told Jess as if making up his mind about something more important than the weather.

Jessica had only a second to wonder before he swept her up in his arms and ran up the steps as if she weighed little more than a feather. For a moment she was breathless with shock and a novel excitement that threatened to leave her blushing and overwhelmed in his arms. All his warmth, strength and certainty suddenly seemed hers to command and…and nothing was less likely.

'Put me down,' she demanded.

'You'll fall over if I do,' he informed her coolly.

'Then I'll fall over,' she said flatly.

'Not on my steps you won't,' he said as if that ought to settle the matter.

'I concede that would be mightily inconvenient, but we are at the top now, so *will* you set me down?'

'Please?'

'Why, what do you want?' she replied childishly and felt the high ground of ladylike disdain fall away.

'For us to be polite to each other for once, Hedgehog,' he retorted, reverting to another youthful taunt for his aunt's awkward godchild.

'And you think this is a good place to start?' she said, cross with herself for letting a note of hurt invade her words.

'No,' he conceded, shifting her in his arms as he seemed to decide his duties as host bade him finish what he'd started.

Jessica suddenly felt she would pay too dear for

the fleeting pleasure of being in his mighty arms like this. 'Please will you set me down now?' she almost pleaded as they finally arrived in the Blue Parlour the family always used and he looked for the best place to deposit the awkward female he had literally swept off her feet.

'Your wish is my command, Miss Pendle,' he lied, as he deposited her on a sofa, then bowed with an overdone flourish that was obviously intended to defuse the tension that had drawn tight between them.

'Hah! That's a likely story,' she said and saw relief in his eyes as the world shifted back on to its proper axis.

'True, although anything reasonable you happen to want just now is probably within the limits of my patience,' he said with a wry grin she did her best to resist.

He turned to greet his aunt. 'Forgive me for leaving you behind, love, but I thought you'd feel better if your favourite godchild was safe in your parlour where you can fuss over her in peace while she recovers from her journey.'

'I am prepared to wait for Jessica to put off her

bonnet and spencer before I do that,' his aunt almost scolded him as she swept forwards to deal with the former while Jessica wriggled out of her spencer. If she didn't demonstrate some independence right away Jack might hustle her out of it himself and ruin the effect all the lovely distance she'd put between them was having on her jumping nerves.

'Jack, take these into the hall for Jessica's maid to deal with when she has settled in,' Lady Henry commanded and Jessica almost laughed at the sight of his Grace the Duke of Dettingham meekly acting the lady's maid.

The thought of him doing so in truth, helping her strip off her creased and travel-worn gown and all that lay beneath, struck her like a bolt from the louring clouds outside and all desire to laugh vanished abruptly.

Jack paused in the grand hallway of his ancestors and wondered if the sky was due to fall on him in the near future. Confound it, but he needed to pay a visit to his mistress if the mere feel of cross-grained, touchy little Jessica Pendle in his arms threatened to set him afire like some lecherous old satyr. He caught himself savouring the faint scent lingering on her spencer jacket that was so uniquely hers. Was it the hint of rosewater or something more sophisticated that seemed to warn his sixth sense she was by? If it was, then at least he might have enough warning to avoid her in future, he told himself, for a pricklier, more distracting guest to be inflicted with just at the moment he found it hard to imagine. The reason he'd been so glad to see her was yet another mystery he didn't care to examine.

He laid her plain jacket and austere bonnet on a gloriously carved Carolinian chair as if they might sting him and fought to still his senses before he returned to the Blue Parlour to play the genial host. As if things weren't already tangled enough without him suddenly wanting Jessica in every way a gentleman should never want a lady like her, he reminded himself disgustedly. Luckily he turned back towards the Blue Parlour in time to escape being caught musing over Jessica's outer garments like a besotted lover by his butler and half the footmen in the household, streaming across the marble hall with enough tea and pastries to feed an invading army.

'Ah, there you all are,' he greeted his younger cousins with no surprise at all and some relief as he heard them thunder downstairs at the merest hint of treats.

'Would that we were,' the eldest of them said theatrically and he eyed Miss Persephone Seaborne sternly.

'You will not mention Richard's absence, or distress your mother in any way you can avoid, during this confounded house party of hers, now will you, Percy dear?' he asked, meeting her willow-green gaze with a very direct look.

'Of course not,' she said as if he was some sort of monster to even think she might.

'Promise?' he asked, inured to the imitation of a wronged angel she could turn on and off at will.

Persephone sighed loudly, looked long-suffering, then nodded.

'Out loud promise?' he heard himself wheedle, because he knew her far too well to leave her the slightest room for manoeuvre.

'I promise not to jeopardise the noble task of

getting you off our hands and into those of some deluded female who might be persuaded to wed you, despite your many and varied faults,' she told him pertly.

'With you and Miss Pendle in the house, I stand little chance of being swollen-headed, however much the ambitious mamas fawn on me and their daughters fall over themselves to become my duchess,' he told her wryly and noted the speculative glint in her eyes with an internal groan.

Let the little devil get even a hint of the odd feeling he'd had just now that Jess belonged in his arms and he'd never take an easy step during this house party for fear of her match-making schemes. Since they'd argued heatedly from the moment they had met, he couldn't imagine anyone less like the comfortable wife he'd pictured when he finally agreed to this totty-headed scheme of his grandmother's to marry him off and silence the scandal-mongers than Jessica Pendle.

'Don't forget how much depends on me finding a duchess, Percy,' he cautioned her seriously.

'Do you think it will work, though?' she asked anxiously.

At least he didn't have to pretend with her that this scheme was anything more than a desperate attempt to persuade Rich to come home, even if he was beginning to have very large doubts about the whole mad idea of marrying to please everyone but himself. He suspected his grandmother would be very glad to see him wed for the sake of the duchy, but he had seen the list of candidates for the post and was rapidly losing any enthusiasm for the business himself.

'Rich is sure to come back once he knows there's little risk of him ever inheriting my titles or obligations,' he told her uneasily, cursing his cousin for putting them through so much by absenting himself so determinedly that it was nigh three years since anyone admitted to having seen him.

'What if he isn't doing this of his own accord though, Jack?'

'Then we'll know one way or the other,' he said grimly.

'And you will have put your head on the block

for my heedless brother for nothing. Those silly gossips are plain evil, Jack, and you should not regard a word they say. Sometimes I wish I could challenge one or two to a duel since they hide behind their sex to spread rumours about you and Rich and suffer no consequences for their spite. If you offered for one of their repellent daughters, I dare say they would bite your hand off as soon as let you withdraw it, even if they truly thought you capable of the horrible crimes they only dare hint at.'

'Such is the way of the world and I truly do have to wed sooner or later, love. I'm seven and twenty and will be left on the shelf before long if I'm not very careful,' he joked with an inward sigh, knowing a single, solvent duke would be a magnificent prize on the marriage mart even if he was ancient, blind, senile and truly a murderer.

'As much chance of that as the moon truly turning blue,' Persephone said, looking unconvinced.

Luckily she gave up trying to challenge his sudden desire for a wife and turned towards the chatter and gaiety in the parlour so they could both forget they didn't know where Richard Seaborne was or had been for three years.

'I hope you scrubby brats left us some cake?' Persephone demanded of her younger siblings as she entered the room.

Hard not to contrast the welcome she received with Jessica's stony reception of himself, Jack concluded as he followed his lively cousin in. Jessica smiled a wide and rather enchanting smile and Persephone rushed towards her long-time friend and ally so they could embrace and coo over each other as if they hadn't seen each other for years rather than a few weeks. He felt an odd gnaw of discontent; how strange to feel excluded by a pair of headstrong, awkward females he should be only too delighted to leave to their own company while he went wife hunting. Cook's bounty provided a welcome distraction to his uncomfortable thoughts, but it was soon disposed of and the children dragged back to the schoolroom by their long-suffering governess.

'So when are the rest of your guests due, your Grace?' Jessica asked brightly.

'Tomorrow,' Jack replied gloomily.

'Well, the weather seems set fair, despite Godmama's dire predictions, so at least it won't cause any delay in their journeys,' she said as if that was a good thing.

Damn Rich! When the rogue finally came home and Aunt Melissa lost that haunted look, as if her worst nightmare was about to come true, he'd beat the living daylights out of him, after he'd reassured himself the care-for-nobody wretch was hale and whole and rackety as ever.

'Excellent,' he said hollowly. 'Entertaining them will be much easier without the wind and rain we have endured so far this summer,' he added pompously, as if he was Squire Countryman, obsessed by his crops and the weather to make or mar them and barely able to spare time to pick himself out a wife between haymaking and harvest.

'How *are* you planning to keep them all amused?' Jessica asked and his aunt rattled off a list that should keep an army of eligible young ladies busy for the rest of the summer, let alone a fortnight.

Jack left them discussing final arrangements

for the guests' comfort and escaped his duties one last time before the hoard of *ton* beauties and their various chaperons descended on them. Half an hour later he was galloping his latest acquisition over the hills above Ashburton, trying to pretend to himself everything was well with his world and Jessica Pendle's arrival meant no more to him than all the other young ladies due to intrude on it tomorrow would do.

'Trust Jack to slide out of his obligations the minute he could,' Persephone said disgustedly when his escape was commented on indulgently by her mother, who seemed determined to take the 'boys will be boys' attitude to his sins.

'There's no need for him to stand on ceremony with me and he knows it,' Jessica said as if she agreed.

'You defend him, yet you two were at daggers' drawn within half a minute of setting eyes on each other as usual, were you not?' Persephone asked.

'We always bring out the worst in each other,' Jessica admitted. 'Since his Grace must be on his best behaviour for the next two weeks if he's going to find himself an amenable bride, I probably should not have come.'

'Much better if he found one who wasn't going to agree with his every word, if you ask me. He's not the sort of man who will be content within a marriage of convenience for long,' Persephone replied with a look Jessica didn't trust one bit.

She shuddered at the idea of Persephone contriving devious ways to throw her at Jack's head and even had qualms about him being forced to be brutally honest with her. Jack Seaborne was a fair and honourable man, under his arrogant, infuriating confidence that he was lord of all he surveyed even when he was away from his wide domain. Having to make it clear to a lady he'd known for so long that he wouldn't be making her an offer would pain him nearly as much as it would her.

'You would have thought his parents' marriage would have given the deluded idiot a hint there is more to married life than finding a wife in much the same way he'd go about mating his racehorses,' her friend went on in a voice too low to reach Lady Henry's ears now she was consulting Hughes about when to serve dinner and the possibility of his Grace being home in time to eat it at a reasonable hour. Even sunny-tempered Lady Henry Seaborne would have indulged in the vapours or a storm of shocked maternal outrage if she'd heard such unsuitable remarks on the lips of her eldest unwed daughter.

'I don't recall them very well from staying with you at Seaborne House when we were young, but I do recall gossip that the late duke and duchess fought like cat and dog. Perhaps Jack's intent on finding a more peaceable wife,' Jessica said, hoping her air of lightly amused indifference would convince Persephone he was welcome to such a milk-and-water creature as far as she was concerned.

'Which only proves my point, don't you think?'

'I might, if I only knew what it was.'

'That arranged marriages are insipid at best and Jack is the last man who should consider making one. He has such a passionate, headlong temperament under that haughty indifference he shows the world and would be bored with such an empty-headed automaton of a wife before the marriage feast was over, let alone their bride visits.'

'His Grace is also a wealthy and tolerably handsome nobleman, who would be hard pressed to find a lady who saw past that to the man himself. If they were still alive, no doubt his parents would have found a rich and lovely noblewoman who would understand his life, then contrived to throw them together long ago,' Jessica argued.

'Not they,' Persephone denied with an emphatic shake of her head. 'They would pick rival candidates and make Jack's life a misery until he ran off with a farmer's pretty daughter to prove he wasn't going to be dictated to.'

'Then since he can please himself who to marry, no doubt he'll choose himself a conformable and agreeable wife he can be comfortable with.'

'Such a pallid creature would never suit him,' her friend said stubbornly and Jessica couldn't help picturing Jack living with a female who forever agreed with every word he said and shuddered at the very idea.

Considering the vitality and impatience Jack Seaborne had struggled to contain ever since she first laid eyes on him, Jessica thought her friend was right. After such a stormy childhood, maybe it should be no surprise if he chose serenity over ungovernable passion in his own marriage, but it sounded so very dull.

'Whatever we think, his Grace will go his own way—he always does,' she said with a shrug and tried not to think of how she would feel if the Duke found himself a wife of character as well as beauty. Glad, she told herself stoically and did her best to look serenely content with her own lot in life.

'Not if I can stop him he won't,' her friend countered darkly, an intent look of purpose on her face.

Jessica shuddered to think what schemes Persephone might come up with over the next weeks to prevent Jack marrying a sweet little nonentity and wished herself at Dassington with her sister and the new baby.

'One day you're going to meet someone you can't manipulate or charm into doing whatever you want, Persephone Seaborne,' she warned lightly.

'I already have, Jessica dear. You and Jack are two of the most stubborn and infuriating beings ever set on God's good earth to plague the rest of us.'

'Funny, that's exactly what we always thought about you,' Jessica countered with a smug grin that turned into outright laughter as Persephone did her best to look meek and mild enough to disprove such a slander and failed.

Jessica used the excuse of being tired after her journey to retire early that night, although as Persephone pointed out when she turned up at Jessica's door once Martha had left it, her journey had been so stately even her own formidable grandmother could not have been fagged by it. They spent an hour or so curled up on the luxurious state bed, where queens of England had slept so often nobody was quite sure which one it was named for any more. Jess recalled nights when she and her sister Rowena had sat talking like this, or stolen downstairs to watch the adults, then raid the larder before going back to bed with their booty and telling each other tall tales about the guests gathered below. Rowena liked her bed and her husband in it far too much to leave it nowadays and it wasn't as if she wished her sister anything but happy, yet being the last spinster sister had felt very lonely at times.

'Which of the hopefuls on Mama's list do you fancy will win Jack's noble hand in wedlock then, Jessica?' Persephone said, interrupting her reverie with an unwelcome reminder of exactly why there was a party of guests arriving tomorrow.

'What list?'

'The one of his potential wives, of course. Which lady do you back to win the ducal chase?'

'None,' Jessica said decisively, 'I feel sorry for whomever he settles on. She will be watched and whispered about every minute of the day without me joining in the speculation. It's quite enough to make even the most rampant husband-hunter turn tail and run for home, if you ask me.'

'I'm sure you underestimate them, Jess.'

'Maybe, but I won't speculate about his intentions towards one lady or another.'

'I dare say,' Persephone said with an odd look Jessica suddenly didn't want to interpret.

'Never mind Jack, didn't you meet a man you could marry this Season, Persephone?' she asked to divert her friend from this dangerous topic. 'You seemed very pleased with Mr Harmsbury's company for a while.'

'Did I? That's an impression I shall make sure I correct if I find myself called upon to endure it again, then.'

'Oh, dear, what did he do?'

'He tricked me into walking with him in the Park when I thought we were to meet a group of friends. The wretched man thought to compromise me into marriage when a few rough kisses and a rushed proposal of marriage didn't win me over. Not a mistake he will make a second time with a lady of character, I suspect.'

'And how did you bring on such a turnabout?'

'You have brothers; I expect yours told you as well as mine did exactly how to disable a man long enough to escape him when they finally thought you were grown up enough to need to know. It really works, Jessica, should you ever need to try it.'

'Unlikely, but I would need much longer to run, would I not?' Jessica said bitterly.

'Your injury has always troubled you far more than it does anyone else, you know,' Persephone informed her with such matter-of-fact common sense that Jessica wondered if she did indeed make too much of her slightly halting gait.

'How tiresome of me,' she said with a rueful smile.

'No, but it is infuriating for those of us who would have you put a far higher value upon yourself than you seem prepared to do.'

'More than tiresome, then; everyone will be happier when I have finally settled to a life of single blessedness and retired from the social scene.'

'I never heard anything so ridiculous as your notion of buying yourself a neat little cottage and settling down to keep bees and a pig or two, presumably whilst driving yourself about the country in a donkey cart distributing flannel petticoats to the poor, whether they want them or not. Anyone would think you were five and fifty at the very least, not over thirty years younger.'

'Should I burden my parents with a spinster daughter, hire myself out as companion to a bad-tempered old lady or become a governess then, Persephone?

'None of those; you should find yourself a loving husband to convince you, as the rest of us seem unable to, that you are his lovely and desirable wife, despite that damaged ankle you seem to think so much more important than the rest of you.'

Jessica stayed silent, unwilling to admit she had decided against falling in love at too early an age to launch into it like some headlong débutante now.

'I'm never going to be content with less than love and neither should you be, but it can't be so very difficult to find a good man,' Persephone announced, as if nagging herself as much as Jessica now she was on the subject.

'I am content with naught,' Jessica said calmly enough.

'No, it's not enough to sit back and never try

to find the gentleman you could love. It can't be enough when you consider how much such a wanton act of neglect could affect our futures.'

'What if you find him and it proves impossible?'

'Then he's married? Jessica, how shocking of you,' her friend teased, but looked horrified by the very idea all the same.

'No, because he doesn't exist,' Jessica insisted loudly, even as the sixteen-year-old Jess she had locked away in a dark corner of her mind jumped up and down and shouted that he did, he so much did that her wild young self might have thrown herself on the ground and drummed her heels in grief and frustration at the purpose behind this whole horrible house party, but mature Jessica slammed the door of her internal cell and threw away the key, even if it cost her dear to do so.

Meanwhile Persephone looked as if all her best and worst fears had been confirmed at the vehemence of Jessica's answer.

'You're in lo—'

Persephone couldn't say more since Jessica had slapped a hand across her mouth to stop her.

She stared into her friend's clever green eyes and shook her head in solemn warning.

'No, Persephone, don't speculate and don't plot one of your wrong-headed schemes. I am not in love and I can assure you nobody is in love with me.'

Persephone waved a hand frantically in the air and Jessica took her hand away with another warning look.

'I never thought you were such a coward, Jessica Pendle.'

'And don't think you can make me fly into a temper and swear to prove you wrong, Persephone. It might work on Seabornes, but it won't with a Pendle. We keep our counsel and our tempers far better than that.'

'Nonsense, I've seen you practically incandescent with rage over something Jack said too many times to count and don't tell me that was in your salad days, because he only has to make a flippant comment now and you poker up like an ironwork.'

'Ah, but he is uniquely infuriating, you tell me so at regular intervals,' Jessica managed with a shrug of would-be indifference.

'So is my brother Rich, but you considered him a good friend when he was still here to be one, did you not?'

This was very thin ice to be skating on and cunning Persephone knew it from the glint of self-satisfied mockery in her eyes.

'Perhaps it's because your brother is not an arrogant, to-hell-with-the-rest-of-you duke that I don't find him as infuriating as his cousin,' Jessica replied calmly.

'Or a devilishly handsome rogue with a wicked gleam in his eyes, eyes that most young ladies of the *ton* would love to have focused on them?'

'You underestimate your brother; he's very handsome indeed and it's the older sisters of those very young ladies his eyes glitter at the sight of, although I could hardly expect you to notice that, considering you're his sister and last time he was in town you were barely out.'

'I'm barely two years younger than you, Jessica dear, so don't try to pretend I'm a schoolroom miss who doesn't know a hawk from a hand-saw to get out of an uncomfortable situation,' Persephone warned half-seriously.

'I'm not in any difficulty. I have merely been exchanging foolish gossip with my best friend, or at least I considered you my best friend until tonight, when you seem to be growing into a younger version of your grandmother, the Dowager Duchess.'

'Now that's cruel and unjust, Jessica, as well as downright evil and witchy. I will never be like the Dowager if I live to be a hundred.'

'Consider it a timely warning.'

'And you know what you can do with your untimely warning, don't you?' Persephone replied and heaved one of the royal pillows out of the royal bed and proceeded to pummel her former best friend with it until Jess fought back and they were both breathless and laughing, as well as more than a little shamefaced about the quantity of the very finest down now wafting gently about the state bedchamber.

'So you won't plague me day and night for the name of the man I once thought I could fall in love with then, Persephone?' Jessica almost pleaded.

'Only if you take back that hideous accusation

about my grandmother,' Persephone insisted so solemnly that Jessica wondered if she had inadvertently touched a raw nerve and her friend really did fear she might become like her famously irascible granddam one day.

'Do you promise?' Jessica asked, unconsciously echoing Jack's stern demand earlier in the day.

'I promise,' Persephone said almost solemnly.

'Then I admit I can't think of anyone less like the Dowager than you are, Persephone Seaborne, and consider it highly unlikely you will ever resemble her in any essentials, since you have a loving heart and I don't think she has one at all.'

'Only pride and an abacus,' her friend agreed a little bit too cheerfully for Jessica's taste and she eyed her suspiciously as Persephone yawned artistically and declared herself far too weary to stay and argue the night away any longer.

She then hugged Jessica warmly, bade her have a good night's sleep and promised to spirit her off to Ashburton village in the morning so they could avoid the fluster and fuss of arriving guests under the guise of visiting Jack's tenants. It wasn't until she whisked out of the Queen's

Room and shut the door safely behind her that Persephone smiled wickedly and uncrossed the fingers of her left hand.

# Chapter Four

Jack Seaborne stood as if he'd frozen in place on the fine flags on the terrace outside the nearly always silent and deserted staterooms, where he automatically came to brood whenever being the Duke of Dettingham seemed a little too much to bear. He suspected he gave a fine impression of man turned Greek statue, with the caveat he was fully clothed and not given to striking poses, but Jack didn't care how he looked to a mythical observer as he cursed softly and puzzled over that almost-admission his cousin had just got out of Jessica. Who was this man she might have learned to love? And why on earth did it suddenly seem to matter so much that she forgot about him?

He racked his brains for the fool's identity, but

came up with a blank. Yet he had done such a fine job of avoiding her for so long he only had second-hand evidence to rely on, so he supposed there could have been some mysterious idiot in her life who didn't notice she was almost in love with him and Jack would never have known of it. He wanted to pace the flags outside Jess's window as he fought a rush of what felt uncomfortably like jealousy. As he'd made no attempt to boost Jessica's marriage prospects for some odd reason, it hadn't even occurred to him to introduce her to the odd respectable and decent man of his acquaintance, so there was no reason he would know if she had almost fallen in love with one of them.

Something in him was revolted at Persephone's idea that Jessica ought to marry a good enough man, who would overlook her slightly halting gait and win the soft heart and quick mind she guarded so well. The thought of the wild and spirited Jess he remembered wed to a man who would make allowances for her and find delicate ways round her slight disability made his fists tighten and a picture of himself punching such a self-satisfied idiot on the nose formed in his mind. The terrible idea that Cousin Rich might be her mystery man occurred to him and it felt as if the bottom had fallen out of the world at the same time the sky began to fall on his head. Individually he loved them both, so wasn't it a shame the very thought of them paired together in holy matrimony made him feel sick as a horse?

Any illusions that he was in some way superior to ordinary mortals, as well as in command of his family because of his ducal authority, would have flown into the night on the spot, if only his cousin Rich hadn't already demolished them by disappearing like smoke on the wind three years ago, then stubbornly refusing to be found. Now he couldn't even keep the thought of Rich and what felt uncomfortably like his betrayal in his head for his racing thoughts of Jessica Pendle and the giant question of who her unattainable love might be. He hardly dared move lest Jessica heard him, looked out of her open window and realised how easily a listener could hear anything said within. He must wait for her to go to sleep before he could risk creeping away.

It was a shame he couldn't pace while he thought, he decided, since he needed to burn off some energy. Tomorrow he would face a clutch of hopeful young women he found oddly interchangeable and somehow he was supposed to pick out one to spend the rest of his life with. That ought to concentrate his thoughts, but somehow they kept drifting back to Jessica and this impossible love of hers. He didn't want love himself and certainly didn't want to love his wife, so why the notion of Jessica forming a passionate alliance, either within or without marriage, made him want to hit something he had no idea. Even if he wanted to court the sort of heartache his parents always managed to inflict on one another, he wouldn't allow himself to fall in love with a female who showed every sign of indifference whenever she wasn't ripping up at him like a fishwife.

So he didn't want to marry her himself, but the idea of some other man doing so seemed utterly repellent. Which made him what? A dog in the manger, he decided disgustedly. It was nothing personal, he excused himself to a hopefully sleeping Jessica, he didn't want to marry any other well-bred female either, but needs must since there was the succession to consider, and at least he need not commit his heart and soul to any one of the interchangeable young ladies about to arrive at Ashburton. Somehow he knew that if he were ever to decide he must court and win Jessica, he would have to offer her a lot more than a grand title and vast possessions before she'd accept him, and he didn't have more to offer his duchess.

Committing everything to one person meant tragedy and loss for everyone about you, he reminded himself as he recalled how it felt to be a sixteen-year-old orphan, furious at his father for not wanting to live without his mother. They said it was a riding accident, that his Grace had been distracted by his grief, dismounted too close to the edge of the old quarry and slipped on a patch of unstable turf so that he had gone over the edge before he could regain his footing. Jack knew differently, having tried to live with an inconsolable lover who had lost his one and only, passionate, turbulent love and found the world intolerable without her for six months.

His father had drunk, fought and raged the nights away after his wife died in that late, disastrous attempt to give him another son. Jack shivered as he recalled how his father had blamed himself for that, when the doctors had insisted she should not risk another pregnancy after his own birth. It had taken years to get out of the way of thinking it was his own fault for causing his mother whatever damage she suffered at his birth so that she had died at her second attempt to birth a baby. Even now his eyes stung at the thought of his fiercely devoted mother and father restraining their passions sufficiently to avert that outcome for so long and marvelled at the depth and breadth of their love.

Not that their passionate relationship made the idea of such unreasonable emotions any more attractive, he reminded himself. He might be the product of a great love match rather than a dynastic marriage, but those extravagant feelings hadn't brought much comfort to his parents, or even their son, when they were too busy quarrelling, making up, then swearing undying love for each other to notice they even had a child most of the time. With the eyes of maturity he saw what a terrible strain it must have been on both of them to love so deeply and have to deny themselves the full expression of that love and the urgent desire that went with it. To love so much, so urgently that you would stop short of risking your lover's life by loving them to the full must have been an agony as well as an ecstasy to his father. All the same, such love was not for him. He intended to be here to love his children, even if he didn't have it in him to do the same for their mother.

All of which did nothing to tell him why the idea of Jessica and her theoretical lover made him feel like kicking something so hard it relieved the roar of denial in his head. He regarded her as a particularly annoying extra cousin, didn't he? Since she was clearly halfway in love with another man, he had better learn to think of her in that way if he didn't already, but somehow that role didn't fit her either. She was just there, Jessica Pendle—annoyance, challenge and sparring partner, or at least she had been when he was young and furious enough with life to need her to be just that. Now she was just as vexing, but so different from the wild Jess she had been once upon a time that he'd almost deceived himself she was the nonentity she'd pretended to be for far too long. He struggled with that urgent need to pace once more as it occurred to him that a Jessica somewhere between the two extremes sounded almost too good to be true and worth fighting a few battles for against the demons that drove him to seek a marriage of convenience.

If only she wasn't wedded to the idea of eccentric spinsterhood, since she couldn't have this unattainable lover of hers—she would have made him the ideal wife. If she was in love with another man, yet certain there could be no future for them, wouldn't she make him a duchess in a million? He knew her well enough to be certain she would never betray him, even if this paragon of hers suddenly became available after all. He liked her, despite her prickly reaction to him, and she was as lovely as he'd tried to convince her she was that day in London, to very little avail so far as he could tell. As a duchess she would be gracious and dignified and beautiful and he could always rely on her to care for his family and his tenants if he had to be absent. Her children would be as full of character as she was herself and he would certainly enjoy begetting them on her, he decided, as he felt his loins quicken to an uncomfortably rigid eagerness at the very thought of bedding her.

If only he could persuade her to accept a convenient arrangement on both sides he would be well content with his life and avoid the sort of passionate lunacy his parents had inflicted on him. Yes, if he could use the next fortnight to prove to Jess how well they would suit, then he would look forward to marriage with her, rather than see it as a burden to be taken up for the sake of his family. Here in the shadow of the great house, as the moon finally deigned to come up, it sounded such a straightforward idea, until the real human frailty of both himself and Miss Jessica Pendle were thrown into the equation. Well, she would be a challenge, he decided with a wolfish grin. It was time she learnt the extremes of pleasure she was denying herself with that silly scheme of becoming the archetypal spinster. With a house party in residence he would hunt her as cunningly as the most skilful predator. Suddenly the next few weeks felt ripe with possibilities as delicious little vignettes of Jess warm and luscious from his passionate kisses, lodged in his mind and refused to be reasoned away.

It all jarred into irrational fury when he came up against the image of her looking like that in another man's arms, but he managed to push the idea aside at the memory of how bleak she had sounded when she denied all chance of that girlish obsession of hers succeeding. Jack stubbornly refused to feel guilty about the man; he'd clearly had his chance with her and either walked away or not had the wit to know it was there in the first place. Such idiots didn't deserve that she should spend the rest of her life avoiding marriage because they existed. Jessica deserved better, and who knew what he deserved? He hoped he deserved a wife who would not bore him to Bedlam and back, he hoped he deserved Jessica, Duchess of Dettingham, as much as she did a better life than the one she had just mapped out for herself.

Yet what a fool he'd been not to see Jessica was his duchess until now, even when she'd been right in front of him that last night in London—somehow setting the rest of the world in its rightful place the moment he'd laid eyes on her amongst all that heat and chaos. If she was in the least bit taken in by his worldly advantages of title and wealth he would have had a head start over her tardy lover, but instead they would be an obstacle to be got over. Yet a spark of awareness, the flash of mutual shock and possibility he had felt between them earlier today when he'd lifted her into his arms, was a start. And at least she knew the worst aspects of his stubborn personality before they began.

Even the thought of coolly composed Jessica Pendle wild for him and passionately abandoned in his arms held such a powerful allure for him he wondered how long he'd been lying to himself. He considered a picture of her as she had been in that London ballroom and found himself becoming a critic—a connoisseur of the female beauty he should have seen long before. He wondered how much to blame himself for being so blind and how much Jessica herself for playing down her looks so skilfully. How could he not have noted the softness of her autumn-leaf brown hair until tonight, or longed to touch it and find out if it was as live under his hands as it should be under the light of dozens, if not hundreds, of expensive wax candles, but somehow seldom was in any of the London ballrooms she frequented?

Because Jessica dismissed the very idea her hair was a potent attraction, along with her excellent figure and fine-cut features enlivened by eyes of the most unusual shade of sea-green he had ever beheld and then there was the sensuous curves of her lips… Yes, well, best not dwell on those just now or he might climb in through her window and terrify the poor girl as he crassly attempted to discover if they were as lush as he thought, when they weren't set in a disapproving line at the very idea of the current Duke of Dettingham, that is.

Jack decided he had given her ample time by now to get into bed and succumb to the tiredness she had claimed earlier. Refusing to even contemplate the idea of watching her sleep naked in his arms, after exhausting her with his lusty attentions and their mutual passions, in case he really did leap through the window and scare her half to death, he crept from the terrace as carefully as a thief in the night. At least tonight the house wasn't half full of strangers who might be wakeful on their first night in a strange house and see his Grace the Duke of Dettingham acting like a criminal.

By the time Jessica and Persephone returned to Ashburton the following afternoon they were both feeling guilty about staying away so long. Clearly Lady Henry agreed, since she hardly gave them time to put off their bonnets before pressing them into action.

'Ah, here is my eldest daughter Persephone and my dear goddaughter, Miss Pendle,' she exclaimed rather manically when they entered the rarely used State Drawing Room. 'I believe you met Lady Freya Buckle and Miss Corbridge during the Season, my dears?' Lady Henry asked,

clearly desperate to get at least two of her guests off her hands, so she could catch her breath and deal with whatever minor crises had arisen from playing hostess to a large influx of guests. 'These young ladies have no wish to retire to their bedchambers for the afternoon to recover from their journeys and would like to view the pleasure gardens closest to the house. As my daughter and Miss Pendle are home at exactly the right moment to explain the finer points of horticultural interest, I hope that will keep you entertained until the other young people are ready to join us, my dears?'

'Yes, indeed, I believe the gardens of Ashburton are unusual,' Lady Freya replied, as if not quite sure she approved of the unusual.

'So far as I can see, the Seabornes pride themselves on refusing to follow current trends and bend fashion to suit themselves,' Jessica said as noncommittally as she could, but the idea of this arrogant little lady taking over the gardens as well as their owner and his house and bending *them* to her taste filled her with revulsion.

'We do like our own way,' Persephone confirmed with a cool look that contained a warning about more than Lady Freya's flimsy kid slippers. 'Many of the paths are made up of raked gravel,' she announced, as if a lady might require hob-nailed boots to make the tour in comfort, 'but if we stick to the terraces and the yew walk you will not come to grief, Lady Freya.'

'Indeed, I like to go my own way as well, you see?' Lady Freya replied just as coolly and Jessica wondered if Miss Corbridge felt as if she had strayed on to a very polite battlefield as well.

'I dare say,' Persephone replied with a regal sniff and they set off on a stiff and truncated tour of the garden, during which Miss Corbridge and Jessica did their best to fill the rather strained silences with amiable small talk.

'I prefer the picturesque style,' Lady Freya remarked disapprovingly on being shown the basic design of the formal gardens from the famous top terrace of Ashburton's south-facing gardens. 'This is all very artificial.'

'So is the illusion of a mythical Arcadia made so fashionable by Mr Brown and more lately Mr Repton,' Persephone declared; if Lady Freya didn't know war had been declared, she was more optimistic than Jessica. 'I know my cousin the Duke considers this fashion for some sort of false paradise in miniature a conceit,' she went on airily.

Jessica wondered if Jack had ever thought much about the rival merits of the 'natural' landscape and the more obviously contrived ones around him at Ashburton in his life.

'His Grace and I,' Persephone went on, 'believe a natural-looking landscape, constructed at enormous cost to look as if it simply grew that way by accident, is as false as the most elaborate knot gardens or neatly clipped topiary. Although Grandfather employed Mr Lancelot Brown to improve the outer parkland and also commissioned Mr Adam to design follies from which to enjoy it, he insisted the deer park and enclosed gardens behind the house remained exactly as they were. We are very glad he did so as well, since they are so beautiful even Grandmama can't quite bring herself to declare them outdated.'

It should be a master stroke; if the famously aristocratic and abysmally rude Dowager Duchess of

Dettingham approved of Ashburton's mishmash of styles and historical eras, how could the mere daughter of an earl declare them less than perfect? Very easily, it seemed. Clearly, Lady Freya would be a formidable force once she became a real power in polite society.

'How many years is it since her Grace came here as a young bride?' her ladyship mused. 'Sixty or more, wouldn't you say, Miss Seaborne? Much ought to change during such a period of time, don't you think?'

'No,' said Persephone irascibly and who knew what might have come next if Jack hadn't appeared on the terrace as an unlikely peace envoy.

'Good afternoon,' he said cheerfully and impartially, but it was clear to Jessica that Lady Freya considered the rest of them all but invisible in the shadow of a single duke under the age of thirty. If that duke were not Jack, she might have admired the girl's single-minded determination to secure herself a brilliant marriage.

'Your Grace,' the lady exclaimed, sinking into a curtsy so deep Jessica wondered if she might stick and have to be lifted back up with a block and tackle.

'Lady Freya, Miss Corbridge,' he greeted his guests with an elegant bow and managed to hide his amusement as Lady Freya managed to stand without falling over. 'And Miss Pendle and my dear Cousin Persephone, how did you find my poor pensioners today?' he asked and Jessica felt an inexplicable urge to laugh with him, which she hastily smothered with a preoccupied frown.

'Very well, but I believe Godmama has need of my assistance. As you are here to help Persephone explain the mysteries of your gardens to your guests, I shall go and help her, your Grace,' she said.

'Dear me, does my cousin truly need help with such a task, Miss Pendle? Have you lost the use of your tongue, Persephone?'

'Not at all,' Persephone answered quite happily and Jessica wanted to glare at the scheming traitor. 'Mama says my tongue will run all day unchecked. Are you bored with fresh air and the pure country scents of our famous gardens yet,

Miss Corbridge?' she asked with that air of innocent interest.

'Not in the least, Miss Seaborne,' pretty Miss Corbridge replied obligingly. 'Lady Henry Seaborne promised the gardens at Ashburton were out of the common way and I'm intrigued already. We cannot give a creditable account of what we have seen without exploring a little further.'

'True, so shall we carry on with the tour my mother will expect us to have enjoyed when we get back to the house?' Persephone asked majestically.

Lady Freya was out of sight before she could think of a good reason not to obey her hostess's unspoken demand to be left to make arrangements for her guests, then have a much-needed cup of tea and a quiet sit down.

'No, you don't,' Jack murmured as Jessica went to follow the others and, as he had a firm grip on the skirts of a favourite gown, she had to remain despite Lady Freya's fury.

'Let me go,' Jessica demanded furiously as soon as they were out of earshot. 'I will make a lifelong enemy of that girl if I remain here when your aunt specifically asked me to help keep her amused.'

'The haughty minx is determined on a duchess's coronet and I'm equally certain it won't be mine, so if you stay with me she cannot double back and swoon into my arms in the hope of being compromised.'

'But that's why she's here, isn't it?' she asked, now thoroughly bewildered by his contrary behaviour. 'I thought all these young ladies were here to be considered as your potential duchess.'

'Well I've considered Lady Freya and decided I have no wish to wed a noble fishwife. Do you hate me so much you would have me shackle myself for life to such ambition and arrogance, Jessica?'

'Don't call me by my given name,' she said as it was easier than answering such a question.

'You have always been a member of my wider family and will always be Jessica to me.'

'When we were children, perhaps, but not now,' she argued, 'and not when you have a large party of guests who know we are not related.'

'They will accept you are my aunt's goddaughter and that's nearly as strong a bond as blood to the Seabornes.'

'They might accept you believe it so, because you're a duke and think what you like. I am only the eighth child of a viscount, subject to the petty rules and quick judgements afflicting humbler beings.'

'You weren't meek as a girl,' he said with a reminiscent smile that did unfair things to Jessica's insides. 'Then you would damn the rules and tear off on your pony into the hills every day until such stuffy guests departed.'

'And look what happened to me and poor Mercury last time I behaved so heedlessly,' she said painfully and turned to leave him if he would not leave her.

'No, you are for ever running away from awkward questions. So why did you change your whole life because of that one disobedience among so many? I only want to know what happened to that wild girl,' he said as if it truly mattered to him.

'She died,' she said harshly.

'Nonsense. She stands in front of me now, a little diminished perhaps, but I see the untamed minx behind your sea-green eyes whenever you're at your most stubborn. Now and again I even catch a glimpse of a bold spirit of adventure under the starch and propriety Miss Pendle uses to keep the world at bay. I wonder how she will fare if you insist on setting up as the parish spinster. Will the wild woman burst through in a rush of rebellion, or will you finally manage to turn yourself into a travesty of all you could be, if only you would let yourself?'

'None of your business,' she snapped and fought his slackened grip on her gown with a furious swipe at his broad masculine hand.

'Ah, but it is my business. My very personal, intimately crucial business,' he murmured so silkily she was shocked into halting her headlong rush away from the terrace to note the revolutionary threat in his words and that soft, too-certain undercurrent in his dark baritone voice.

'No, my hopes and fears are not your concern. We're nothing to each other, your Grace, and are about to matter less than nothing,' she claimed as boldly as she could whilst somehow still here on the terrace—where anyone could see them on this side of the house, this terrace being visible from the whole south side of the mansion and built to show off the glorious views beyond.

'You have seldom been more wrong in your life and by the end of this fortnight I will prove it to both our satisfaction,' he stated.

'No, for I am right and you're more wrong than you ever were in your life if you believe otherwise,' she countered.

'So you always claimed in the past, but were proved wrong.'

'That I wasn't,' she defended herself stoutly.

'Oh, but you were,' he said and kissed her briefly, a quick, devastating caress of his wicked mouth that was unexpectedly soft on hers. Disobedient fire shot through every nerve and impulse she had.

She knew colour flared high on her cheeks because she felt it flame when he raised his head to watch her as if she might explode, which was fair enough, since she was wondering the same thing. Try as she might to resemble cool and composed

Jessica Pendle, she could still feel the heat and shock of his lips on hers, and now that he'd drawn back to watch her with hawk-like eyes she knew her hand shook so badly she hastily clenched her fingers into an impotent fist.

'You confounded *duke*, you,' she spluttered when she finally found the breath.

'If you think that's the prerogative of all dukes, I'll make sure you don't encounter any others,' he said and she heard the rumble of laughter in his deep voice and wanted to spit furious fire at him for it.

How could he take anything about the last few minutes less than seriously? She almost hated him for making a mockery of her, especially where anyone might see them and then gossip about how lame and shelf-bound Miss Pendle was casting out shameless lures to the Duke of Dettingham, of all people.

'I will bite and slap every single one who dares lays a finger on me from this day forward,' she vowed furiously, ready to do either if he came even one step nearer.

'Now that's more like the real Jessica Pendle

we all knew and loved so long ago,' he drawled and she sucked in a very deep breath, unclenched her fingers and met his mocking gaze look for look, despite the titanic effort it cost her.

'And you are still the arrogant young fool I didn't want to know and certainly never loved,' she lied without conscience, 'and I refuse to dance to your tired tune.'

'It would be a dance to our music, Jessica, not mine,' he said cryptically and walked away, leaving her with a hollow dread in her stomach that felt a little too much like fear and a sharp heat rather lower down she certainly wouldn't be analysing when she considered this stupid scene in the cold light of day.

'I'll not dance to any man's tune,' she called after him as he walked casually away, his long legs eating up the yards, a part of her that she refused to acknowledge wanting to scream frustration at his going.

'Jessica, if you don't help me entertain all these giggling girls, I swear I shall succumb to the vapours and take to my bed,' Lady Henry informed her goddaughter three days later.

Jessica herself was ready to scream at the incessant chatter of the potential duchesses. Until today she had managed to take no part in the entertainments arranged for the Seabornes' guests. Jack had got his aunt to invite this gaggle of girls so he could pick a wife and if only he would get on and do so the young ladies wouldn't be trying so hard to impress, eyeing each other suspiciously for a sign he favoured one above another.

'Since he's supposed to be playing host, where has Jack got to?' she whispered.

'A very good question,' his exasperated aunt muttered back grimly. 'Givage made a fuss about a mysterious night visitor one of the grooms saw in the back lanes last night and I expect that's where he and my nephew are now. Jack said someone was after the deer, but this is hardly the time of year to poach or transport it. Our deer are not exactly meek and tame beasts to be herded off to market and, at this time of the year, the meat wouldn't just be ripe and ready for the pot by the time they got it to a market where nobody asked questions about its provenance, it would be downright rotten and stinking to the heavens.'

'Then he was probably lying to allay any worries we silly females might think up,' Jessica replied, knowing she was only echoing her godmother's thoughts.

'I hate it when men are so ridiculously overprotective. Especially men I can easily recall as squalling babes in their cradles,' Lady Henry said crossly and Jessica decided she wouldn't like to be in Jack's shoes when his aunt eventually got him on his own with a stout door between them and the rest of the world.

'I don't take it well when they keep information from us because they believe we're not strong enough to bear it either. Such masculine idiocy always infuriates me almost beyond enduring,' Jessica admitted.

'Which is exactly why you're so perfect for...' Lady Henry's voice tailed off and she looked hunted, before garnering inspiration from the sight of Lady Freya glowering at one of the marble-and-gilt side-tables as if she hated it and its noble owner. 'For helping me amuse these children so they won't pull caps with one another, at least not before the picnic is ready and their chaperons see fit to leave their chambers and face a gaggle of over-excited young people at last.'

Telling herself it was ridiculous to suspect her godmother's motives because Persephone had chosen to throw her at Jack's head, Jessica suggested charades and even Lady Freya agreed, to her own and everyone else's surprise.

'Wherever can the duke be?' Lady Freya reverted to type and loudly demanded of nobody in particular when it was over and they began to assemble for the promised ride to Ashbow Castle at last.

Unable to avoid this ride and picnic since her godmother's very good impression of a hostess at the end of her tether, Jessica had been forced to grit her teeth and hurry into her riding habit. She ignored Lady Freya's question and thanked the groom who led out a skittish mare always available for Jessica to ride when she was at Ashburton. She fervently hoped they would get a chance to gallop, before Lucia lashed out at

Miss Poole's stolid gelding from sheer boredom or Jessica snapped something short and to the point at Lady Freya.

Calming the precious chestnut thoroughbred as best she could, she tried not to tell Lady Freya exactly what she thought of her manners and her brash questions. It was absurd to worry that Jack might have an enemy capable of stirring an absurd rumour into life and then do him physical damage if the gossip didn't bring him down.

'Have *you* seen his Grace this morning, Miss Pendle?' the girl asked in that over-loud voice she considered commanding.

'No, pressing estate matters must have kept him,' Jessica answered more calmly than she felt.

'Nothing should be more pressing than entertaining guests.'

Jessica looked pointedly at Lucia's impatiently flicked back ears and advised Lady Freya not to crowd the Duke's favourite mare if she valued her safety. 'Perhaps you're right,' she let herself say absently as she moved away, since Lady Freya seemed constitutionally unable to do as she was bid, and blessed the sound of the older ladies issuing from the house in a surprisingly animated group.

'Do you not think it odd, Lady Clare,' Lady Freya appealed to the still-young dowager viscountess, whilst carefully ignoring her very pretty daughter as if she should not exist, 'that Miss Pendle believes his Grace was called away on urgent estate business, yet nobody knows about it?'

'I think his Grace is a very busy gentleman,' Lady Clare replied repressively and Jessica began to like her very much.

'I doubt he would confide in a chance-met acquaintance rather than an honoured guest,' Lady Freya muttered darkly as she finally gave up and moved away.

Jessica imagined what sort of a mistress the girl would make for poor Ashburton and felt as if ice flowed over her instead of bright sunshine. She would demand the lovely old place be modernised and re-painted and re-plastered until it was unrecognisable. The maids would all leave for less demanding posts within a se'enight and even Hughes, the stately butler, and Givage, the land steward, would give their notice inside the month. Lady Freya would make Ashburton a mausoleum and drive Jack back to his clubs and his mistress. Not that she should care, Jessica assured herself, so it was extremely unfortunate she still did.

# Chapter Five

'You all seem to be ahead of me, ladies and gentlemen, so I must be a very tardy host,' Jack observed genially when he finally entered the stable-yard as if he owned it, which seemed fair enough, Jessica decided whimsically, considering he did.

She spared him a slight nod and was glad Jack was too late to lift her into her saddle and tacitly remind her of the shivering desire he'd awakened in her last time he was close to her. His kiss had been so hot and sweet and frustrating she'd ached with some unnameable longing for the rest of the day and she needed no reminders.

Miss Clare and Lady Freya competed to engage Jack's wandering attention, but he frowned at the stable clock as if he doubted it was telling him the entire truth and Jessica wondered what he'd discovered and if it explained his abstracted mood. Luckily her godmother distracted them, herding the chaperons and less-energetic young ladies into the waiting carriages, so her grace and good humour covered Persephone's lack of enthusiasm and Jack's preoccupation.

'Such a fuss over one of the maids dropping a cold pie on the kitchen floor as you can, hopefully, only imagine, my dear,' Lady Henry Seaborne confided in Lady Clare and the two ladies were soon deep in an animated discussion of the shortcomings and fits of temper indulged in by chefs as their carriage joined the procession.

Most of the gentlemen tried to ride as close as they could to Miss Persephone Seaborne, dressed in a light-green summer habit that picked up the lights in her unusual dark-chestnut hair and provided a fine foil for her willow-green eyes. Jessica tried to fade into the background and kept spirited Lucia apart from the mêlée, lest it prove too much temptation to lash out at some lesser beast.

'I fear I must ask you all to fall back, gentlemen,' Persephone said sweetly as her gelding curvetted and offered to kick one or two of their mounts. 'Mercury is not familiar with your horses and, like Miss Pendle's chestnut, only runs easily with his stable-mates.'

Wondering how Persephone had persuaded her easy-tempered mount to give credence to her tale, Jessica nodded sagely in agreement and suggested they ride a little further back together until Mercury calmed down.

'My lovely lad will probably never forgive me for maligning him in such a way, but I truly couldn't stand any more, Jessica,' Persephone murmured when they were far enough away not to be easily overheard. 'I tried to fake a megrim, but Mama threatened to physic me and you know how she saves her foulest medicines up for imaginary ills. I wish I'd held my nose and swallowed her dose now, though, for this promises to be a thoroughly uncomfortable afternoon.'

'At least we're out in the fresh air and I haven't been to Ashbow Castle for years. I dare say it won't be half as bad as you expect,' Jessica replied hopefully.

'Don't lie, you know it will be every bit as

awful as I expect, if not more so. That silly Lady Freya will act as if she owns Jack by right of birth all afternoon and the others will faint and giggle even more than they usually do in order to get his attention. If they ignored him, it would probably intrigue him far more; you certainly do and he's always far more interested in where you are than he is in any of his hopeful harem.'

'You can't call them that,' Jessica protested, trying to be scandalised on the young ladies' behalf. 'Anyway, I don't ignore him and I certainly don't want his attention.'

'Then you're doomed to disappointment,' her so-called friend muttered and fooled Jessica into seeking him out only to see Jack glance back at her as he held a conversation with Lady Clare and his aunt and controlled his own powerful mount without seeming to think about it.

'Miss Clare seems very agreeable, don't you think?' Jessica asked, desperate to change the subject.

'In an empty-headed sort of a way,' Persephone replied grudgingly.

'Well, we can't avoid your cousin's guests for

the rest of the day on such a feeble excuse as Mercury's skittishness. We could ride beside one of the carriages now the road is wider and I'm sure even you can be civil for half an hour or so, Persephone.'

'I'm not,' her friend argued, but caught up with the pack and joined the tail of coaches meandering down the highway to Ashbow all the same.

'Your godmother rescued us from a most foolish predicament last night, Miss Pendle,' Mrs Corbridge told her when Jessica rode beside the Seaborne barouche for a while. 'Lady Ware mistook the way and we were all wandering about the corridors like lost souls when Lady Henry Seaborne found us lost lambs and guided us back to our rightful places. If not for her ladyship, we might even now be stumbling about this great place like a flock of very confused sheep.'

Jessica laughed, then wished she hadn't, as she felt Jack focus intently on her once more as if she was scorched by little licks of pure fire. Curse Persephone's mischief-making and that interlude in the garden for making her so conscious of him and drat her fine skin for showing it on her hot cheeks.

'I fear you are feeling the sun, Jessica,' Persephone remarked. 'Why don't we two take a turn off at the next crossroads and ride up through the woods to avoid the worst of the noonday heat? We'll be perfectly safe in the rides and Jack's woodsmen always keep them clear,' she urged, clearly longing for an excuse to escape the chattering throng so they could canter, or even gallop, in peace.

'An excellent idea, Miss Seaborne,' Lady Clare exclaimed. 'Dear Caroline often finds the heat sadly trying, too. I'm sure she would be pleased to join you in the shade for a while, suitably accompanied, of course.'

'And I shall come along to make sure you are all quite safe,' Lord Clare insisted and Jessica almost laughed at the horrified expression on her friend's face when Persephone realised she wasn't going to escape the viscount that easily.

'I am perfectly well, Mama; indeed, I shall enjoy some more sunshine after spending so many gloomy days in London,' Miss Clare insisted.

Jessica wondered cynically if Miss Clare liked the sun, or wished to stay here because Jack could not abandon his duty as host.

'My head groom and his boy can be trusted with my cousin and Miss Pendle's safety, Clare, since you are so mindful of your duty by your sister and Lady Clare,' Jack broke into the debate to inform his guest with bland good humour.

Much to his own disappointment, if his expression was anything to go by, Lord Clare rode back to the rear of the procession and hungrily watched Jessica and Persephone trot into the Ashburton woods with only the groom and his son in attendance.

'We would have time to ride to Ludlow and back in the time it takes that dreary procession to reach Ashbow,' Persephone said with an urchin grin and urged her lively gelding into a gallop as soon as they were out of sight and earshot of her cousin's guests, Jessica's Lucia hot on her heels and Brandt and his son hurtling along behind them.

Knowing they had plenty of time to spare, they rode up through the wide rides to the wooded hillside above Ashburton itself. Pausing by mutual consent to look down on the great house and its gardens in the distance, they took in the grandeur and beauty of it from afar as Brandt and Joe sat their horses just out of earshot and talked of who knew what.

'I shall miss it sorely,' Persephone admitted with a sigh.

'Why should you, it's your home?' Jessica asked, preoccupied with her own conviction that this might be the last time she saw the lovely spectacle of Ashburton in the full glory of its wide setting between the Welsh hills and the last edge of England.

'Not when Jack decides to wed. His wife won't want five cousins always on hand to disturb their peace, if we count Rich, of course, which I feel we should even when he's not here.'

'Of course you should,' Jessica agreed without hesitation, 'and if the lady doesn't like his family, Jack won't marry her. You are close as his brothers and sisters would be if he had any and he would never evict you just to keep his wife happy.'

'Let's hope he doesn't settle on Lady Freya, then. If she had her way, Mama and the rest of us would be put out of the gates and left to walk to Seaborne House as soon as she had his ring safely on her finger.'

'I don't believe he will choose her ladyship,' Jessica said without too much fear of being confounded, since she had seen his look of distaste when Lady Freya was impartially rude to everyone below her in rank or fortune.

'It's my opinion that he won't choose any of them,' Persephone said with one of those knowing looks Jessica was beginning to hate.

'Even though your grandmother and the society hostesses will accept no less than a Duchess of Dettingham if he's to be free of these ridiculous stories?' Jessica asked, forgetting what those stories were until she saw pain in Persephone's eyes and wished she'd kept her tongue between her teeth.

'Even then,' Persephone said. 'He's a fool to

give up his liberty on the chance Rich would come back if he married.'

'Then you realised as well why Jack's choosing to marry now?' Jessica was surprised into asking.

'Of course I did, the self-sacrificing idiot.'

'I can't argue with that,' Jessica said with a helpless shrug and they turned their horses towards Ashbow by mutual consent.

The closer Jack got to making his choice the more raw and rebellious her feelings became. She had no idea what they even were and didn't dare take them out and examine them too closely. Fearing the headache Persephone had nearly claimed for herself might close in if she let it, she gave Lucia her head and they tore down the hill, then up through the woods to Ashby Hill, arriving at the picnic site in time to join that sedate entertainment.

Jack's staff had set out long before his guests, with barrels of ice to preserve the ices and other fragile delicacies and the steadiest wagons available to make sure all was right and ready. Jessica limped towards one of the mighty stones fallen from the keep of the original Norman lords of

Ashburton and sat with the odd civil nod and murmured greeting as she managed to avoid Jack altogether.

Ashbow Castle had been built in supposedly lawless times to put the rebellious Welsh or unruly English off the idea of outright rebellion. Jessica thought the first Earl of Dettingham wise to site his magnificent new mansion several miles from the original fortress. It was the perfect place for a summer picnic, with a pleasant breeze and none of the heavy sultriness threatening in the valley, but Ashburton New Place had an unrivalled position on the side of a wooded valley, with the lovely panorama beyond, but sheltered from the worst of the wind.

Content to sit and dream for once, she knew many of the guests wandered off to explore the ruins and the hillside beyond, but it wasn't until Jack appeared at her side that she realised they were all but alone. The servants were packing the remnants of the picnic into the wagons and the visitors had strolled off in easy groups; even Lady Freya had been dragged off by her mother to examine the outer bailey and Jessica could hear her complaining about it all the way there.

'I refuse to leave you sitting about like patience on a monument,' he said with a smile that threatened to melt her bones with longing as she got to her feet.

'I was quite happy until you disturbed me,' she protested half-heartedly.

'I know, but I wasn't and now I've done my duty and spoken to every débutante and dowager Aunt Melissa thrust under my nose and deserve a reward,' he said, looking virtuous, and she realised they were deep inside the Castle ruins only when he drew her through a series of twisting corridors and into a surprisingly complete chamber that might once have been the lord's private solar.

'And a walk with me is your chosen reward?'

'No, that would only add to the frustration of the day,' he told her huskily and she was trying to unknot the meaning behind his words when he turned her away from the fine view of the hills and valleys beyond and drew her into his arms.

'No, Jack, we mustn't…' she managed before

it was too late and his mouth came down on hers and magic simply seemed to engulf her in its wake. 'Ah, Jack, you must not,' she murmured distractedly when he raised his head long enough to gaze down at her as if he couldn't quite believe they were here kissing like lovers either. 'Don't stop,' she encouraged him shamelessly and he gave her a familiar mocking look, as if to tell her he had no intention of doing so and many versions of Jack and Jessica suddenly melded into the here and now and took away what little breath she had left.

This was the right one—how they ought to be. How they should have been since that moment of startling awakening when she was sixteen and he not quite one and twenty. He opened his mouth on hers and subtly coaxed her lips apart to accept his tongue within it and all the reasons this could not be floated away on molten pleasure. She opened to him without shame or hesitation, parted her lips so he could plunder with a greed that fed her own intense enjoyment.

His arms held her so close it seemed as if they were made to fit together and she sighed in wanton contentment as her body melded itself ever closer to his, seeming to know exactly what to do when her mind didn't. He sucked in a deep breath, gazed into her eyes for a long, wondering moment, then pressed fleeting kisses along her slender brows, teased more down her pert nose, then seduced all along her jaw and found the tender skin just below her ears. She shuddered with delight at the whisper-soft seduction of his mouth she had never believed could cause such tingling arousal in her wild once-upon-a-time dreams of kissing Jack long ago.

'It's like coming home and exploring a wondrous new-found land all at the same time,' he whispered and it was probably just as well he didn't wait for a reply, since she wasn't capable of making one.

His mouth trailed quick, hot kisses down her neck and into the hollow at the base of her throat and she gasped when he opened his mouth against the pulse beating so wildly there and licked so delicately at it that she shivered with delight and anticipation of more seduction to come, even if she had very little idea what that more might be.

Impatient of the thin lawn shirt under her light riding jacket, he flicked tiny buttons open and settled his mouth on the silky smooth skin revealed, button by button, until a gap opened deep enough to reveal the tantalising valley between her suddenly fuller and heavier breasts, and it seemed to Jessica they knew of their own accord that something delightful was about to happen and came to attention at his tantalising touch.

On the edge of bewilderment, Jessica was relieved to fall back into enchantment instead when he trailed a long finger even further down, then found the aroused tip of one engorged breast to flick it experimentally and give a hum of masculine satisfaction when she gasped with delight and her nipple peaked even more urgently under his teasing fingertip.

A half-sweet, almost painful rush of heat and tingling awareness of him as a man and her potential lover pulled and dragged at her innermost core and she keened and moaned as he grew impatient of those tiny mother-of-pearl buttons and bent his head to replace his questing finger with his plundering mouth and suckle on her through the fine lawn of her blouse. Jessica knew she had wandered into some wonderful new dimension as an even stronger surge of fierce pleasure shot through her and she had to bury her own mouth in his springing black curls to muffle the moans of encouragement her hungry lips wanted to utter.

The thought of all those eligible young women so close by crept into her moment of earthly paradise. It leached some of the enchantment from this wondrous lesson in how much a man could please a woman, if he chose to lavish pleasure on her every sense and rouse this heady, aching desire for more. Reminded of how close they were sailing to the wind, she tried to suppress her soft sigh of pleasure and failed. Her legs wobbled perilously from sheer sensual excitement as he left one breast for the other and she felt her deserted nipple tighten under the kiss-wet lawn as the faintest waft of a warm breeze cooled it, even as he was heating the other and her into something close to desperation.

Jack's mouth was more urgent, promising further delights to come and Jessica let her head fall back against the sun-warmed stone at the side of the ancient window, feeling as if she was attuned so closely to him that speech was redundant. As he began to raise his head to kiss her once more, she leant into the warm stone at her back and felt him come with her, almost as hard and unyielding as the stone as he pressed closer to keep her mouth connected to his and she finally took in how powerfully a woman could affect a man. His hands were skilful and even more arousing as his breath caught and she felt what she did to him. It distracted her from the eternal 'how?' and 'wherefore?' virgins must ask themselves, even when they passionately desired not to be one any longer.

Jessica hadn't thought more pleasure could exist after the deep and almost visceral passion he'd aroused in her with even the most casual of kisses up to now, but suddenly she knew she'd been a fool to think there were any boundaries to this limitless wanting. Yet even as she found out there were no edges to her own fiery and abiding desire for him, Jack was caressing fine lawn back into place, flicking tiny buttons into their equally tiny buttonholes and smoothing his suddenly soothing, ordering hands over her disordered, wanton person to make her fit to be seen by the wider world. And all she wanted was for that wider world to disappear.

It was shock she was feeling and she would soon come back to her true self, she decided as she attempted to make sense of the new world he'd built, then demolished so easily it couldn't have mattered that much to him in the first place. She turned her face aside to guard her raw feelings; far below them a herd of cows was being taken in for milking by the patient herdsman and the hovering dairymaids and she was astonished to hear an echo of the herdsman's dog barking for the sake of a good bark. If she could hear so much drifting up from below, what if their softly inarticulate, almost-lovers' noises had been audible over the sound of buzzards mewing high above and those distant cows lowing? Fighting a desire to hide her face from the very sun itself and refuse to leave this time-worn sanctuary, she tried to reassemble a façade of calm indifference to protect herself with.

'Don't shut me out, Jess,' he whispered unsteadily into the heavy wave of burnished brown hair that had tumbled down on to her shoulders during their passionate tussle in my lady of the castle's once-upon-a-time private chamber.

'You can clearly shut *me* out between one second and the next,' she protested.

'You think that was easily done?' he asked and she looked up and met his eyes, now a hot and flame-shot green, and finally believed it had cost him something after all.

'It was very convincing,' she muttered bitterly.

'You're spouting nonsense, Princess, and have no inkling how I burn for you if you think stopping was simple,' he said curtly, pulling her back into his arms so her whole body came against his and she could feel for herself the steel of tensed muscles, the latent power of his mighty masculine frame and his potent, rigid and unmistakable arousal. 'Now tell me I don't want you,' he challenged into her mussed and lover-tousled hair, as if he dared not risk the touch of her skin under his mouth again, for fear of what it would do to his self-control.

'You can't want me, Jack, I'm not the right duchess for you and I won't be your mistress,' she declared, getting to the true heart of the matter, only to hear him laugh softly in her ear, then pull away to grimace wryly at her, as if she'd said something so ludicrous it was almost beyond contradicting.

'I think we just proved how wrong you are about not being my duchess; as to the other, I should wait until you're asked and you'll wait a very long time,' he told her.

'Very well, then, to put it even more plainly— you should not want me and can't marry me,' she said stubbornly, reluctantly pushing him away so she could wind her tumbled mane into a knot at the base of her neck, then cover it with the fine silk net Martha had insisted on for her ride.

He raised his eyebrows, as if silently arguing with her right to know what he should and should not do, when he clearly did want her acutely. 'I can and I will.'

'The suitable misses and their chaperons out there would be shocked to their core if you wanted one of them in such a way,' she objected a little desperately.

'So would I, for I feel no more for any of them than I would for a roomful of silly schoolgirls, Jess, and never will. Before you decide to list all the irresistible diamonds of the first water my aunt and your mother somehow failed to put on their list of suitable duchesses, you should know pushing me away will not make me want one of them instead of you.'

'It must; I'm a dull spinster and they're all young and lovely and here to be flirted with while you settle on the one who'll make you the best wife.'

'Say just one more word along those lines and I'll drag you out there and announce our betrothal before you can find breath to argue with me,' he said fiercely. 'I won't have you set yourself lower than they are, Jess. Even if I didn't want you in my bed and at my board, I would still abhor hearing you put so little value on yourself.'

'How many offers do you think I have had in my five years in polite society, Jack?' she asked angrily.

'As many as you encouraged or wanted,' he replied austerely.

'None,' she countered.

'Exactly,' he said as if that proved his point and not hers. 'What self-respecting gentleman would offer for a lady who patently didn't want to be offered for?'

'He would if he loved me,' she argued defensively.

'You made sure there was no chance of that by pushing all the eligibles away.'

'Don't flatter yourself that was because I was in love with you,' she sniped.

'When you glowered fearsomely at me whenever I approached after your official emergence into polite society? I'm not that courageous! Your chilling frown of disapproval could be used as a secret weapon against the French, if some brave soul could perfect a method of bottling it and sending it in their direction at the crucial moment.'

'Don't joke,' she said flatly, suddenly feeling very weary of this pointless argument.

'It's no joke, Jessica. I'm deadly serious,' he

promised, leaning his brow against hers, as if he couldn't get close enough to her.

'Serious that I could serve as a deterrent to Bonaparte's crack troops?' she asked, so tempted to waver and let him make the biggest mistake of his life she almost couldn't bear not to.

'Seriously in need of you as my wife, Jessica,' he told her and raised his head far enough to look deep into her eyes while he said so with all his promises and potential to be her husband sincere in his gaze.

'Not seriously enough, then.'

'How would you know?' he asked, as if she was hell-bent on torturing him, rather than saving him from making the biggest mistake of his life.

'Because I would make us both look ridiculous—a limping duchess who spent five years sitting on the sidelines while younger and prettier girls danced and flirted and married ahead of her. Oh, how the gossips would laugh at both of us and only think how endlessly they would speculate about how I managed to trap you so effectively that you had to marry me to silence a potential scandal.'

'You're a fool, Jess, and almost foolishly blind to your own attractions with it.'

'I'm not nearly silly enough to say yes just because you know me and think I would make an acceptable enough wife, Jack. You couldn't insult me more deeply.'

'You think not?' he asked in an aloof and chilling tone that made her shiver, despite the warmth of the midsummer sun and the memory of the heat they had generated between them so recently. 'The worst I could do to you would be so much less than what you have done to yourself, Miss Pendle. Once upon a time you were a free spirit, a rebellious, ungovernable brat who would never have let herself be put at less than her true value by anyone, be they king or commoner. Now you are so quiet and polite you fade into the furniture and, because of a mere limp, you won't take your proper part in the world. That's not caused by false humility is it, Jess? You just won't take part in a game you think you might not win.'

'You know so much about me? Then know this as well, Jack Seaborne—the half-wild girl you claim to prefer would have spat in your eye rather than listen to your half-hearted proposals. That Jessica would not accept a marriage with no love to go with it, and neither will this one. Whether I limped or not, I would still have refused to be any man's "good enough" wife,' she told him furiously.

'At least I've managed to rouse you to some sort of passion,' he drawled as if they were simply in the midst of one of their uncomfortable encounters in the London ballrooms she had so dreaded for the last five years. 'And seen you with your lovely hair down your back and those turquoise eyes of yours flashing with temper again at long last, so at least I *know* the real Jess is still alive and well underneath even if you're not quite sure. I want that Jessica Pendle. I will wed you and no other.'

'No, you won't,' she said implacably and, deciding her hair was as neat as she was ever going to get it while he was watching her, she abandoned her attempts to tidy it. 'Passion isn't love.'

'No, it's better,' he offered as if that ought to do.

'Not to me,' she told him proudly, daring him

to argue as she flounced out of the ancient chamber, not even noticing she had managed it as fast as any other female could have until she was out in the afternoon sunshine and felt the breeze tug at the wisps of hair still trying to escape the knot she'd done her best to confine it to.

'Did you think I would gallantly lurk in the shadows while you pretended you've been tangling with a stray hawthorn bush rather than a duke?' Jack asked softly as she sighed with relief.

'How foolish of me if I did,' she said quietly and managed to catch her godmother's eye before anyone could remark how unkempt she looked. 'I tripped and fell,' she lied blithely.

'Oh, my dear, have you hurt yourself?' Lady Henry asked, with a sharp look at Jack.

'I escaped very lightly when I think of what might have happened,' Jessica replied with a dagger-glance at him of her own.

'You really should not wander about a ruinous building with your disability, Miss Pendle,' Lady Freya informed her with a scornful look.

'Why would that be, Lady Freya?' Jack asked

so smoothly Jessica shuddered on the other lady's behalf, even though she was oblivious to danger.

'Well, I should think that perfectly obvious,' her ladyship replied with the single-minded determination of someone who knew she was wrong and had no intention of admitting it. 'Miss Pendle should resist the impulse to ape those of us better able to cope with uneven paths and fallen boulders, if only for her own good.'

'Miss Pendle is the best judge of what she can or cannot do and knows my home and estate far better than you, Lady Freya. We Seabornes all know better than to tell my aunt's goddaughter what she should do or where she should go, so I suggest you follow our example in future,' he said coldly and Jessica shuddered at the sound of him nailing his colours to the mast in fine, impulsive Seaborne style and suppressed a pained groan.

'That's all very well, Jack,' Lady Henry interrupted strategically, 'but Jessica may be suffering in silence as we speak. No matter how much we value her and admire her independence, I would still be happier if she was back at Ashburton being attended to by her maid.'

'I am not hurt,' Jessica insisted.

'Nevertheless, it's high time we made sure all is packed away and turned for home,' Lady Henry declared implacably and soon there was such a fuss about missing plates and mislaid young ladies that Jessica was able to find Brandt and accept his help to mount Lucia once again, before anyone could suggest she rode home in one of the carriages like an invalid instead.

'And where did *you* get off to so mysteriously?' she asked Persephone once they were riding a little apart from the others again.

'Never mind me—how did you get in such a state?' Persephone countered.

'I tripped over a hidden stone and tangled myself in a bramble,' Jessica lied.

'Would that hazards such as that left me with a glow in my eyes as if I'd been somewhere wonderful,' Persephone teased knowingly.

'And then you would have to come back again,' Jessica said rather sadly and her friend sighed and shook her head as if despairing of such a hopeless case.

* * *

Somehow the rest of the day seemed an anti-climax after the excitement of journeying to the ruins and indulging in fine food, fresh air and gossip. Having only picked absently at the food and done her best to avoid gossip, Jessica ate her dinner with appreciation when the time for it finally crept round. She even managed to limp a little more than usual to give colour to her story of a clumsy fall among the ruins. Apart from a barbed comment from Lady Freya about how it must be such a strain for someone like her to ride such a spirited mount, which Jessica ignored, she seemed to have got away with that scandalous interlude among the ruins.

Even so, she was tired and even a little stiff and glad to seek her bed when the older ladies declared themselves exhausted. She wasn't sure whether to be glad or sorry when Persephone retired to her own room and stopped there. Although she found her friend's conviction she would make the ideal wife for Jack trying, she didn't want to lie in bed thinking about his wondrous kisses, followed as they had been by that ridiculous proposal to bring her hurtling back to earth.

So of course she lay in the luxurious comfort of the Queen's state bed and found she could think of nothing else. If they had taken their amorous encounter to its logical conclusion he would have been her lover by now. Jessica was racked by a shudder of delight at the very idea and stirred restlessly between the fine linen sheets as she wondered if it really had grown suddenly very warm in this lofty bedchamber, or if it was just the thought of Jack's mighty body next to hers that sent her temperature rising so sharply. She doubted there would be much sleeping done if he had the effrontery to join her here, and she the idiocy to let him, but she had learnt enough today to yearn for the feel and sight and scent and potent promise of him naked and awesomely aroused in her splendid bed, if only for one night.

If only she was a more sophisticated lady, she could have laughed off his proposal whilst not shutting her bedroom door in the face of such an experienced lover. At the advanced age of three and twenty, surely she might allow herself one of those without all and sundry lining up to censure her and badger her into a hasty marriage with the man in question? She sighed and considered what her father and all her brothers and brothers-in-law would have to say about that scenario, and realised they would defend her honour to the death, even if she was twenty years older than she was now and truly at her last prayers. Once upon a time, Jack and Rich would have considered themselves part of the bristling masculine pack determined to defend her from harm, real or imagined. Now Rich had been gone so long none of them knew what they could ask of him any more, and Jack was the very man all those quixotic gentlemen would think they had to defend her from.

How very odd life could be at times, she decided, and rolled over to find a comfortable spot among her luxurious nest of the pillows. Should she have accepted Jack's offer, despite the fact he clearly didn't love her? It was the question she had tried not to ask herself ever since she turned him down and now she had nothing else left to occupy herself with to put off answering it. He would be a good husband to her and this afternoon had shown her there would be great pleasure for both of them in their marriage bed, so could that be enough for her?

Growing up surrounded by adults being or falling in love with each other, she supposed she had been very privileged in some ways, but it had also left her with expectations that were unlikely to be met. It was the custom of her kind to make matches of sense and mutual advantage, not love. She had been offered such a marriage by the man she had done her best *not* to love all her adult life and had turned it down without a second thought. Yet, now she was lying so alone in her splendid borrowed bed and longing for him, she was far less certain she'd done the right thing.

When she considered marrying him, then falling all the way into loving him, it felt absolutely right to have refused him, though. It was all getting very confusing. The mere idea of Jack taking a mistress so he could lavish such powerful feelings on her, rather than saving them for his wife, made her ache with loneliness and jealousy. It would break her. Yet she was three and twenty and quite determined not to marry anyone else, so if the chance ever arose to share this wide and generous bed with him, outside the prison of matrimony, of course, she resolved to take it. Having come to that momentous decision Jessica promptly fell asleep, before her conscience could stir and let her know it would still only ever be half a loaf, even if it might seem better than never having any bread at all just now.

## Chapter Six

High above Ashburton there was a vantage point that would have made the great house indefensible against a determined enemy in the days of the Marcher Lords; Jack had plenty of time to brood on Jessica Pendle and his other troubles as he watched for the night visitors haunting Ashburton of late from the Burton Heights. Givage, with his nephew and chosen successor, had insisted on stationing himself near the North Gate to spot anyone entering through the least used and largely forgotten entrance to the estate, despite his rheumatics and Jack's argument that he could safely leave the task to his deputy. Jack's head groom and his son Joe were in hiding near Ashbow Castle, which seemed a likely haunt of night owls and Jack did his best not to know how Joe knew all the best places to lie up.

Jack cursed the rogues who were using the darkness to impinge on his territory and keeping better men out of their beds for most of the night. That was the least of their sins, of course, who- ever they might be. It seemed he had an enemy and the cowardly rascal had already lashed out with this silly story going the rounds about him and Rich. Jack sensed a darker threat building against him and his than mere scandal and he'd be a fool to sit and wait for the next blow to fall. Anyone who thought he could move against any member of the Seaborne family and get away with it would soon discover he had a tribe of ti- gers by the tail. Before he mobilised his formi- dable network of power and influence, he must know who to crush into powder, which was why Jack and his most loyal supporters were spending half their nights huddled in the darkness as they attempted to at least identify the sneaking cow- ard and protect Ashburton from his incursions.

Jack wasn't quite the arrogant and insular no- bleman his elusive enemy seemed to think, but it seemed as well the sly villain should keep on believing it. So by day he did his best to appear no more than a self-satisfied nobleman who considered it his privilege, even his right, to call the finest young ladies in the land to his house so he could take his pick. By night he was free to trap his opponent and if he resorted to his study and locked the door on the world during a long day duchess hunting, nobody knew he was catching up on his sleep. At least once they knew who the tricky devil was, he could neutralise the threat and get a decent night's sleep for once, he decided with a grim smile.

He shifted silently on the hard ground and frowned at the peaceful huddle of Ashburton's bulk in the fitful moonlight as he examined that conclusion more closely. Without Jess in his bed he would never sleep easy. He recalled that wondrous and ultimately unsatisfying interlude among the ruins of Ashbow this afternoon with her and barely bit back a frustrated groan. He was so close, a hairsbreadth away from attaining the woman he wanted, yet they were caught up on a mere word she wanted and he couldn't bring himself to say. Could he blithely lie to her and pretend he knew what so-called love was? No, he decided with another groan bitten back and stored up for use against his enemies.

His fists clenched in the darkness. Jack decided he wasn't a patient man and furtive night reconnaissance left him too much time to brood. He did his best to think of something else as his body informed him how completely Jessica Pendle had enchanted his senses, how deeply she'd wound herself into his wants and needs until the very thought of her made him rampant with frustrated passion. It was an unwelcome novelty to want so bitterly and be denied and he supposed gloomily it might be good for his soul. If he'd been one of the fabled Marcher Lords he would have had to fight for everything he had wanted in life so far, whatever his birth. Instead he'd been sheltered from the struggle for power and fortune that had driven his forebears on.

Growing up with the burden of all they'd gained resting on his shoulders he hadn't thought it such a privilege, but with the right duchess at his side he could finally leave behind the lost, grieving boy he'd once been and fully embrace his rights and responsibilities. He recalled his naïve horror at the ruthless husband hunters of the *ton* openly determined to drag him up the aisle, before he'd learnt to avoid them with a bored shrug and a cynical smile, and he shuddered for his more innocent self. Little wonder he'd bolted for the distractions of clubs and theatres and courtesans and won himself that rakish reputation. Those night-time brigands might be out to relieve him of as much of his inheritance as they could get their hands on, but at least none of them expected to marry him.

And he'd had Rich and Rich's father to share some of it with then. He realised how deeply he missed both as he recalled Lord Henry Seaborne's succinct advice to his son and nephew not to trust anyone to guard their backs but one another, to always make sure their mistresses were clean and stayed faithful while they were paying their bills and to make certain any dice they gamed with were not weighted. He could almost hear his uncle encouraging him to do anything he could to secure himself a bride like Jess now, short of lying. He couldn't swear eternal, unreasonable love for her; she wouldn't marry him unless he did and he would not lie to her, of all people. That was it: stalemate.

Gazing frustratedly into the night, he already knew his enemy would make no move tonight as the darkness began to lighten so far towards the south at this time of year as to astonish a man who hadn't seen too many dawns of late. He almost stretched his cramped limbs and began the long trek back to Ashburton and his neglected ducal bed straight away, but dawn would make him more visible, as well as any potential foe, and Jack knew he was a mark. He was slithering back into deeper cover when movement nearby made him freeze and lie still.

Tense and eager, he flexed his cramped limbs and muscles against the hard ground to ease them until he was ready for action. A blackbird let out a sleepy experimental trill and Jack visualised the rest of the choir stirring and stretching and warming up for the dawn chorus. A swift swooped low over his head in search of unwary insects and he heard the uncanny shrill of its mew as it called to the rest of its family to join in. He almost felt the acrobatic swirl of its sharp wings, but if there was anything else out there in the pre-dawn stillness he could neither hear nor see it.

'It's me, your Grace,' Joe Brandt whispered from far too close by and Jack wondered anew about his under-groom's talent for creeping about in the dark undetected. 'Pa sent me to tell you we saw someone over at the ruins just now.'

'Maybe he followed you,' Jack muttered.

'No, he went off towards the village with Pa hot on his heels,' Joe said laconically. 'Not even an old dog fox would know he was there if Pa didn't want him to,' he reassured his master with a grin in his voice and Jack wondered how he'd never known creeping about in the night was a Brandt family tradition.

'Then we might as well go back to Ashburton and get some sleep,' Jack said and got to his feet, feeling as deflated as a débutante who'd gone to the ball full of rosy expectation and not been asked to dance even once. 'Go home and tell your father you're both excused duties until noon, or

I'll want to know why he can't trust Amos with his precious nags.'

'Aye, your Grace,' Joe said with another un-repentant grin as he faded back into the shadows before Jack could invite him to walk back at his side. Speculating whether Joe was certain of a cosier welcome back to his bed from one of the village girls than he could expect himself, Jack grabbed the gun that provided his excuse for being abroad at such an hour and disarmed it so there was less risk of shooting himself in the foot during his weary walk home.

How Rich would laugh at him for embracing town hours and this new habit of not emerging from his bedchamber before noon. The grin that had lifted his mouth out of sternness straightened and his lips thinned as Jack recalled how long it was since he'd heard his rackety cousin laugh about anything. Which made it all the more urgent to secure his duchess.

Rich was gone; he had wilfully set himself apart from his family and everyone else who loved him. Rich had been his best friend and partner in any mischief going when they were too young and silly to settle to more than enjoying themselves, but their lives had diverged now. Jack took the responsibilities of great estates and managing the wider Seaborne family assets more seriously than he had even three years ago. He'd gradually grown into his role as Duke of Dettingham and head of the family just as his Uncle Henry had always said he would, but Rich had grown more wild than ever, even before he'd disappeared.

What his cousin needed was a purpose in life, and Jack sighed at the notion of Rich settling to anything as mundane as gainful occupation and a family and shook his head. Wherever he was now, Rich clearly needed to cleave his own path through life and it was time to sit back and let him, if only they could all assure themselves that he was safe. Meanwhile Jack had a duchess to secure and a life of his own to lead and it was high time he got on with both. Any guilt he might feel about doing anything in his power to get Jess up the aisle, then in his bed for the rest of her life, was outweighed by her ludicrous scheme to become an independent old maid. He shuddered at the very idea of her enduring such a narrow and excluded life and plotted ways and means to avoid it all the way home.

By late morning Ashburton's usual serene calm had been disrupted by Lady Freya's rudeness to everyone except Jack and a polite battle between Miss Clare and Miss Lloyd that probably wasn't about the coffee stain now adorning Miss Clare's best morning gown at all. The truth was that the young ladies were fretful about which of them might be the 'Dear Duke's' favoured candidate. He was so blandly charming to all of them, whenever they reminded him of their existence by dropping their reticules at his feet or contriving to trip over imaginary rucks in the carpet, then conveniently land in his strong arms, that the tension was beginning to invade the very air itself.

After enduring the role of peacemaker for far too long Jessica told the still half-furious and half-tearful Miss Clare that her figured muslin was even more charming than the sprig one she had begun the day in, agreed with Lady Ware that the manners of some modern young women left a great deal to be desired and slipped away from the house before anyone else could talk her into a headache. With luck the whole party of guests and family would leave without her very soon now for wherever it was they were going today and she could enjoy the labyrinth of inter-connected gardens in peace for once.

She eventually settled on the herb garden as an ideal place to avoid casual strollers and, if she closed her eyes, she could almost imagine herself back home with the familiar scents and textures of stillroom herbs all around her. She sank on to the bench in the rotunda at the centre of the high-walled garden and leant back against the gener-ous pile of cushions left there for the comfort of any visitors to chance on this most tucked-away and outlying of the walled gardens. The air in the neat little summerhouse was filled with the scents of aromatics basking under the mid-day sun and trapped here in a heady medley by the high walls. Jessica gave a sigh of contentment.

Deciding it was safe to lounge about in a most unladylike fashion so far from the house, Jessica shifted to lie full out among the exotic welter of both silk and velvet cushions, closed her eyes and let her thoughts drift. Once she thought she heard the faint sounds of carriage wheels in the distance when the light breeze shifted direction for a moment. Hopefully Jack and his guests had now departed on one of Lady Henry's excursions without her. She wasn't willing to go and find out if she was right, but, pleasantly conscious she was playing truant, she closed her eyes and lazily took in the peace and quiet of this lovely corner of Jack's estate.

The stable clock solemnly tolled eleven o'clock and she relished the idea of having a whole afternoon to herself. Today she wouldn't have to watch Jack court his belles while their mamas looked on with delight or disappointment, depending which one he was considering today. The sooner it was all over with the better, she supposed, then ordered herself not to think about him and his bevy of beauties and closed her eyes in an attempt to blank him and the disturbing memory of their heady encounter in the ruins from her mind.

* * *

Hard to believe she had managed to do so, she decided as she opened them hazily some unmeasured time later and vaguely remembered him striding into her dreams as if he owned them. Difficult to credit she could sleep in this exotic nest of luxurious fabrics with the drifts of perfume from the lavender, sweet attar from the apothecary roses and sharper scents of kitchen herbs and more astringent aromatics in their full midsummer abandon all around her. Even to avoid the idea Jack might come home all but engaged to one of his fair guests she wouldn't have thought she could drift off here like some exhausted harem favourite. She fought the tangles of sleep and did her best to forget those dreams along with that shocking notion. Not knowing if she'd been dozing for five minutes or five hours, she tried hard to gather senses that were finally awake enough to warn her she was no longer alone.

'You?' she observed as she finally opened heavy eyelids, her gaze still half-dazed with dreams of him.

'Me,' Jack replied as if even he was surprised.

'You should be with your guests, or busy with some crisis on your estates, not hobnobbing with a nonentity like me,' she said with a drowsy smile.

A frown twitched his dark brows together and instead of going away as she told herself she wanted him to, he strolled closer and sat himself beside her so she couldn't get up without an undignified struggle.

'I've grinned and grimaced and capered for my guests quite enough for one day. They have gone to Hereford to take the waters, or sip tea at an excellent tearoom my aunt knows, and then shop relentlessly. Young Clare and Sir Gilbert Ware were happy to escort the party while I dealt with the manager of my Cornish estate, who arrived unexpectedly soon after you performed your vanishing trick. I probably won't dismiss the man if he runs off with my entire rent roll after he gave me an excuse to escape. And I won't have you categorise yourself a nonentity, since we never entertain any of those at Ashburton, my dear Miss Pendle.'

'Don't mock me,' she ordered him crossly.

'Not you, but I do deplore your quest to constantly belittle yourself, Jess.'

Forcing her mind to sharpen when it wanted so badly to soften and dream for once, she met his eyes steadily. 'And I shall never join the chase and allow others to belittle me instead, your Grace.'

'What chase would that be?' he asked silkily and moved so close to her supine form that her heartbeat bounced about like a child's ball and her breath came short.

'It's the closed season for most country sports, Miss Pendle.'

'Other than spinster baiting and duke hunting, your grace?' she demanded, driven by a fervent desire for both to be immediately outlawed.

'Open season has certainly been declared on the latter pastime,' he told her with a bitter twist to that fine, latently sensuous mouth of his and she almost put out a hand to smooth it into something more tractable, but just stopped herself in time. 'And if anyone tries to bait you whilst under my roof, they will answer to me. You are Aunt Melissa's much-loved goddaughter and belong here as the rest never could, Jessica. Nobody should forget that fact, least of all you.'

Her turn for a rueful, slightly bitter smile as the irony of that statement hit her. 'I shall preen myself on it day and night,' she managed to joke and told herself it was a relief when he chuckled and seemed ready to return to the half-mocking, half-affectionate relations they'd once enjoyed.

'I know you far too well to expect even a superior look when Lady Freya Buckle tells you she has known my family for ever, or Miss Clare tells Persephone they have been best friends since they were in their cradles,' he said.

'Lady Freya would certainly come up with such a tale if she thought it might depress my pretensions, although Caro Clare and Persephone never could stand each other even when we were children and I doubt she would demean herself with such a lie, even to set down a rival, which I am not, by the way. Although I can't conceive what possessed you to invite Lady Freya and her mama here,' she observed unwarily, 'since she would make you a nigh-unendurable duchess.'

'Ah, but duchess hunting takes great finesse

and cunning, my dear. Leave her out and there would have been far too much speculation concentrated on the other ladies Aunt Melissa invited here.'

'Maybe, but we'll all regret your unwillingness to decide on a front runner soon, with her here to sour our tempers and try our patience,' she warned and shivered at the very idea of having to endure Lady Freya's barbed tongue for much longer. 'I shall have to develop an interest in cataloguing your grandfather's library, since I can't imagine her setting foot inside it for a handsome bet,' she informed him, wondering if she could get away with it.

'Then I shall find an excuse to work there as well,' Jack stated.

'It won't work if you're going to be there, too, and you know very well it would cause gossip if you closeted yourself in there with me.'

'I'll seek out every hiding place you find and make sure you can't use any of them to pretend you're not really here,' he warned. 'And I can't help but wonder if you're ever going to forgive me for whatever it was I did when we were children and help me out of this wretched situation, Jess?'

Jessica turned to look at him more intently than she had dared to since she arrived at Ashburton for this visit. Even yesterday afternoon, when she had been held so close in his arms, she hadn't quite dared fully meet his eyes for fear of what he might see in hers. In London she'd noticed how troubled he was, but there was a new tension about his extraordinary eyes—even a couple of fine lines developing about his mouth, as if he had had to hold it under stern control far too often—and his air of weariness tugged at all her resolutions to resist him.

'What help could the Duke of Dettingham need from a crippled spinster without looks or influence?' she finally forced herself to ask.

'Your sunny disposition?' he teased.

She made herself look up at him as if she had a dozen better things to do than listen to his ill-timed jests, so he sighed and leant over to bridge her still-supine form with his outstretched arm, then looked into her eyes as if to emphasise the importance of what he had to say. She tried to look cool and sceptical despite the heat and overwhelming physical presence of him, so close to her body she could feel him through the thin muslin of her gown and the flimsy underpinnings even a lady allowed herself to wear on hot midsummer days. Telling herself she must not be wantonly glad only a few whispers of gossamer separated her from all that heat and potent masculinity, her only defence against becoming a houri seemed to be to remain coolly ladylike and look slightly amused.

'You have a clear head and sound judgement when you choose to use them. Use them for me, Jessica; tell me what people are saying about the Seabornes. What they really think of me and mine when I am not by to be charmed or revolted by their opinions and prejudices.'

'You want me to spy on your guests?' she asked incredulously. 'No, worse, you would have me make your Judgement of Paris for you, like some unpleasant female pander.'

His look of offended surprise chased the lingering melancholy from his face, swiftly followed by revulsion and a fearsome frown.

'I should have known better,' he said sharply. 'I ought to have recalled how little you always thought of me and stayed as distant from you as you are intent on remaining from me, should I not, Miss Pendle?' he demanded hotly.

She flushed with mortification, even as she cravenly refused to meet his eyes and meekly agree she might have wronged him, especially with him looming over her like some judgemental god. 'Probably,' she told him in a tight little voice even she had a job to recognise.

'Certainly,' he snapped and leant even closer to look deep into her eyes as if trying to find a glimmer of humanity in them, then he kissed her as if he'd decided it was the only way to remind them both she was a woman with warm blood in her veins.

Jessica held her breath as if it might protect her from the feel and taste of him; the sheer physical fact of his mouth on hers. Then, when she had to let it go and take in air at last, she seemed to breathe in the very essence of Jack Seaborne himself along with it, which only made his warm masculine fragrance of lemon and sandalwood, both simple and exotic at the same time, seem even more purely him. His lips teased and tested hers and the infinite temptation of feeling him do the same to the rest of her made her raise one hand in incoherent, unseen protest before she let it steal round his neck and pull him down even closer. One more taste, she promised herself, a moment of bliss she could comfort herself with when he was wed and as distant from her spinsterly self as the planets.

At first his mouth almost mocked, as if he wanted to punish her for trying to hold herself aloof from him, then demolish the very idea she ever could. She gasped air into her lungs in a moan as her traitor mouth softened under his. There was that same hint of incredulity in his kiss there had been yesterday; the secret shock that this was them again, almost addicted to being Jessica Pendle and Jack Seaborne, best and worst of friends as they always seemed to have been, simply kissing each other as if that was all that mattered.

Finding her luxuriating at the heart of a garden full of sun-hot scent-drenched aromatics, he would probably want any woman who tumbled so shamelessly into his arms, she told herself desperately. Sensible Jessica groaned out loud, but he seemed happy to take that soft almost-demand to let her escape this perilous enchantment as a demand for more instead of less.

'If you hate me, why do you turn hot and sweet as molten caramel in my arms?' he asked as if almost as puzzled by that conundrum as she was.

'Because I'm an idiot?' she managed to ask between one kiss and the next.

'A lovely, luscious idiot,' he muttered and deepened his kiss until words were beyond both of them and she gave up on them with a soft sigh of pleasure.

Soothing his large hand under the curve of her spine, then shaping her narrow waist with a murmur of masculine appreciation, he shifted so he lay beside her and gently cupped the soft curve of her breast, as if he could wait every moment it took for her to become as eager for every touch as he was. She gasped in wordless argument since words were currently beyond her and she was frantic for more, so he teased long, strong fingers a little higher, circling above and below her aching nipple, lingering, savouring every step along the way, yet with the huge promise of more to come that made her shudder with delight and arch into his touch with shameless invitation.

He gave a stuttering moan as if she was driving him hard too and took the swollen fullness of lips as if he couldn't resist the wanton response of her eager mouth as he delved and pleasured them both so urgently it felt as necessary as breathing. A wild heat, almost too driven and desperate to endure and at the same time much too hot and promising to renounce, made a blazing need at her feminine core and demanded appeasement only he could give her. She writhed against the pleasure–pain of it and moaned an inarticulate demand she hoped he understood.

Apparently he did, since at least he flicked a lazy, knowing fingertip over the peaked hardness of one of her nipples, then swallowed her soft cry with his mouth again, his tongue plundering deep within her eager mouth as that knowing touch flickered infinitely gently, terribly tantalizingly, over her needy breast.

Uncaring where they were and what all this might lead to, she revelled in becoming a truly mature, sensual woman, luxuriating in her man's arms for probably the last time in her life. Sensible Jessica had another try at pushing that sobering thought to the forefront of her mind, but the restless, adventurous, even-wanton Jess wasn't listening. Jack used that teasing, sweetly torturing hand to palm her breast and gently, sensuously circle and explore it, then praise with a more thorough, more all-engrossing attention her other breast as that stung with his desertion. At least it would have been all-engrossing, if his other hand wasn't bound lower, towards the feral heat that only burned more fiercely at his boldness.

'No, Jack,' she managed on a last gasp of sanity.

'Jessica,' he exhaled in a voice shaken and shot with desire until it seemed potently hers alone, his tone kept solely to seduce Jessica the lover, Jessica the woman. It was entirely seductive as well after feeling like Jessica not-quite-good-enough, since her accident. 'My Jess,' he added as if that solved everything.

'We can't,' she managed to whisper between

lips that felt almost too kissed and probed to move except in responding to his kisses.

'Why can't we? We'd be perfect together.'

Sure he was taunting her, his words made her shy away as if he'd bitten her.

'You never even thought of me as a potential wife until the very minute you landed that first kiss on my mouth that afternoon on the terrace,' she accused.

'That's not true; I've thought about little else for far more than a mere minute, but we've certainly achieved a lot in a short time,' he replied, irony in his deep voice and a hurt she dare not examine just now in his suddenly defensive gaze.

'Not enough to trap you into marriage,' she assured him with the revulsion the very idea sparked in her and obvious in her voice.

Evidently she lacked practice in the so-called gentle art of lovemaking, although to her way of thinking it was more swept along in a runaway carriage than a gentle wooing into heavy-limbed pleasures that ladies were not supposed to know anything about. No doubt a lover of such repute as his Grace the Duke of Dettingham had long ago attained total sensual self-confidence, but for her it felt like the discovery of some sort of primeval force previously unknown to the world.

It would transport her into a world she didn't understand even now, however much she longed to lose herself in it. She shuddered at how close she felt to being so enchanted by Jack as her lover that she would let him talk her into being his duchess as well. She would be the Lame Duchess; gentlemen in their cups would mock Jack for marrying her and the tabbies would gossip and speculate that she must have compromised herself so utterly that the mighty Duke of Dettingham had had no choice but to marry a quiz.

Even with that disaster in mind to hold her back, she still longed for him to sate this huge need inside her in some way only he could. With the Lame Duchess capering about at the back of her mind, she still couldn't bring herself to rip herself out of his arms and demand he leave her as Miss Pendle, spinster, once more. She wasn't innocent enough now to think he didn't want her, as the evidence of urgent need was emphatic against her side, his rigid arousal a stark reminder of the pleasure she could have with him in her bed for the rest of her life as that pool of sweet madness at the heart of her quickened to slake it somehow.

He was half-prone and half-propped up on his elbow beside her so he could watch her as if trying to see what went on in her head. All she had to do was reach out a bare few inches and caress his cheek or stretch up to kiss him and she could have what they both wanted so much. She felt the heat of it across her own cheeks in an echo of the hard flush on his high cheekbones. His torso heaved as he sucked in an unsteady breath and she knew some of her thoughts and temptations must be clear in her eyes as his heavy-lidded gaze told her he wanted it, too, all the more so for knowing exactly what the 'it' was.

'It would never be a trap for me, Princess, more of a delight,' he drawled as if he meant it and a wicked voice in the back of her mind argued it would be all she had ever longed for in her life put together.

'"Violent delights have violent ends,"' she

quoted bleakly, since he'd robbed her of words of her own with that lovely, heart-wrenching promise that he could be right tugging at her good resolutions.

'Been reading too much Shakespeare again, lover?' he asked and the tenderness in his voice, the attempt to joke her gently out of her mood of desolate rejection, tempted her so badly she had to look away and remind herself of reality.

'Yet in poor Romeo and Juliet's case it was all too true,' she said bleakly.

'They were very young and silly, and we are neither. We'd make a much better fist of being lovers, my Jessica, given we're not quite so young and nowhere near as foolish.'

'We're not in love,' she argued softly.

In his eyes she saw the conflict between lying that he could love prickly, abrasive Jessica Pendle, now she'd responded to his kisses and caresses with such encouraging enthusiasm, and the reality of it all. She was three and twenty and the least likely candidate for his duchess if he searched the whole kingdom.

'We could be lovers and friends and trust each

other before any other. That sounds like a far better marriage than one based on fire and sweet little lies and fury to me. I will never betray you, Jess,' he assured her.

'Only think what sort of duchess I would make, Jack. I'd lead you a dog's life and all your friends would mock you for making such a misalliance.'

'Then they would not be my friends and could go hang. I'm very weary of falsity and flatterers and you've never held back from telling me exactly what you thought,' he said, as if that was more important than some ephemeral emotion. 'And you'll be a very fine duchess,' he said as he let his voice sink back into that husky rumble that made goose-bumps break out down her back. 'One I'll desire fiercely for the rest of our days and long for whenever we're apart for the odd hour or two.'

'I'd never thought to marry at all, Jack, and certainly not as a personal favour to a friend,' she persisted with a rather wobbly smile.

'Then think of it now,' he pressed. 'I've been chased by the husband hunters since I was sixteen and came into the title far too young to realise why I was suddenly the most desirable spotty youth in England. I want to marry someone who won't care if my title goes to a mysterious lost heir or I lose my fortune tomorrow. Won't you give me that, Jessica? The satisfaction every passionate husband wants when he knows his wife wants to walk at his side for his own sake, not because of his goods and chattels and this tiresome title?'

'I might prefer you without them and I don't recall you being so very spotty,' she corrected smartly, as if defending him from detractors he very likely didn't have. 'Or particularly desirable for that matter,' she corrected herself stalwartly and gave him a sharp nod as if to make up for the over-supply of encouragement she'd handed out just now.

'Something time has clearly dealt with,' he reminded her wickedly and she fought the urge to kick him in the shins as she had once done, before being banished to the nursery and fed bread and water for the rest of the day.

'Although it has equally clearly done little to abate your arrogance or vanity, your Grace,' she informed him repressively from the disadvantage of her supine position as she wondered why she hadn't simply got up and walked away as soon as he mentioned marriage again.

*Because you can't bear the thought of his gaze lingering on your limping gait and lack of the gliding grace as you walked away,* she scolded herself silently.

'Then you should clearly consider marrying me to depress my pretensions, my torment,' he said with amusement and that terrible Seaborne determination not to be bested glinting in his eyes.

'Haven't you listened to a single word I have to say, Jack?' she demanded impatiently. 'I'm the last female in England you should consider marrying. I'm three and twenty, a cross-grained spinster who is about to retire to the countryside and breed cats. Not even the most hopeful of match-makers would put us together; if you hadn't caught me unawares that day on the terrace, you would never have seen me as more than an irritating acquaintance.'

'Now there you wrong me, Princess. I've thought about you that way since you were sixteen years old and I had such a hard time calming my wayward response to the fiery female temptation you represented that I resorted to swimming in the lake with most of my clothes still on. I had such a scolding from my uncle for it that I'm sure he knew exactly why I had to cool my ardour.'

'I had no idea,' she said blankly, remembering how she had been furious with him and the world in her half-child, half-woman confusion.

Sent to bed with no supper, she'd been glad of the solitude after flying at him in a rage and kicking him that day. Jessica had known she would never walk or run without thought or self-consciousness again; her heart had been so sore about his perfection and the sense of loss it provoked that it had been kiss or kick him and the latter felt preferable, then.

'I'm not sure if it's your worst fault or greatest virtue that you're unconscious of your own allure, Jessica. You're a dangerous woman.'

'So dangerous my father has to fight off besotted suitors in mobs and I dare not go abroad for fear of causing a riot,' she scoffed, trying not to let a weak tear fall as she considered how untrue that was.

'No, so dangerous because you hide behind prickly pride and that waspish tongue you use to set such shallow fools at a distance. Do you think I haven't noticed your gowns are made in a style more suited to a dowager than a lovely young woman? Or that you act as if your youth deserted you before you even made your come out? I would be forty times a fool not to know you hide in dark corners and make sure nobody notices you're young and lovely. Is it just that you despise or fear the social world, Princess, or are you a coward?'

'I'm certainly not afraid,' she spluttered indignantly. 'I admit I don't feel at home in the polite world and would prefer one where I'm valued and of some use.'

'That place is here with me,' he insisted.

'No, it's not; I would be a bad-tempered and awkward duchess at best.'

'No, you would be real, Jessica. If you doubt how much I need that, come and mingle with your fellow guests tonight instead of sitting on the sidelines pretending you're not really here. Then tell me afterwards you sincerely think any of those lovely young ladies are up to the task. If a maid fell down the stairs or the boot boy got stuck up a tree he should never have climbed in the first place, they would have the vapours and retire to their room for the rest of the day instead of coping with it and getting on with life. Not one would know what to say and do with the needy and sick and the dying who look to me for help and comfort.

'You could face down the gossip and lies that hound any man of power in this land with that regal look of contempt you use so effectively to keep the world at bay if you chose to. I need you, Jess; won't you say "yes" instead of forever practising that chilly "no" on me?' he begged.

# Chapter Seven

There was such sincerity in Jack's voice and that admission he wasn't always comfortable in his ducal shoes had caught her on the raw and made her pause. She gave him a thoughtful look and wondered—did he truly need her? Very likely Jack needed someone to unburden himself to, a listener and perhaps even a lover, but not specifically her, surely?

'I can't do it, Jack,' she told him finally and, when he would have argued, held up her hand to ask for his patience. 'No doubt we'd rub along well enough if you endured the derision of your peers and I ignored the whispering and spite caused by such as me catching such as you, but there's only one thing that would make it all possible for me and that's the one thing you can't give me.'

'Now you're talking in riddles,' he said with a wry grin that still refused to take her 'no' as seriously as he should. 'What is this marvellous quality I so signally lack?'

'Love,' she said starkly, refusing to plead for something he didn't feel.

'Oh, love,' he said hollowly.

'Yes, unfashionable of me to demand such an unlikely emotion from my husband, is it not?' she asked and wondered at the brittleness in her own voice.

'To the devil with fashion, but why would we put all our hopes on a fleeting infatuation all wrapped up with Cupid's bows, Jessica, when we could have a lifetime of mutual respect and delight in each other? You can't deny we're as compatible as a man and woman can be after what almost happened just now. Would you truly throw away all we could be for the sake of a romantic delusion? I can't believe I'm hearing such blithe nonsense from you, of all people,' he exclaimed.

'Why do I deserve love less than any other woman?' she asked curiously.

'Because you should know better,' he said as if the answer had been goaded out of him and she should never have asked it in the first place.

Rising hastily from the intimacy of the extravagantly cushioned bench, he began to pace impatiently, as if it was the only way he could stop himself shaking her. So why must her senses note how the sun-warmed herbs gave up their scent ever more sensuously wherever he brushed them when he was obviously far too preoccupied to note such wonders of nature himself? Because her senses were as dazzled by him as the rest of her, she realised in a horrified daze.

Of course she wanted his love or nothing at all; it was what she'd secretly longed for ever since she'd decided not to love him at sixteen. How stupid of her not to let herself see that self-denial of any other future for what it was until now. She was in love with the wretched, arrogant, demanding, wonderful man. It made her feel alive to her fingertips and contrarily as if she was being tortured by some perverse fate, sitting laughing somewhere about this faulty human who had just been offered all she'd ever wanted.

'Then I should accept second-best?' she said and rose to face him, and if she had to storm away ungracefully under his cool gaze, so be it. 'And certainly never demand such an untidy emotion from you or any other man?'

'I meant that you are a woman of sense. How much better it would be to build our lives on this powerful attraction we have for each other, coupled with a mutual respect and our many shared interests, than to chase after a chimera that would fade and die as soon as we were foolish enough to try and grab hold of it,' he argued.

'Then that chimera, as you call it, wouldn't be love in the first place, you idiot.'

'You're the fool, Jessica,' he said bleakly, 'to throw away everything we could have for an illusion that could drive us both mad. You didn't have to watch my mother and father rip themselves into pieces over love, did you? Staying with Uncle Henry and Aunt Melissa, you would have been exposed to the more reasonable Seaborne variety of it. You haven't the slightest notion how it feels to be a child caught in the middle of all that boundless passion, Jessica. I do and I grew up swearing I would never let myself love as they loved, argue as they did—like a pair of wild beasts trying to tear each other apart. They'd storm away from each other as if they hated the very one they loved to distraction, only to turn back and fly into each other's arms in front of anyone who happened to be nearby, as if there was nobody else on earth who mattered but each other.' He stopped speaking for a while and she could sense the hurt of the boy he had once been that his mother and father had let themselves be so absorbed in each other that they couldn't spare him enough love to control their fiery emotions in his presence.

There was a bleakness in his eyes that made her long to go to him and tell him it wasn't the whole story of love he'd seen, or not even most of it from the sound of things. Her parents loved each other deeply, her sisters and most of her brothers had found such a love within their marriages and they were all blissfully happy.

'When my mother died in childbed, even though they'd been told all along another babe could kill her, he couldn't go on without her. My father didn't fall over the edge of that quarry in a moment of rash distraction; he threw himself over because he couldn't live without her any longer. His son and his duchy were not enough, even his duty and the rest of his family meant nothing by the side of losing the woman he apparently loved more than life itself. With their blood in my veins how could I love any woman like that and risk leaving a child she gave birth to alone to bear what I had to? I can't love anyone like that, Jess, I refuse to,' he declared stonily.

'So that's why you went about looking for a duchess in such a chilly and calculating manner? Well, you're wrong. Love doesn't have to be like that. Indeed, it is not like that for my parents and most of my brothers and sisters. They love their spouses and their children and if they lost them they might feel as if half their life had been chopped away, but they love the rest of us enough to carry on, just as your Aunt Melissa did without your uncle. Surely you don't mean to deny that they loved each other very deeply indeed? You will be a craven liar if you do,' she pointed out.

'I don't doubt their abiding fondness for each other, but they didn't have the passion my father and mother had for each other.'

'No, your uncle was a Seaborne, too. I suspect they had the strongest of passions in private, but they were mature enough not to parade it in public,' she said before she could bite her tongue on the implied criticism of his parents.

'I expect you're right, but I'm still the man who grew up with an ungovernable passion ruling my life and I don't want that for myself or for my children, Jess. I can't let myself love in case it takes me headlong to the devil as it did my father.'

'And nothing less than love would persuade me to marry any man, Jack, least of all you,' she stated softly.

'Well, that puts me properly in my place, does it not?' he said with such blandness that she heard how much she'd just hurt him with that clumsy denial even as she could see it in his closed expression.

He was so close she could easily reach out and breach the chasm of misunderstanding yawning between them after her hasty words. She stopped herself with an effort that made her nerves scream and met his stormy green-and-gold gaze.

'I hope so,' she made herself say.

'Be careful, Miss Pendle, you might get yourself a reputation as a tease if you try such a risky strategy on another man. Don't offer less than marriage to the next man you lure in with those promises in your eyes of undreamt-of delights, will you? It might make him as dangerous as you nearly made me,' he jeered.

'I think it unlikely,' she said distantly, thinking of all the lures she had never cast out, all the hopes she had always refused to raise, and now she realised why. It had all been because of this stubborn idiot she loved against all common sense.

'So do I; you've never been a trifler with men's hearts. I beg your pardon. Why not accept me and simply enjoy all we could have together, Jess? What point questioning it when it's strong enough to bind us together for life and we could be happy?' he tried again.

'Please don't say any more, Jack. Find yourself a more suitable duchess among your eager candidates and leave me be,' she pleaded from the heart.

'I can't,' he groaned and undid the distance between them by taking the hand she raised to fend him off and kissing it as if she was infinitely precious to him.

Rampant sexual hunger burst through her defences and fire shot through her as he pulled her up from her seat on the bench and into his arms once more.

'I can't accept one of them as my duchess and pretend not to want you instead, Jessica,' he protested as if he meant every word. 'Call me a weak fool for wanting you so badly if you like, but don't deny us. Don't fool yourself we could ever become old acquaintances who once wondered if they might be more. The thought hurts like a knife through the heart I'm not supposed to possess. Don't you dare pretend you could sit and smile while I wed another, or politely congratulate me on my first-born when he or she had nothing of you in them. You're mine, Jessica.'

'Oh, Jack,' she managed, tears glistening in her

sea-green eyes as they met his burning gaze and saw sincerity blazing back at her. 'How can I be?'

'Because you are you,' he murmured as if that explained everything and he kept his eyes open and compelling on hers as he lowered his head to give her a promise as much as a kiss.

It was heat such as she had never dreamt of even after what had gone before. A delight she couldn't suffocate with any amount of denials and refuse to kiss him back. The need she'd struggled with last night resurfaced and whispered wild temptation. She might not marry him, but for a short while, for now, could she accept him as her lover? A flash of guilt made her lower her eyelids against his hot, questing gaze, for if she accepted him as her lover he would consider she'd implied a promise to be his wife that she would not keep.

Luckily he lost patience with gentle persuasion before she could delve that lie for what it was and flattened his palm over the incurve of her waist, then briefly spread it over her concave belly and lingered as sweet heat made her breath gasp and her lips part even more urgently. She felt the terrible pleasure within increase until it was nigh unbearable and she wanted to press her legs together to at least try to abate the fire within. He seemed to know a little too much about that fiery sensation he'd awakened so urgently and left unslaked and let his hand settle for a moment on the apex of her, where she thought she ached the most.

On fire for him again, as if their argument had never interrupted this sensuous journey into everything she suddenly most wanted to know, Jessica caressed his neck, then tugged at his cravat and his waistcoat buttons in an attempt to get closer to him, as close if not closer as the fine lawn shirt currently in her way was to his skin. She felt him smile against her mouth as he shifted to wrench it out of his breeches and let her questing hands explore underneath. He found the lacing at the back of her gown and loosed it to give easier access to her eagerly roused breasts and the tightly demanding nipples that would have given away her bemused state of need, even if her heavy eyes, lushly kissed lips and shameless fascination with his masculine body did not.

She hummed a sort of wild approval and only just resisted the urge to clench her thighs even tighter to fight the hot drive within her. He let her wanton body slide down his as if it was boneless, then joined her back on that soft silken nest of cushions inside the summerhouse. Lost to anything but him now, she let her thighs part as he sank down beside her again and his exploration grew even more breath-stealing as she felt warm soft summer air on her calf, then her thigh, and his expert fingers trailed up her leg until they were beneath her muslin skirts and lawn chemise and found the naked need of her and she let out a long moan of welcome.

This time she felt against her well-kissed mouth rather than heard him gasp at the warmth and wetness he found there, heard him shush in stuttering breath as he struggled with himself to draw back, to let her go. She managed to blink open heavy-lidded eyes to watch him fight his primitive, masculine urge to take a willing woman who wanted him as much as he did her. Her last chance to claim her lover, she decided in a daze of delighted incredulity. Her only chance to make love with the man she loved, so it was no contest at all for her.

'Anyone might come along and find us,' she managed to say, hearing the words as if from a huge distance when she only wanted to tangle her tongue with his or use it to lick and explore and test his skin, slightly salty as it was with wanting her so much.

Then she would kiss all the way down his heaving torso until she found out exactly how much the breath-stealingly handsome Duke of Dettingham wanted her, she promised herself as if laying aside a fantasy against the drought to come; for now she, Jessica Anne Melissa Pendle, wanted him so much she didn't quite know how she was to get him wherever they were meant to fit, but if she didn't do so soon she thought she might expire for lack of him there.

'Locked the gate, wanted to speak to you in private,' he assured her as he petted and roused and feasted on her as if he couldn't help himself either and sounded as if words had almost become a burden to his ready tongue.

This garden was secluded from all the others

by high walls and distance from the house. The rise and fall of the land, the old bay trees and carefully trimmed myrtles and the venerable old lemon trees, dragged out of their orangery for the summer, meant nobody could see into it even from the hills above the house. As a trysting place it could hardly have been bettered if they'd searched half the county.

Jessica gave a soft sigh of contentment before leaning into his muscular frame and finding out for herself just how badly he needed her. She thought later that he might still have drawn back if she hadn't pre-empted him by exploring him as intimately, if less knowledgeably, as he was her. She clicked her tongue at the barriers between her curious fingers and his very aroused male member. She'd heard the maids whispering how a man went hard at the very sight of a pretty girl he found desirable and even harder if he thought he could have his wicked way with her. Jack was like sheathed rock under her wondering touch and, impatient of his breeches flap and his gentlemanly pantaloons, she fumbled with the buttons and ties until she reached her objective and sighed with greedy satisfaction.

Now he was obviously huge and very aroused; she looked at his rampant need incredulously for long moments, then saw the fever in his deeply emerald eyes, the flush of heat on his high cheekbones, and knew for certain that she wanted whatever that velvet sheathed rod of very obvious masculine need could do to her as well. Wantonly she licked her lips, bit white teeth down on to her full lower lip and smiled straight into the intensity of his blazing gaze. Oh, he wanted her and intended to have her, no need to even ask if he'd gone as far beyond reason as she had.

Bending his head just enough to take her lower lip with his mouth, then find a way past her neat white teeth with his tongue, he suckled on it and let it go before repeating the caress. That heat within her blazed into intense life, ground at her until she moaned a protest into the very emphatic rhythm of claiming and renunciation his mouth on hers set up. She shifted a little and, arching against him, let her swollen breasts abrade the open wings of his plain silken waistcoat. Feeling the sensuous contrast of her naked skin on his clothed torso, she gasped with delight as he raised her on the cushions just enough to get full access to her gently rounded bottom, then round to her most secret cleft as he wound a spell higher and harder with his wicked, questing fingers. For a moment she resisted as she felt his mouth close on hers again, his tongue plunge and withdraw, plunge and withdraw in a suggestion of the drive she felt stir like wildfire at her secret core, but even more urgent, ever more ravenous.

Suddenly the need was too much and she parted her thighs, gave up guarding her last iota of modesty and heard a hum of masculine satisfaction as he plunged a long finger inside her and felt her close about it. It needed only the rub of another long finger on the secret nub she'd hardly even known she had until today, then he sent her over the edge of some sort of precipice and she spun out into thin air and a heady wave of nothingness, of weightlessness almost, and she let out a pleasured moan as she drifted on it in his arms.

Coming back to the here and now, she looked up into his hot green gaze and down at what little of herself she could see from this odd position and wondered for a fleeting moment if that was it; if that was the secret that bound man and woman to each other all down the ages, the mystery of the marriage bed women dreamt of and dreaded in equal part, depending on the man they were to share it with. No, she suddenly knew. A man did not, could not get so hard and driven and downright rampant just to watch his woman spin off over that cliff of delicious lightness in his arms. Come to think of it, he was still hard, driven and just as rampant, and somehow that wasn't right either.

She wriggled on her silk cushions, let her thighs splay just enough for him to watch hungrily as his manhood sprang to even more attention under her fascinated gaze and she lowered her eyelashes to send him a come-hither look she had never dreamt herself capable of until today. There was something so special and unique about doing this in the gentle shade of this sun-flecked building, with the haze of heavy fragrance and herby sharpness in the air all about them and the somnolent buzz of distant bees and preoccupied birds occasionally singing as they foraged for their young. The air and dappled light on her bare skin was almost as great a novelty as his hot-eyed fascination with her, just her, for one long, golden afternoon.

Almost despairing of his self-control, she stretched out an almost idle finger and rubbed it down his quivering shaft and he launched himself at her as if she was his last hope on earth: desperate, beyond reason and passionate for her, Jessica Pendle. Suppressing the reality of who she was and what they were to each other, she almost wept as he tentatively touched her, as if testing to see if she still wanted him after all. As if she could ever stop. Then she shifted, so he could feel for himself how very much she really craved him, and sighed a long, satisfied breath as he butted the blunt head of his erection against her softened, needing core at last. Spreading her legs yet more to show how welcome he was, she held her breath as he entered her, heated her, slid into the very heart and soul of her as he showed her how pleasurable it truly was to have a man inside her, at long last.

'I have a man inside me.' She echoed her own thoughts gleefully, mouthing the words so he could feel them even if he couldn't spare enough of his senses to truly hear them. 'I have you inside me, Jack Seaborne,' she went on with such smug satisfaction he grinned boyishly at her, almost sheepishly, and sighed with infinite pleasure at that very pertinent fact. *My love*, she added in her head and thrust aside the disparity between love and wanting for later, when it was cold and lonely and real in her life, not hot and driven and as right as breathing to have him inside her, thrusting ever deeper until she wondered how much more pleasure a woman could take without swooning clean away.

'Trust me?' he whispered as he came up against the feeble barrier of her virginity at last and hesitated over it, even as she felt the impatience of his much-tried member and the unknown drive to completion beginning to eat away at this lazy sensuality he'd gifted her with until now.

'Always,' she murmured, frowning that he even had to ask as she managed to clench muscles about him that she hadn't even known she had until this moment.

Any danger he might withdraw and leave her wanted, but technically untaken, vanished at that wicked little shimmer of her sleek, wet core and he roared on through her maidenhead as if he couldn't stop himself if his life depended on it. Ravaged, pleasured and just a little stretched and sore, she rode the wave of urgent need for a long moment, then experimented just a little once again.

'Witch,' he muttered, heavy eyed, beyond remembering anything but her softness welcoming his hardness, revelling in it as if she knew what was coming, which he was in a very good position to know she didn't.

Jack knew something had been released within him in Jess's arms this afternoon, something he hadn't even known was there until she called it forth and set it into full and glorious life, burning within him, driving him, causing huge changes in how he knew the world. Primeval, he decided; it was a simple, complex thing that had been in him probably since the very first moment he set eyes on her all those years ago. *'Mine!'* that new Jack bellowed into the darkness as he drove and strove and felt himself let go into her, only her.

For a moment a sense of panic clutched at him. He was her first-ever lover, as well as her last, and he hadn't let her climax first as a gentleman should; hadn't shown her gallantly into exquisite pleasure before he took his own in his driven haste to claim her as his in every way there was. Then he felt the beginning of her climax around him, saw the flush overtake her delicate cheekbones and even her rosy-tipped and glorious breasts as her eyes widened at the huge promise she suddenly knew was hers and suddenly he could forget himself after all, lose himself, obliterate himself ecstatically in the ultimate pleasure with her. He settled his hungry mouth on hers, coiled his powerful body in long, almost tortured thrusts into her hot silky depths and flew. That was the only word he could find in his pleasure-soaked mind—he just flew with her, into her. They wrapped new forged wings about themselves and soared into Jessica and Jack, one special being, or rather two special beings, made infinitely more extraordinary by each other.

Jessica willed herself to soak in all she could of this wondrous singing world in his arms. She felt the mighty pull of shock after shock of infinite pleasure rack her and every pump of his body and reflex of her core around him reminded her so sweetly that he was within her, sharing in that joy, causing it, pulsing, thrusting and revelling in it as his body spasmed in a great final surge and his seed soared into her, that she was infinitely glad. As she drifted back to the fact of this golden afternoon in his Grace's herb garden, she knew she should feel chagrined, or even horrified that he had spent himself inside her, as if he had no more choice about that fact than she did in wanting it. She didn't, however, feel anything of the sort. Instead she hugged the chance of his child to herself and gloated over it. For perhaps a fortnight she would have the lovely illusion to carry about with her that she would bear his child nine months from today, that she would have someone to love when this lovely afternoon was the light and yearning of her empty life, the memory that warmed it.

Until reality dawned, she let herself lie under him, revelling in the weight of her lover on her stretched-out torso for the brief moment she knew he would allow her to take it. She sucked breath into her lungs, panted her still-roused breasts against his chest as she wantonly enjoyed the pulse of life running so sure through both of them, as if they were as necessary to each other as air. Sweet little aftershocks ran through her as he raised heavy lids over warm green eyes and she marvelled that she could ever have thought him truly hard-hearted. Except in one particular very potent area, where it was very desirable for him to be so hard of course, she reminded herself wickedly, and once more a quiver of pleasure shook through her and him still inside her and he sleepily chided her as a sweet wanton.

They lay like that with most of his weight rested on his arms as he laid the rest against her stretched and pleasured body for perhaps another infinitely precious minute, while gentling aftershocks of delight still shook her now and again and he seemed almost unconscious with the sheer pleasure of what they had just done together. It couldn't last for ever, and at last he raised his weight from her and straightened his arms and pulled back a little, so his even now half-roused member at last left her clinging sheath. He brushed a kiss on her pouting lips and rolled over with her in his arms, so she lay half across him instead and he smiled up at her as if she was all he had ever wanted.

'I think those were indeed the "deepest and strongest of human emotions" I could experience, my dear,' he managed to say huskily—trust him to quote her own silly sayings back to her.

'It was a start,' she said with a wry smile as she let herself play with his midnight-dark curls and wished she thought it truly could be the be-ginning of love.

'You are a very demanding lover, Miss Pendle, if that is as high as you rate today's performance,' he informed her as he propped himself on his elbow once more, so he could look down into her face as if learning the look of it with passion and delight, heavy-eyed and gloating, still on it.

'And that's the pot calling the kettle black if ever I heard it,' she replied, shamefully glad that his eyes seemed to first cling to the sight of her lush mouth, still swollen from his kisses, then move down her exposed throat to gaze fascinated on her rose-tipped breasts that even to her looked full and generous and almost self-satisfied as her gaping gown utterly failed in its mission of covering Miss Jessica Pendle from the eyes of the nobility for once.

'Somehow I think there's nothing I would ask of you that wouldn't be met with eager encouragement today,' he drawled, the apparently idle hand he wasn't using to prop his chin on whilst he inspected her with those glowing green-gold eyes wandering in the wake of his gaze and making her feel as seductive and seducible as the heat building in his eyes once more told her he found her.

'What time is it?' she asked reluctantly, wondering if either his guests or one of his household might come looking for him and find a very unexpected scandal instead if they tried the door of the herb garden and found the master of the house was locked inside it with Lady Henry's lame goddaughter.

He sighed and seemed to renounce the idea of seducing her all over again with extreme regret. 'Time I made a discreet exit before someone comes looking for you and fails to find you at the same time as they can't find me, I suppose,' he admitted with a wry grimace at being the lord and master of so much that he rarely had time to be absent from it all without someone noting the fact.

'Then we will have to do something about your scandalously ruffled appearance, my lord Duke,' she told him with a smile she hoped told him she understood he had responsibilities far beyond satisfying her so extravagantly twice.

'Try that and we will neither of us get out of here before we're due to dress for dinner and we don't want a scandal marring the announcement we will be making tonight do we, my dear?' he said so tenderly she almost gave in to the inevitable and simpered and meekly agreed to become his wife as ordered.

'There will be no announcement. I refused you, Jack,' she said starkly instead.

'What a poor memory you have. I, on the other hand, distinctly recall that you just refused me absolutely nothing, Jessica,' he argued as he subjected her to a cool scrutiny that made her feel guilty and humiliatingly naked under his now-angry gaze.

'I still won't be your wife,' she said, stubbornly setting her chin aloft even as she scrambled for ties and lacing and looked about for the hairpins he must have pulled out of her heavy mane of hair while her attention was elsewhere.

'You won't be any other man's wife either after that,' he said and she flinched at the reminder that a man expected a single lady to be chaste and virginal on her wedding night.

'I was never going to be anyway,' she said with a shrug that dismissed all the hopes and dreams of her kind as if they were not relevant to her, which indeed they were not. He hadn't altered any of that by making her his lover.

'So you decided, as soon as you recovered from the fever and agony you must have felt after injuring that ankle and spending a night out on the moors under your fallen horse and soaked to the skin, that you would never have the things all of us secretly crave and perhaps even expect as our right, didn't you?'

'Yes,' she agreed simply, as she finally got her shift back into its accustomed place and twisted around so he could deal with the laces of her gown, since he had undone them in the first place and she couldn't reach them without wild and un-dignified contortions.

She held her breath and fought a shiver of de-light as his long fingers brushed her back even through the fine layers of lawn and muslin now between them. Somehow she had to make him see that to assume she would marry him because they had made love was an arrogance too far even for the Duke of Dettingham.

'I was reckless and stupid and the poor animal paid the price for both of us with his life, but I knew I would never run or even walk as others do so easily again, or dance or be expected to flirt lightly with young gentlemen who might want to marry the passably pretty youngest daughter of a viscount. If I didn't already know it, those young gentlemen soon made it clear that I fall sadly short of their ideal.'

'Young puppies,' he muttered disparagingly.

'Were you, Jack? I really can't remember,' she said softly and felt him flinch even as his hands came down on her shoulders to turn her round and face him.

'I never meant to slight you, or imply you are less now than you were before your accident, Jessica,' he insisted so solemnly that her heart threatened to soften against him at the worst possible moment. 'I was just a heedless young idiot with half the world at my feet and didn't dare speak to any young lady for longer than a minute in those days, lest she or her relatives decided it was a sure sign I must want to marry her. To think that my determination not to be tricked or badgered into marriage when I felt too young to even know who I was could rob me of you for the rest of my life—now I just don't have enough words to tell you how I regret not realising from the outset that you were different from all those idiotic young duke hunters who saw me as a passably acceptable youth with a delightful title they could much more readily fall in love with than the boy who went with it, Jessica,' he told her as if he was in court swearing it in front of a judge.

'I can easily see how such shenanigans might put you off the company of young ladies of any variety,' she conceded, wondering if that early experience of being the focus of ambition had made him even more resistant to loving any woman he might choose as his duchess.

'It certainly didn't put me off you,' he said with a self-deprecating grin. 'I told you how acutely you affected me that last time you came here with your parents when you were sixteen and I was nearly one and twenty. If I avoided all but the most formal contact with you when we were in London, it was probably because I was afraid of you.'

'You were never afraid of anyone in your life,' she scorned.

'I'm certainly afraid of you now, Jessica, afraid you'll whistle all we could have down the wind because I can't offer love along with everything

I am. Afraid I'm not fit to be a good woman's husband.'

'You're fit to be any woman's husband,' she defended him from himself so fiercely she nearly groaned out loud when she saw his satisfied smile. 'Except mine,' she added hastily.

'I think we just established how fit and ready I am for that task,' he murmured as he brushed a wicked kiss on to the incredibly sensitive spot where the back of her neck met her spine and shivers of delight ran up her backbone.

'If only that was enough to prove to me we should wed, Jack, but it needs more than compatibility in bed to make a good marriage.'

'It seems a good place to start,' he replied half-seriously. 'That went far beyond mere sexual compatibility; it was a banquet of the senses— wildfire and champagne compared to a rush-light and bad ale.'

'I'm not the one making it less than it is, Jack, you are.'

'Then don't say no; if you believe so deeply in this love of yours, give me a chance and I'll learn to say it for your sake, Jess. I must be halfway there already to beg like this. Love has never been something so wonderful it could be better than what we just shared for me. More of a falsehood wrapped in misery than the blessing you seem to think it.'

'I've seen too much love in my own family not to believe in the something wonderful, whatever you happen to call it,' she replied as she wavered between agreeing to be courted, in secret, until they convinced each other one way or the other they could love each other, or that she might and he never would.

'Then don't deny us the same chance, Jessica,' he pleaded and she heard the real urgency in his deep voice and wavered.

'Perhaps, but promise me there will be no announcements and certainly no public flirtation to bring the wrath of Lady Freya down on me, Jack,' she cautioned.

He gave a sigh of something like relief, even if it was laced with exasperation, turned her about and rested his forehead against hers as if he had to share his relief that she hadn't shut him out completely. 'I would have battered your defences down night and day if you'd refused me even this much hope, you know that?' he murmured and she saw from the flash of heat and steel in his eyes that he spoke truly.

'Do you think I don't know you by now, Jack?' she asked softly and felt a wave of tenderness for the great, handsome idiot wash over her as she pulled far enough back to raise a hand and smooth his sable hair into some kind of order, since she had mussed it up again without consciously knowing what her hands were at.

'I hardly know myself since you came to Ashburton,' he said ruefully.

It seemed as if a tentative new path had opened up for them after all, even if she wasn't sure it would lead them to duke and duchess, lovers or as divided and distant as they were before they began.

'Well, that's two of us; I certainly don't know myself when I'm with you now,' she replied with a cautious smile and a shake of her suddenly aching head.

'Then don't leave me, Jess,' he said bleakly,

then turned on his heel and strode away, saving her a struggle for dignity as she forsook him.

So she let her shaky legs wobble and sank back on to her nest of cushions to try to collect herself. Compared to the woman who'd entered this seemingly enchanted garden this morning, she felt a very different Miss Pendle indeed. After last night's wild dreams and her passionate yearning for Jack Seaborne in her bed, she supposed she ought not to be surprised she had allowed him to take the ultimate liberty and become her lover. No, she had to be truthful with herself; she hadn't just allowed it, she had blatantly encouraged him and adored every kiss and caress and arrogantly annexed freedom along the way. Searching her conscience for objections, she realised she didn't have anywhere near enough for her peace of mind. How had he shifted her world so radically she'd agreed to be secretly courted by the Duke of Dettingham when her way of life had been set, recorded and unchangeable until today?

# Chapter Eight

Jack strode away by the most circuitous route he could think of to reassemble his racing thoughts and make himself into a cool and collected duke who was fit to be seen once more. Doing his best to avoid the more obvious haunts of any other stray young ladies who might have managed to avoid the exodus and be lurking, he resorted to the Circle of Hades, with its statue of the grinning, greedy, open-mouthed king of that place guarding a crumbling grotto and a mercifully faded and rather badly executed fresco, put there by a misguided ancestor who wanted to ape Sir Francis Dashwood and his notorious Hell-Fire Club. It was a part of the whole, he supposed grudgingly, but at least the garden's unsavoury reputation meant he could brood over Jessica's intransigence here without being twittered at by simpering young ladies.

There was still no news of his cousin Rich either, he recalled with increasing frustration, nor any sign of the agent he'd dared trust with finding him meeting with success. And whoever was creeping about the estate at night had managed to evade Brandt. Now the only woman he could think of as his wife had turned him down, not quite finally, and he ached for her. He felt bruised and battered somehow by that refusal of hers, even if she had agreed to let him persuade her further. As if he could walk away from the irrational, magnificent female after that astonishing sensual encounter in the herb garden. He had to fight an impulse to march back and carry on persuading her using every underhand method he could come up with, but it was too soon.

He paced more vigorously instead and hoped no ladylike ears were attuned to his savage curses as he considered other ways of unpicking this confounded conundrum Rich had set him. How could he flush his heir out of hiding and take the shadows from under his beloved aunt's eyes if he couldn't bring himself to marry and free Rich of that burden of expectation he dreaded so much? Yet how could he marry anyone other than the ardent, infuriating Jessica Pendle, who stubbornly refused to marry him? Any sensible lady would consider herself bound to wed him after he'd taken her maidenhead with her willing and very passionate co-operation, scruples or no—but not his Jessica.

So why was she really being so mulish? He strode restlessly about the garden and decided it was a good place to curse and pace like a madman, since a madman had clearly made it, or caused it to be made—the thought of any of his noble ancestors digging their own soil or building their own grottos, even one in as dubious taste as this one, almost made him laugh.

How could she think he would tamely let her go? The very idea of another man ever watching her with lust in his damned impudent eyes, let alone touching her on any intimate level at all made him long to take a sledgehammer to this particular ancestor's creation and personally demolish everything the wasteful idiot had had built to relieve his fury. He would have to find Rich another way if he couldn't persuade Jessica she was the only woman he could ever marry now he'd finally realised his perfect duchess had been under his nose all this time. He told himself she was a rational female, on every other subject but marriage, and would be sure to see sense in the end. All he had to do was keep seducing her until she realised a lifetime of mutual pleasure in his bed was a far better notion than the barren alternative she seemed to have mapped out for herself.

That resolution made, he let himself remember her ardently innocent response to him, and the stridently demanding arousal of his body at the very thought of her lying wordless and passion shot in his arms again shocked him nearly as much as the primitive roar of possession that he only just stopped himself shouting out loud. He had to fight his inner beast not to march into the herb garden and ravish her until neither of them remembered their own names. Yet she'd turned him down. How could he fully make love to her again unless he was sure he could convince her to marry him? If she refused to even consider it without that sweet little lie he couldn't tell her, she might conceive his child, then run away with that precious burden—and how could he endure the catastrophe of losing both Jess and their child?

The very thought of losing her made him think seriously about finding that sledgehammer after all. Jack paced the unhallowed paths of this misbegotten garden and worked on methods of persuading Jessica to accept him so they could make babies to their hearts' content. She was his, to the last stubborn inch of silken skin and shining hair on her lovely head. What a dance she'd lead him when he finally persuaded her to say yes, he decided, with a smile he might have called nauseating if he'd seen it on another man's countenance.

Jessica got through the rest of the day with her reputation unscathed more or less by luck. Glad that the other ladies were tired, too, if for a very different reason, and didn't seem in the least bit curious about what she had been up to while they were enjoying a pleasant excursion, she managed to cite a little too much walking about the coun-

tryside while they were gone as an excuse to
seek her bed early. Yet once safely there, with
her door secure against any stray dukes who happened to be wandering about their own house in
the middle of the night, sleep was impossible.
How could she sleep when her whole world had
changed so radically today she hardly recognised
it any more? She was astonished neither her godmother nor Martha had noticed any difference
in her when it felt to her as if the Jessica Pendle
who had got out of this elaborate bed this morning was a very different one to the Jess who was
lying sleepless in it now.

Martha had been surprised when she'd asked
for a bath before dressing tonight, of course, but
that was easily explained away by stiffness from
that careless exercise she was supposed to have
taken and Jessica wondered guiltily if she had
more talent for deception than was quite comfortable. But she had taken some careless exercise after all, so it wasn't a complete fiction. Heat
stung her cheeks as she recalled the nature of it
and she burned for Jack's amorous attentions in
the most shameless fashion. If she had said yes to

him, she supposed it would have been tacitly accepted that he would be sharing her bed tonight, even if his family and staff kept up the pretence he was tamed and docile enough to wait for his wedding night to seize his bride and possess her in every way to their mutual satisfaction.

And so much of her wanted to be seized, to be so overcome by their need of one another that the choice she faced now would simply fade into an assumption that they would marry. Then she would find herself walking up the aisle to say 'I do' without ever having to admit that was all she really wanted out of life. She tossed and turned on her luxurious feather bed and told herself a little self-denial would be good for her—maybe even for Jack as well—except it didn't feel good. Last night she had been haunted by dreams and fancies of how it would feel to have Jack as her very male and powerful lover; tonight she knew exactly how it felt and wanted him in her arms, in her bed—in fact, any way she could have him, she realised with another shamefaced blush at her own headlong wantonness.

So why didn't she unlock her door and let him

in? Maybe he wouldn't come anyway; she had said her 'no' and he might be gallant enough to accept it after sober consideration, so why would he come to her and try to alter her perceptions of love and marriage? Because she wanted him to, she realised as frustration ground at her slightly sore feminine core and she wriggled against the cool linen sheets to try to find a position where she could fool herself she might sleep despite it. Yet what would it feel like to sleep next to Jack? a sneaky little voice asked in her head. Like all her birthdays had come at once, wanton Jess replied, and she pushed her hot face into the pillow on the other side of the bed where he might have slept after mighty exertions, if he were only here, and tried to cool her hot cheeks on it.

Try as she might, she couldn't be ashamed of herself and something told her that if Jack really did come knocking at her door she would spring up and eagerly unbolt the door before he could raise his hand to make a second soft tap on the splendid carved-oak panels of the Queen's Chamber. Yet the hours ticked by and there was only silence outside while her bedclothes became ever more tangled with her restless thoughts and longings, and the Duke of Dettingham stayed sternly in his own elegant wing of the house. Cliché though it might be, she felt she'd made her bed and now had to lie lonely in it for the lack of a single word.

So why did it matter so much he should say it? He'd promised her marriage and his fidelity and he was a man of his word; he clearly wanted her and she wanted him so much that the restless need ground and prodded and pinched at her until she wondered if she would ever sleep for the lack of him. Couldn't that be enough? There would probably be children as well and the thought of them made her smooth her hand over her flat belly and marvel that one might already be growing there after that magnificent consummation in the herb garden. She gave a soft sigh at the very thought of growing big with Jack's child and lay back against her pillows to stare at the rich-silk canopy over her head and dream of little lords and ladies, running about Ashburton as they squabbled and grew and laughed together. It was something she wanted so much that tears stung her eyes, but loving their children together could never be enough for her if she weakened and married Jack.

Whilst they wanted each other with this fevered urgency she could never imagine waning, it might be enough. For the time while they learned each other's habits and quirks and battled now and again for this or that, maybe it would be enough. Then the time would come when Jack grew bored with domestic disharmony and his wife being forever pregnant or preoccupied with their family, then he would feel trapped and irritated by their marriage and she would gradually see less and less of him as the business of the estate and the vast Seaborne interests and the company of clever men and less occupied women absorbed him. To endure such a life, when she felt as if Jack had put the moon and stars within touching distance for her today, would surely be worse than the arid single life she had mapped out for herself so blithely before she came here.

So she had her answer, even if she didn't like it very much. She would not marry the Duke of

Dettingham unless he could convince her that he truly loved her, and that seemed about as likely as day becoming night, so she would not marry. Ever. For a determined spinster she had some very shocking needs, wildly seesawing emotions and bitter frustrations to cope with, but she turned over once again, buried her head in her pillow and assured herself the worst of them would pass once she was away from Ashburton and its arrogant master. She heard the hour strike three in the distant stable-yard and knew there was no chance of Jack visiting her tonight, when it would be light again so soon at this, the peak of the summer.

Jessica thumped her misused pillow as if it had sneered at her neediness and told herself it didn't matter that he clearly didn't need her as she needed him, then burrowed her head into it to hide her tears and try to pretend to herself she wasn't crying because Jack didn't love or even want her. She was tired and it wasn't every day a virgin lady became a wanton houri in a handsome, eligible and nigh-irresistible duke's arms, so surely she was allowed to be a little overwrought? It wasn't as if he loved one of the other young ladies here to be picked or rejected as suitable duchesses either, even if he might well marry one of them now she had turned him down, so how could the lack of his love hurt her when they wouldn't have it either?

Because it was a golden future they could have had, a dream she should never have let herself dream when more than half of it coming true depended on a man like Jack. He was untameable, aloof, uniquely himself, handsome as the devil, clever as a fox and strong as a Titan for her, but she couldn't deny those attributes added on made him a lover most females would cross countries and ford raging torrents to earn in their bed. His duchess would be a very lucky woman and sensible enough to realise half a loaf was so much better than the life without any bread at all that Jessica would now have to resign herself to all over again. It was so much easier not to miss what you had never had, she reminded herself mournfully as she finally succumbed to sleep, because being awake suddenly seemed so unattractive.

\* \* \*

'Good morning, Miss Pendle,' Jack greeted her the next morning as if he felt as sunny as the morning outside.

'Good day, your Grace,' she murmured unenthusiastically, helping herself to toast and coffee, then finding a seat as far away from him as she could get without moving out into the next room.

'And I wonder what plans my aunt has for it,' he remarked genially and Jessica wondered sourly if he had already begun his campaign to charm another woman into becoming his duchess, since so many of them were present and seemed willing to hang on his every word.

'Botanising in the park, I believe,' Miss Clare said unenthusiastically.

'Sketching in the gardens,' Lady Freya said, pulling a wry face that almost made her look human for once.

'Helping arrange the flowers,' Persephone put in as if trumping an ace.

'Such heady delights,' Jack said with the careful blankness of a gentleman who knew he would be elsewhere and far better entertained.

He and Lord Clare and Sir Gilbert Ware were due to meet some of the local gentlemen for a tour round the model farm Jack had set up on the estate, to try out new methods of agriculture and perhaps encourage some of his more-conservative tenants to believe the sky would not fall on their heads if they altered methods that had been in place very nearly since Adam was a gardener. She recalled Eve had spun while her husband gardened and wondered if she had found it as mundane as modern females did when they were sidelined for the more interesting toil of men.

'And what do you do, Miss Pendle?' Lady Bowland asked as if she had her stern eye on shirkers like her after yesterday.

'I believe I am to prick out patterns for the new seat covers Lady Henry plans for the chairs in the winter dining-parlour, Lady Bowland,' she replied as politely as she could manage while fighting the strong desire to tell Lady Freya's mama to mind her own business.

'Well, that is a useful and suitable occupation and you can hardly be expected to make more strenuous use of your time, can you, Miss Pendle?'

'Can I not, your ladyship?' she managed to say calmly, because her ladyship was clearly suspicious of a lady who had contrived to be left behind at the same time as their host cried off his engagements yesterday.

Luckily she could not know how very right she was, so Jessica ate her toast, sipped her coffee and waited.

'Not with your unfortunate disability,' her ladyship persisted.

To Jessica's silent astonishment, Lady Freya looked more uncomfortable than Jessica felt at the Dowager's attempt to set her in her place, wherever that might be. A lifetime of keeping company with Lady Bowland and Lady Freya's pompous elder brother might easily make the girl believe herself better than anyone not born a Buckle, so maybe there was hope for Lady Freya after all. Jessica decided she would have become a rampant husband hunter herself if she had been immured in Sussex in their company for the first eighteen years of her life, if only to find an acceptable way out of it.

'Are you planning a vigorous walk yourself then, Lady Bowland? Or perhaps you have in mind an adventurous ride about the countryside to enliven that sketching party for the younger ladies?' Jack asked, so coolly polite it was all but an insult.

'Why, no, your Grace.'

'Then why would Miss Pendle's slight limp exclude her from any or all of the activities just outlined so succinctly for today?' he persisted despite a pleading look urging him not to jump to her defence from Jessica and what she judged, from a well disguised wince, to be a hearty kick under the table from his cousin Persephone.

'Because she cannot do as other young women do,' Lady Bowland persisted and even Jessica wished she would let the matter drop now.

'Can you not, Miss Pendle?' Jack asked her as if surprised to hear it.

'I do not dance,' she said concisely.

'If that's the summary of your limitations, then you're not missing much,' he said with such a rueful, intimate smile she couldn't help returning it like a besotted débutante.

'No indeed,' Persephone said, leaping gallantly into the speculative silence. 'Last time I took to the dance floor I had both feet trodden on by different young gentlemen with less natural grace than an elephant. Then someone stepped on the hem of my favourite ball gown and ripped it so badly it went to the ragman.'

Luckily the other young ladies launched into counter-tales of their misfortunes on the dance floor and Lady Bowland's spite and Jack's defence faded into memory as Persephone had intended. Yet most of Jack's guests treated her differently after that uncomfortable scene. Lady Bowland was rude and dismissive as ever, but the other chaperons and even their beautiful charges took more notice of her than usual. It finally dawned on her they'd begun to suspect that *she* might be the next Duchess of Dettingham and were determined not to offend such a potentially powerful lady, even if it meant giving up hope of standing in her shoes.

'How could you?' she demanded when she managed to drag Jack into his study as he came in from his early morning ride long before his guests were stirring.

It was now three days since their wondrous meeting in the herb garden that haunted her almost-sleepless nights and any dreams she did manage to have. Eyeing him in all his vigorous power and glory and deciding he'd managed to forget all about it and sleep like the innocent he probably never had been, she stamped her good foot and glared up into his wickedly alive green eyes and smelt man, a hint of horse and the fresh morning air on him and ordered herself not to want him.

'How could I what, Princess?' he asked as he threw his hat and gloves on the table and annoyed her even more by hitting his mark even from ten feet away while coolly facing her wrath—her *justified* wrath, she corrected herself and reminded herself she hadn't come in here to admire anything about him.

'Let them all think I'm going to marry you,' she raged.

'Because I am?' he suggested, the laughter he

so carefully confined to his gold-shot eyes somehow even more wicked for being so unashamed.

'No, you are not. I told you "no"—how much clearer could I be? No, I won't marry you. No, I won't be picked over and inspected by your guests before they shake their heads at your inexplicable fancy to take a quiz for a wife. No, just no, Julius Seaborne,' she finished on his true name in the hope he would realise she meant it.

'I love it when you rage and rail at me as if we were already wed, my dear,' he drawled and obviously hadn't listened to a word she said.

'I am *not* your wife,' she shouted at him.

'Not yet,' he countered and pulled her close before she could find something to throw at him and make herself feel better. 'You're right, though, it has been too long,' he informed her before lowering his head to kiss her so urgently it seemed she'd been wrong about his nights and his dreams after all. 'Far too long,' he managed to say as he raised his head only long enough to breathe, then kissed her again.

'I didn't say anything about that,' she managed

to murmur when breathing became a necessity again.

'But you knew I was waiting,' he said as if he could be vexed at her for taking so long to stop doing so.

'Waiting for icicles in hell?' she asked and who cared how much she'd given away about her impatience for him when he was lavishing open-mouthed kisses down her throat?

'Waiting for you to heal, lover,' he told her, hot eyed and unapologetically aroused.

'I wasn't wounded,' she said defensively.

'You were a virgin and have no idea how hard I have had to fight not to batter your door down every night since we made you otherwise together, Jess.'

'Together,' she confirmed, liking the feel and sound of it on her lips.

'Aye, how can you even think of us not being so?' he said as if she was the one who ought to know better.

'Because you will grow bored with me?' she suggested as he somehow managed to undo the cunningly concealed hooks in the side-seam of her bodice and her respectable morning gown suddenly became as loose and open as its owner.

'Does this feel like boredom, Jessica?' he asked as he pushed the sensible cambric off her shoulders and trapped her in the fallen sleeves so he could feast on her breasts without let, or stays, she realised hazily as they fell to her feet with another magical sleight of hand. 'Should I fetch myself a newssheet or order my breakfast to stave off my ennui?' he asked ruthlessly as he freed her hands from their captivity and shucked her gown off completely. Standing in her shift and little else, she shook her head emphatically.

'Don't you dare,' she threatened and felt herself shiver with nerves and anticipation and sheer need.

'I hardly dare breathe for what you do to me, Jess,' he told her in a voice that sounded scraped raw with wanting her.

'Then do it to me back,' she urged and that was the last almost-rational thing she managed to utter for a long time.

He was like a man possessed and she was certainly his woman very much possessed as he bore

her backwards and took her against the oak pan-
elling of his study, only pausing to shrug out of
his jacket and bundle her hastily into it to protect
her tender skin from the hardness of the wood
behind her.

'It suits you better anyway,' he declared on a
wry smile as he tucked up the trailing sleeves so
she could use her hands on him even as he used
his to lift her off her feet and wrap those hands
round his shoulders while he hastily undid the
flap of his breeches.

'You suit me, Jack,' she told him as he hiked
up her ineffective shift and she parted her legs
with shameless eagerness.

'My Jess,' he claimed her as he entered her
at last and three whole nights of wanting him
crashed into one galloping, reckless coupling that
left her gasping out her satisfaction and revelling
in his shout of ecstasy, even as part of her was
very glad indeed that his study was in his own
private wing of the house and nowhere near the
guest rooms on the other side of it.

'Ready to admit you can't live without me yet?'
he asked her smugly as he reclaimed his coat and

looked about for her so-proper gown and every-thing else they had removed in their haste. He looked far too sure that her body was singing with satisfaction and demonstrably wanted him extravagantly, generously and almost insatiably.

'What will you give me in return?' she made herself joke, so torn between the lush, hasty plea-sure of their lovemaking and the sadness of it not being love.

'Me,' he said simply. 'I'm only a man, but take me and let me take you, Jess, to be my lawful wedded wife.'

'What about "to love and to cherish" then, Jack? Are you planning to have that bit omitted from the marriage ceremony?' she asked as she struggled back into her clothing, helped—or hin-dered—by him.

'I'll cherish you every day of the rest of our lives, whether you marry me or no, although if you don't I might also curse the day I first laid eyes on you.'

'And how very much you disliked me on that day,' she said with a too-bright smile that threat-ened to make her teeth ache.

'I was puzzled by you. Females were a closed book to me back then, before my cousins came to live here, along with Aunt Melissa and Uncle Henry, after my parents died. Now I know enough about them to wonder why I didn't retreat in fear and trembling at my first sight of such a naggy female as you proved to be.'

'I'm not naggy,' she sparked back.

'Next you'll be telling me you're not changeable as the wind and challenging as a high sea, either,' he said drily.

'Well, I'm not.' She pouted.

'And I'm the Queen of the May.'

'You're the Duke of Dettingham,' she argued rather mournfully.

'And isn't that most of the problem?'

'No, the problem is I cannot be sure I'm not just the convenient wife who happened to be in your sights just when you needed one.'

'Does this feel convenient to you, Jess?' he argued harshly as he drew her roughly back into his arms so that she slammed up against the rigid muscles and sinews of his legs and encountered ample proof he was already roused again and wanted her emphatically. 'You don't know enough about how men are to realise this isn't just a fleeting passion. There's nothing mundane and little and containable about how I ache for you. I could tear my hair out because you don't know your own power and my response to it is nigh on uncontrollable. Sometimes I think if I could go back and not feel whatever it is I feel for you, as well as inconveniently wanting you every waking hour of the day and most of the sleeping ones as well, I would. It seems likely to send me mad before you come to your infuriating, contrary, enchanting senses and realise we were meant to be man and wife.'

'I'll think about it,' she said smartly and marched out of the room with her nose in the air.

'Virago!' he shouted after her and she sniffed loudly before marching down the corridor without giving much thought to the injury she had always thought precluded marching, until today.

'Idiot!' she muttered under her breath as she reached the courtyard door that would take her over to her queenly domain and refused to sneak out of it like some guilty lover. His Grace the

Duke of Dettingham sounded almost as if he might be suffering from love, as if he were a lesser nobleman, she decided with exasperation and went about the task of reassembling proper Miss Pendle from the skin up as soon as she got back to her own room and thankfully found Martha was elsewhere.

That night Jack absently sipped fine cognac and tried to look as if he was listening to Lord Ambleby's warm story about one of Jack's ancient, and now very pious, great-aunts. God knew what they would all think if they could read his mind, he thought with a faint sigh. Frustration, puzzlement and downright anxiety troubled him tonight and, while he blamed Jessica Pendle for the first and some of the second, he couldn't lay the third at her door with any justice.

His butler had handed him a letter that had mysteriously arrived in the hall when he came downstairs to play host tonight. Nothing about the neatly folded package indicated where it came from and the direction announced his title in a neat hand that could have belonged to any professional scribe or secretary. The seal was of plain red wax and the sender hadn't bothered to press even a plain initial into it whilst still hot. A very plain missive indeed, on the outside, Jack concluded grimly.

The writer had been brutally direct, apart from the withholding of his name. Apparently he knew where Rich could be found, but would only discuss terms for his safe return if Jack met him in the temple pavilion by the lake at midnight tonight. His Grace must come alone and unarmed if he wanted the writer to appear at all. Jack toyed with the idea of disobeying that demand, then rejected it. If his secretive correspondent was intent on making money from Rich's disappearance, it would hardly be in his interests to kill the goose he was expecting to lay a golden egg and he couldn't afford to frighten away even the slightest lead that might help him find his stubborn idiot of a cousin.

Yet could he trust a blackmailer not to take the money and kill Rich anyway? Jack caught himself tapping out a preoccupied tattoo on the highly polished mahogany table and stilled his betraying fingers, hoping his male guests were either too castaway or too caught up in their own concerns to notice he was lost in his thoughts. He would have dismissed the whole thing as an enterprising fraud, if only a lock of Rich's distinctive tawny hair and the silver cravat pin his cousin had won off him after they'd raced their ponies for it when they were hardly old enough to need a cravat to put it in had not been included in the package. Nobody else but Rich would still use the battered thing to skewer his cravat twenty years on, Jack decided, with the mix of affection and exasperation he felt for his errant cousin nowadays. The pin was unmistakable, however, down to the clumsily scratched initials they had decided such a trophy warranted at the time.

'My wife will have my hide if we leave her to the tender mercies of one or two of your guests for very much longer, Dettingham,' Sir Gilbert Ware murmured in passing as he returned to the table from a quick visit to the pot cupboard.

'Aye, it's high time we returned to the company of the ladies, gentlemen,' Jack announced as he got to his feet a good deal more steadily than some and waited for the thought of feminine censure to sober them, before leading the way into the state drawing room his aunt would have retreated to tonight, rather than the much cosier parlour the family preferred when they were alone.

Once there he did his best to play the attentive host, prattled a good deal of empty small talk, even accepted a cup of tea with a false smile of gratitude and fervently wished everyone would leave, if they were local, or go to bed if they were guests. The thought of his cousin roistering happily somewhere and blissfully unaware of the trouble he was causing had often made Jack tighten his hands into impatient fists as he considered how much damage the amiably self-centred caused those around them. Yet after receiving that letter there was little chance Rich was safe and sound somewhere and merely enjoying a refreshing adventure, since he would never part with such a treasured possession as that cravat pin voluntarily. So now Jack had to worry about his rackety idiot of a cousin after all, as well as Jess.

'Jack, have your wits gone a-begging?' Persephone muttered in his ear, after treading rather more heavily on his toe than most gentlemen would consider the slender and incomparable Miss Seaborne capable of doing.

'They must have wandered off whilst I was looking in vain for your manners, dear Cousin Elephant,' he whispered before looking enquiringly in his aunt's direction, to see from her genteelly desperate expression that she was in grave need of rescue. 'Just sort out some music most young ladies can play, will you, Percy? For I believe most of our guests would enjoy a lull in conversation after their busy day, even if it does mean listening to Lady Freya murder some poor musician's cherished efforts once again.'

'Only if you will turn the pages for the little darlings, my lord Duke,' his cousin replied with a limpid smile the younger gentlemen present would have fought for.

Unimpressed by such an idea, Jack grimaced. 'Certainly not,' he murmured as they set up the questionable musicale between them. 'As the suitably dazzled host it's my job to watch in awe as they show off and that requires distance.'

'Awe, my foot,' she informed him with a look that told him she would only co-operate because she was doing her best not to make her mother's task as hostess more difficult than it was already. 'I would rather listen to a pack of hounds howl than endure the caterwauling I know is to come, after hearing them practise while you were safely ensconced in the dining room with your port and tall stories.'

'You must bear your share of the ordeal and even learn to love it, cousin dear. Don't forget you need to enchant some idiot with your perfections some day soon, if you're not to stay on my hands for ever and drive me to Bedlam.'

'Tempting though such a possibility might be, I have no desire to hang out for a title as your precious visitors seem determined to do. I know perfectly well they are borne by fallible human beings, you see, so how on earth could I want such a puffed-up mountebank for my very own?'

'So glad to have been of service and instruction to you, Percy dear,' he said blandly and guided her to a seat so close to the piano she couldn't graciously escape the eager circle of her admirers, then he stepped back to join his aunt and those doing their best not to be the centre of attention, such as Miss Jessica Pendle.

'Have you the headache, Jack dear?' Lady Henry asked softly.

'Not yet, my darling aunt,' he murmured and caught Jessica's quickly hidden smile as she did her best to look as if all her attention was on Lady Freya's plodding rendition of a Tom Moore song he'd thought he liked until now. 'No doubt one will come upon all true music lovers very shortly,' he added in the hope of provoking another of those delightful, almost furtive smiles from his Jess.

She disappointed him, but he could tell it was such an effort for her to keep that impassive façade in place that amusing her somehow trumped having half the room convulsed with hysterical laughter.

'Lady Freya's mama is watching us,' Jessica whispered a warning and he looked up to find

Lady Bowland's gimlet eyes on them and felt all desire to laugh fade and die.

'Now I know how the lions in Prinny's zoo feel,' he murmured and managed to close his ears to the mechanical efforts of the fair pianist as he brooded on what midnight had in store for him once more to distract him from Jessica's proximity.

His thoughts ran on Rich uselessly for a while, then swung back to Jessica like a compass needle to the north. He must be careful with Lady Bowland so intent on his every move, because just the faint scent of lavender on Jessica's gown reminded him of that never-to-be-forgotten interlude in the herb garden in far too much detail. Best not to recall it just now or he wouldn't be able to disguise the effect of such heady memories on his body. So he sat and did his best to listen to Lady Freya's truly execrable playing and only slanted a sidelong glance at Jessica when Lady Clare smoothly ousted Lady Freya from her seat at the pianoforte and tried to look modest when her own daughter took over for a more creditable performance.

Seated as far from the centre of attention as possible, it was still impossible for Jess to cling to the shadows tonight, mainly because his staff had decided there were to be very few of those tonight. All the bees in the county must have been working overtime to produce so many beeswax candles, he decided whimsically, but he was grateful for them as the golden glow caught red lights in Jessica's autumn-leaf brown hair and made him wonder why he'd never noticed how intriguing it was until recently.

Heavy and silken soft, the suppressed life of it left him fighting a wild need to see it loose about her shoulders once again. If he closed his eyes, he could almost feel those heavy waves silken against his skin. Tumbling down the supple curve of her bare back, it would be long enough to veil her neat *derrière* and tease him into even more extremes of wanting and needing her than he did already. Very soon now he would have to grant them both the magical sight of Jessica naked and glorious as nature intended in his bed.

Fully, even rampantly, aroused in the midst of a very insipid evening of suitable débutante entertainment after all, Jack fought the hard flush fighting to paint his cheekbones guilty and advertise his state to the world. He crossed his legs and leant forwards as if listening in fascination to disguise his erection, despite his aunt's impatient frown at such male slovenliness, and fought the dangerous proximity of one Miss Pendle with all his considerable might. This was no time to visualise Jessica as his duchess, in every way. Anyway, he decided crossly as he managed to take another furtive look at the effortlessly composed figure by his side, she looked as cool and unaffected by his presence as if he was some doddering nonagenarian or a piece of Chippendale furniture. Rather less affected than she would be by either of them, he corrected himself scornfully. For one she would have betrayed touching concern for his comfort, for the other perhaps a moment's distracted admiration of the workmanship and line of a fine object.

Shifting in his seat once more to remind himself of the dangers of dwelling on Jessica's presence other than as his aunt's goddaughter, he made a slightly distracted survey of the ladies present and silently cursed them for being in the way. Yet if Jessica had not fascinated him from the moment he'd carried her up the steps, he wondered if any of these young ladies would have roused his interest in them as a potential duchess.

Lady Freya he dismissed with a shudder. He could imagine few fates worse than ending up leg-shackled to her overbearing aristocratic arrogance as he watched her become more like her mother every day. Miss Clare merited a few seconds more thought, as a genuinely accomplished, suitably feminine and even mildly agreeable young lady. The right man would be lucky to call her wife, but he could never have been that man. That only left the lovely Byffant sisters and enchantingly pretty Miss Corbridge in the running, as the others were here to make up his aunt's numbers and Miss Julia Ware was on the verge of becoming engaged—she and her parents were only here to show their loyalty after those tall stories about him and Rich had swept through the *ton*.

No, even if Jessica had refused his invitation, or stayed behind with her parents to await the birth of her latest nephew, he knew he could never have married one of the hopefuls arrayed before him now. Feeling strangely guilty that his aunt and grandmother had assembled a collection of such fine young ladies for him to pick from, when he would marry Jessica or nobody, he wondered how he could inveigle enough suitable young bachelors into coming to Ashburton before they left it to make up for the inevitable disappointment of his fair guests.

It would be such a relief to be wed, when Jessica finally saw sense, after all these years of outrunning and outfoxing ambitious young women and their even more ambitious mamas. Better perhaps if he didn't add that to his list of reasons why she ought to marry him though, he decided ruefully, and began a mental summary of what he could put on that list to while away the time until everyone finally went to bed and left him to get on with his mysterious assignation.

## Chapter Nine

Jessica had noted how often Jack seemed lost in his own thoughts during the evening and when he entered the room with his male guests in tow after dinner and sat down a little too close to her to endure the amateur musicale she was certain only a small part of his attention was on the music. She did her best to pretend enough fascinated attention for both of them and wondered what was troubling him, apart, of course, from his frustration at her refusal to marry him.

She hoped he wasn't furtively eyeing the other young ladies present in order to compare her to them. Her lip curled and her fingers tightened into claws at the very idea of him pressing his urgently male attentions on any one of the ladies present and she wondered for a moment if she would feel more murderous towards him or the object of those attentions if she ever came across him in such a compromising situation.

No question, she decided, the lady would get her face scratched first, but then he would have to deal with her, and if he thought that an easy task he'd better recall how good she was at getting a blow in under his guard before he risked it. She did her best to blank her expression to mere polite interest as she reminded herself she'd been given the chance to win a real live duke as her prize in life. Not that Jack had ever been a trophy to be won to her and she tried to concentrate on the Miss Byffants' rendition of a simple and therefore touching duet. The spectacle of two angelic-looking girls, blessed with sweet voices and an excellent music teacher, finally managed to distract her from the man at her side and she congratulated them at the end as enthusiastically as every other music lover in the room. Luckily for every other such, Lady Henry squashed an attempt by Lady Freya and her mama to regain the limelight with an encore.

'It has grown so late and we have all had such

a busy day that I think we really must save that treat for another time, Lady Freya,' Lady Henry declared firmly and even Lady Bowland somehow couldn't bring herself to challenge her hostess openly.

'Although it was a mere ten-mile drive to dear Pannington's house near Ludlow, I suppose the rest of you have not been so fortunate as Freya and myself in having family nearby to pay a restful visit to,' the dowager countess agreed smugly, as if possessing a son-in-law as dissolute and close to bankruptcy as Lord Pannington was something she should be congratulated upon.

'Speaking of which, we must get home to our family while it is still light enough for our coachman to see the way,' Mrs Delafield declared before her ladyship could embark on the reasons why all connections of the Buckles were automatically wise, good and fortunate.

Through all the fuss of departures and exchanging goodnights with the house party, Jessica remained in her seat. Knowing Lady Henry respected her desire not to attract pitying looks or whispered comments, she waited until the last of them left the room before getting to her feet and exchanging a rueful smile with Persephone.

'What an evening,' Persephone muttered as she tucked Jessica's arm within her own and offered her unobtrusive support.

'I'm sure we have endured worse,' Jessica replied.

'Then I'm infinitely glad to have forgotten it if we have.'

'So am I,' Jessica said as brightly as she could manage and told herself that one day she would really be able to laugh with Persephone about this very trying house party.

'Come now, you two, it wasn't so very bad,' Lady Henry reproached them and shook her head despairingly when they eyed each other skeptically, then rolled their eyes in disbelief at her charitable nature.

'It truly was, Mama,' Persephone assured her emphatically. 'Ah, so there you are,' she said as Jack came back into the room after seeing off his local guests and conferring with Hughes about whatever arrangements needed to be set in place for the next day. 'It was your fault from start to finish,' she told him as if she held him personally responsible for putting her manners to such a test.

'Of course it was, Percy love, but what exactly am I responsible for this time?' he asked wearily.

'For having such an insipid circle of acquaintances,' Persephone accused him as if that was the worst sin she could come up with on the spur of the moment, but it was quite a bad worst all the same.

'That's just the problem, my dear; my real friends are far too interesting to be invited to respectable house parties like this one. I know most of our guests hardly at all,' he drawled and Jessica went back to disliking him with an invigorating snap of temper.

'Presumably they feel the same about you then,' she said coolly.

'Oh, if only that were so, Miss Pendle,' he mocked in return.

'Yet would things change if you became a mere mister, do you think?'

'Not by much, considering they clearly believe me nearly as rich as Croesus, don't you think?'

'I do my best not to at times like this,' she

snapped, flushing under his slow and too bold inspection of her raised chin and the painful effort it cost her to hold his gaze as if he really wasn't worth the effort.

'Since that would seem to qualify you as a docile and accomplished young lady, would you care to marry me instead, then?' he asked her outrageously, seeing as his aunt and cousin were still with them.

'Don't you dare mock me like that ever again, Jack Seaborne,' she demanded in a low, pained voice that surprised even her by its bitterly controlled passion.

'You know I'm completely serious, Jessica,' he replied as smoothly and carelessly as if they were talking about crop yields or a new variety of apple.

'Luckily for you, I know you would never dare do this to any other female of my age and station in front of your aunt and cousin. I used to think I hated you, my lord Duke,' she told him huskily, hardly able to get the words out for the weight of humiliated tears behind the fury that was buoying her up. 'At least now I know beyond any doubt that I do.'

'Do you know, I used to think you did as well, Jessica, but now I know so much better I wonder at my former self for being so simple.'

'We were both mistaken. I don't hate you, your Grace, I loathe you,' she assured him, stepping closer so she could glare up at him from an even less safe distance.

'I'd rather have your brand of loathing than the wholehearted approval of any of the suitable young ladies I've met this Season,' he said facetiously and she saw a kind of desperate sincerity in his green-and-gold eyes before her own hurt and fury reminded her he was mocking her and subjecting her to all this for some perverse reason of his own—revenge, perhaps, for not jumping at the chance to become his duchess like a dog at a bone.

Lady Henry and Persephone's embarrassment made his taunts seem so brittle and harsh that she could hardly bear to look at either one of them and see sympathy or pity in their eyes and disengaged herself from Persephone's protective arm in a sort of driven self-defence.

'Then please consider yourself well and truly loathed,' she said dismissively and went to turn away and leave before he made her cry with fury and thought he'd managed to inflict a deep hurt on her, which of course he had.

'I will,' he said with an odd look in his eyes that she only saw because he refused to be turned away from so easily and grabbed her arm and swung her back to face him again, as if she was the guilty party and he an innocent in all this. 'Only because loathing is the counter-side of something much more passionate, Miss Pendle,' he ground out and she saw how deeply she'd offended and perhaps even hurt him by refusing to marry him.

'This really is most uncivil of you, Jack,' Lady Henry recovered from her shock at so open a quarrel being played out in front of her and managed to protest at last.

'I feel uncivil,' he assured her as if that was enough of an excuse.

'I think we knew that,' Persephone remarked

as if commenting on a play and Jessica sent her nearly as virulent a glare as Jack did, so at least they were united in one thing.

'You keep out of this,' he ordered his cousin and went back to staring down at Jessica with that hint of desperation in his eyes again and she knew that if she let it, her heart would turn over with love and exasperation and ardour for a man who could have been her true mate if only he'd allow himself to be, so she didn't let it do any such thing.

'There's nothing for Persephone to keep out of, or for anyone else not to hear either. I am going to bed and have every intention of pretending none of this has happened when we meet tomorrow, for which mercy you will no doubt be profoundly grateful, once you have slept on our latest disagreement and realised I am right and you could not be more wrong.'

'Don't tell me what I will or will not be, Jessica,' he ordered in a frayed tone she hardly recognised as his. 'I keep my promises and I'll hide this tussle of ours from the strangers in my home, I'll even hide it from our neighbours and friends, but

I won't hide the fact I desperately want to marry you from my aunt and Persephone. And can't you see how much better we would pull in harness together than I ever could with one of those aristocratic young fillies trotted out for my approval tonight, as if they were up for auction at Newmarket?'

'No, I really cannot see how our steps could ever match,' she said as coolly as she could, even while inside she felt as if she was screaming at the truth behind her apparently flippant reply.

'So that's what all this is about?' he said as if he'd just found out she had the blood of the Borgias running through her veins. 'You truly intend to allow a trivial injury, which has no significance for anyone but yourself, to come between me and the one duchess who could make me a better man instead of a bitter and uncaring fool?'

'Of course I do, even if I had the least intention of accepting a careless offer from a careless man, who has grown tired of searching for a wife at the first hurdle and thinks he's found an easy mark in me,' she said steadily enough, for all it

was the basic truth that had always stood between them, from the first moment she realised
how much of her future she'd lost the day she
defied her parents and rode off on a half-broken
colt into a thunderstorm. 'You promised not to
make any announcements and that I could have
time to decide. Now you've broken it.'

'I broke nothing. This is not public and you
can't have it all your own way and twist everything about until it's all my fault. Refuse me because you hate me; refuse me because you believe
I would make you an unreliable husband or because you love another or can't love me, but don't
you dare refuse to wed me because you're slightly
lame, Jessica,' he warned.

'Very well, then, all of the above,' she said
proudly and actually felt her godmother and
Persephone catch their breath at the flare of wild
temper in Jack's now-very green eyes and the reality of actually being present to hear his furious
proposal and her equally stubborn refusal.

'You're a liar, and a damn poor one at that,' he
assured her, his temper suddenly restored to an
even keel as he stood back from her and surveyed

her as if they'd been discussing the weather and very interesting it had been too.

Disconcerted by such a lightning change of mood, she looked to Lady Henry for guidance and received a shrug in reply, as if her godmother was as baffled by her nephew by marriage as Jessica was herself.

'I really have no idea what you mean,' Jessica managed haughtily.

'No, and that's the greatest beauty of all,' he replied and looked not in the least bit chastened by her emphatic refusal, or his aunt and cousin's shock that he could behave so unconventionally in front of them and towards such a cherished guest as well.

'You really should apologise to Jessica for distressing her so deeply, Jack,' his aunt told him as if coming out of some sort of trance after a very odd scene had been played out in this stately room.

'I might, if refusing a duke as many times as she has lately wasn't likely to put her consequence A1 at Lloyds if it gets out,' he said so easily it was clear to Jessica he would walk away from this bizarre encounter with his pride and his heart still hale and hearty, while hers felt as if they were in danger of withering away.

'My consequence, as you choose to call it, my lord Duke, will remain exactly as it is today and was yesterday. I would never advertise the sham of a declaration you just insulted me with. I believe you're considered a gentleman by the rest of the *ton*, your Grace, so I depend on you not to set me up for the general ridicule of our world,' she said coldly.

'You can rely on me to make sure he does not, my dear,' Lady Henry said and looked as if she was having a job not to accuse her nephew of malicious mischief and banishing him to his room as she might have years ago, but hardly could now he was a mature and powerful duke.

Clearly conscious of how impossible that would be, Lady Henry glared at her eldest daughter, who was looking thoughtful about all the possibilities revealing his odd proposal and Jessica's refusal of it might offer.

'Persephone will keep a still tongue in her head, if she wants to retain her mama's good will and her next quarter's dress allowance,' she added sternly.

'Very well, nobody will learn of it from my lips,' Persephone said on a sigh.

'Thank you,' Jessica managed and felt a huge wave of tiredness threaten to engulf her as the tension drained out of her at last and a terrible sense of let-down threatened. 'I will have to trust your training as a gentleman to stop your lips for once, I suppose,' she informed Jack as regally as possible since she then had to limp past him to seize her candle from the store of them laid ready in the hall.

And that really should be that, she assured herself wearily, if only he'd take her 'no' for the finality it truly was. Cursing her damaged foot for not allowing her to run gracefully off to her room and to the devil with her candle flame, she heard his swift steps behind her and turned to meet whatever new torture he had in store for her with enough pride left to get to her room without bursting into overwrought tears in front of him, if she managed to get this battle over quickly enough.

'You forgot your shawl,' he said unemotionally then wrapped the lovely thing about her shoulders as if he knew how chilled she suddenly felt, standing here in the gathering darkness of this midsummer night.

'Thank you,' she managed to say with only a slight catch in her necessarily soft voice as they stood there in the impressive hallway, with the fine Tudor staircase winding its stately way up to the chambers above.

'You're desperately tired, aren't you?' he asked and the genuine concern in his deep voice nearly undid her, as even her fury at him for being so doggedly obtuse hadn't managed to do quite yet.

'I've had an eventful day,' she managed to say in a non-committal tone she hoped would make him finally lose interest in her and seek his own bed.

Instead it spurred him into picking her up in his rather too-compelling arms and striding off with her along the wide corridor towards the Queen's Room. She had been grateful for its privacy earlier in the day, especially after her godmother and Persephone had looked incredulously at Lady

Freya when she openly protested at a lady of Jessica's age and station being given a room slept in by several queens of England, as well as the odd princess and duchess along the way. They had simply ignored Lady Freya's spite as unworthy of comment, but Jessica wished they had listened to that arrogant protest now and she'd been left to struggle up the stairs along with the rest of the guests, because then Jack wouldn't have been able to seize her and overwhelm her, just when she was at the end of her tether and least able to withstand him.

'Please, Jack, put me down?' she appealed as the spicy scent of him snatched away her certainty that she'd refused him once and for all.

'When I get you safely to the Queen's Room,' he said as if he had every right to police her comfort and safety, even in so trivial a matter as this.

'I could perfectly well get there myself, I'm not a child,' she said crossly as he turned down the dark corridor to the state apartments as if he could see every step of the way even though her candle had blown out after he'd manhandled her.

'I know, but that ankle of yours is aching like the devil, isn't it?'

'What if it is?' she answered defensively. 'Any sensible female would feel a little weary after being bothered and besieged and bewildered by you for what seems like most of the day, your Grace.'

'Would they?' he said softly as he shouldered her door open and closed it almost noiselessly behind him and made bad worse. 'Or would they be inquisitive, intrigued and in thrall to what we could become to one another, if only you would consent to marry me, do you think?' he asked her as if he knew all the answers to his own questions and refused to answer any of hers.

Unable to summon a sufficiently crushing retort, she gave an expressive humph of disbelief and tried not to tingle all over as he didn't set her on her feet so much as let her gently slither down on to them inch by inch. His reaction to the progress of her body flowing over his so closely that every curve and whisper was delightfully intimate against his harder planes and angles was as unmistakable as her own more easily concealed one was to her.

'I'm not a shrinking virgin any more,' she protested at his attempts to mesh her ever deeper under his spell by reminding her of the glorious differences between male and female, but not all her attempts at making the extraordinary ordinary could fight the building sense of delight and the more primitive fire he was lighting in her again with this masque of the devoted lover.

'Irrelevant, my dear,' he murmured huskily as he finally set her on her feet and held her for an awesome moment against his mighty, aroused and arrogantly male body.

'I'm obviously not your dear,' she protested, even as her own body clung and fitted itself to his. Since they were already lovers and it knew every intriguing iota of that difference she could hardly blame it, but wished it would show a little more restraint all the same.

'Not yet,' he half-threatened and half-promised and she shifted against him as if her body knew far better than the rest of her exactly what it wanted.

'Not ever,' she said determinedly, doing her best not to hear the note of bitter sadness in her own voice as she reaffirmed what she knew to be true.

'Idiot,' he replied and silenced her with a kiss that smashed through all her barriers and temper and resolutions not to give in.

In the unexpected softness of it, the hint of plea and almost of apology for what he'd just said and done in front of Lady Henry and Persephone, if not for trying to persuade her accede to his will, she felt weak, wanting the rational Jessica take over, and desperately clutched at sanity.

'Don't,' she managed to wrench her mouth from the temptation of his long enough to protest.

'Why not?' he muttered as if nearly at the end of his own tether over her stubbornness, which seemed distinctly unfair when she was being reasonable and he was very far from it.

'Because,' she managed to murmur before heat and passion overwhelmed her once again at actually being in his arms, reeling under the skilful magic of his kiss as she was caught up and held within a magical land of their own once more.

'This is only a dream,' she managed through lips that felt delightfully used by his kissing and unfit for much else.

'Just us, Jessica—not a dream, but us together, as we should be,' he said sternly, his mouth setting in a harder line than wanton Jess could bear.

'To hell with reality then,' she managed and heard him chuckle at her intransigent encouragement, the contrariness of her as she slid further into his arms, closer to his powerfully aroused masculinity in defiance of her own words.

'Not until you accept we are all that *is* real whenever we're together,' he demanded, as if she had been blissfully unaware of him as a man all these years when he was one to belatedly decide to notice she was a woman only days ago.

'I can't,' she said, bitterly and reluctantly, but at least she managed to say it.

'Then neither can I, Jessica darling,' he said with an attempt at humour to lighten the hunger and desperation snapping between them.

'If you were truly in thrall to me, you wouldn't be able to walk away,' she accused him harshly, struggling with the full effects of passionate frustration that had suddenly become so painfully familiar she was glad she hadn't known how fortunate she was in her ignorance all these years.

'Luckily for both of us I'm man enough to do exactly that, before you do something you'll regret in the morning and blame me for it for ever afterwards, Jessica,' he assured her huskily.

'I'm not the one who would wake up tomorrow and find myself saddled with a crippled lover I should never have taken on my conscience, because that's how you would feel, Jack. You would marry me now whether you wanted to or not, even if I protested to the skies that wasn't what I wanted all the way to the altar, so, yes, you're right—I would regret that, bitterly.'

'Kindly allow me the credit for having left the nursery, Jessica,' he said a little too seriously and she knew she'd hurt his pride and run up against that ridiculous idea he'd developed today that she really ought to marry him, love or not. 'I'm not some silly youth led about by my ungoverned passions for the nearest feminine body to sate myself with. We could be far more together than we will ever be apart, but if giving you time to finally take that fact in will make you see sense, I can still walk away tonight. There's another week of such heady gaiety as we endured tonight to be got through yet, so you can have one more night alone to adapt to the idea of becoming my wife if you really must.'

'Don't patronise me, you arrogant great fool. I'm not going to change my mind; I won't suddenly become a swan rather than a limping goose and if you truly wanted to wed me you've had years in which to do it. Do you expect me to believe you took one look at me the day I arrived here, stiff and travel weary and hardly able to stand on my own feet, and suddenly decided I was irresistible?' she accused.

He watched her silently, patiently, and it took all her will power not to clench her fists and give away the strength of her own feelings as compared to the weakness of his. 'Yes,' he finally said as if that trumped all her arguments.

'Why?' she demanded, refusing to admit it could be so simple yet so complex.

'Because I would never be bored with you and I believe that you would be equally well entertained while we sparred, provoked and entertained each other with our mutual eccentricities for the rest of our days,' he said and, when she would have argued again, shot her a darkling look she could pick out even in the moonlight's glow from the open shutters. 'Then there's the fact that we're so compatible that making a family with you will be sheer pleasure, rather than one of my unavoidable ducal duties as it would be with any one of Aunt Melissa's troop of hopefuls.'

'All of which might weigh in the balance with me if you were plain Mr Seaborne and I had no alternative,' she made herself say caustically.

'It seems to me you have far too many of them to be able to see the sense of staying here with me where you belong,' he said with a quick frown.

'Lucky me,' she said wearily.

'Ah, Jessica, just go to bed and dream of me and promise me you'll think again about my proposal in the morning, when you're not so tired that you've become mule stubborn with it?' he said with a weary sigh of his own as he came close again, soothing a gentle hand over her hair and caressing her temples the way she could remember her mother doing when she was young and tired and not over-willing to go to bed. His care of her threatened to undo her just that little bit more.

'I promise to try,' she conceded, doing her best not to let that soothing touch influence her. He'd challenged her, sparred with her, even charmed her at various different times in her life, but his real care for her comfort and tranquillity now was threatening to undermine her resistance completely.

'I'll leave you alone, this time then, lover,' he said softly. 'Please try to understand—I had to ask you again in front of Aunt Mel and Percy. I need them to know beyond any doubt that I won't marry anyone but you. It was the only way I could think of, short of riding off to Northamptonshire *ventre à terre* to beg your father for your hand, to convince you, and them, that I'm deadly serious,' he added as if that explained everything and went after one last kiss that was in danger of becoming far too passionate once again before he broke it with a rumble of male protest she didn't choose to decipher and strode away from her as if she represented almost unendurable temptation.

Jessica noted that he was remarkably soft-footed and lithe for such a large and vibrant male and despaired of herself for being so besotted she even noticed how he moved when he was leaving her now. She didn't know if she most wanted to throw something at his departing back or climb on to her feather bed and do just what he'd ordered her to by dreaming of him in it with her once again and all the dangerous pleasure that would bring.

Glad she'd refused Martha's offer to wait up to undress her when she was perfectly capable of doing it herself, given the simple nature of her evening gown, Jessica got on with the routine of getting undressed and ready for bed and tried to let the ordinariness of it soothe her ruffled feelings and jangling nerves. It had been a long day and, with any luck, she would sleep deeply the instant her head touched the pillow this time.

Trying to blot Jack out of her mind altogether, she finally climbed between the cool linen sheets and settled back on the lace-edged pillows, stretching out her protesting limbs with a sigh of relief. In a few hours she would have to face the likes of Lady Freya and her mother with a serene countenance and her dignity intact once more, so dreaming about Jack Seaborne, the duke every other young lady had come here determined to marry, would certainly not help her with that project.

Jack still had over an hour to wait until his meeting in the dark after leaving Jessica's room. The infinite temptation she presented to linger and seduce her from refusal into acceptance was nigh irresistible, until he realised how insulted and suspicious she would be when he left the instant they finished making love and disappeared into the night. The rakish nature of that idea tugged at his conscience as well, and made him feel more uneasy than the prospect of meeting his mystery visitor. So he used the time to pace up and down his library like a caged beast instead.

What a blind and bumbling idiot he'd been to have lovely, fiery Jessica Pendle under his nose for so long and not notice how sweetly she would fit into his life. He couldn't blame extreme youth for not putting her at the centre of his hopes when he finally decided to wed, that had been a purely Jack Seaborne folly and nothing to do with the shallow ignorance of silly young dukes.

He tried to tell himself courting Jessica was something to put off even thinking about until he'd discovered what mess his cousin Rich had got himself into this time. Finding Rich was important, but it was getting damnably in the way of his campaign to convince Jessica he was desperate to make her his duchess. His impatience with anything that got in the way of that noble undertaking made him frown fearsomely and slow his pacing until he resembled some sort of ominous predator about to set out on a hunt that would spell the end for some unsuspecting prey.

Yet again Jessica couldn't sleep, which seemed blatantly unjust when her thoughts blurred into a disorganised jumble every time she tried to think rationally. Cursing her restlessness and Jack's bull-headed stubbornness, she rose from the comfort of her grand bed and went over to the bay window to pull back the shutters she had closed to exclude the moonlight in the hope that the calm scene outside would etch itself into her mind and let her sleep at last.

For several minutes it seemed her idea would work as her eyes grew heavy and her racing heartbeat slowed, then the cure itself let her down. She blinked, telling herself everyone else at Ashburton tonight was in bed and safely asleep, as she ought to be. No, there it was again, the merest hint of movement in the shadowed garden. At first she thought it was a fellow guest unable to sleep and taking a more extreme version of the cure she had been trying by bathing in the serene moonlight. Then the quiet purpose of that dark figure argued otherwise. What on earth was Jack doing slinking stealthily across his own extensive gardens?

And why couldn't she dismiss his night wanderings as none of her concern and simply go back to bed? Unable to answer either query, she crept into her dressing closet and found her dark riding habit by feel and donned it over the top of her nightgown. Hastily winding her long plait around her head, she pinned it impatiently in place and slipped her feet into a pair of soft shoes. She slipped out into the night, blessing the fact it was so easy from here and hoped Jack was too intent on where he was going to notice her. Tomorrow she might pay for it, but tonight she sped along almost unimpeded by her weak ankle and felt her spirits rise at the awe-inspiring beauty of the silvered landscape.

Perhaps Jack was only restless and trying to walk off wakefulness; if he was half as confused by the events of today as she was, that seemed quite likely. If so, why had he either changed into something dark and suitable for furtive encounters at midnight, or so muffled his immaculate linen as to make sure no hint of the stark white of a gentleman's shirt and cuffs showed by the light of the moon?

It wasn't as if anyone here had the right to challenge him. The Duke of Dettingham could probably walk about his gardens on his hands if he chose to and only give rise to the odd rumour all was not well with his sanity, but even such eccentricities would probably be forgiven so important a gentleman. Not that the fifth daughter and eighth child of a mere viscount would receive such lenient treatment if she was discovered wandering about Ashburton's pleasure grounds in the middle of the night, Jessica reminded herself with a surprisingly light heart.

When she came to the picket gate into the shadows of the wilderness, Jack had left it slightly ajar, so she slipped through despite the shiver that ran through her at the profound darkness beyond. The path winding between thickly planted shrubs suddenly seemed fraught with dangers and a potential home to all sorts of night spectres. Since there was no other way to find out what Jack was up to, she forced herself to take it anyway.

Once her eyes had become accustomed to the shadows, the closely planted wilderness held an unlikely beauty. On a more aimless journey she might have stopped to admire the headily fragrant star-shaped flowers of the exotic mock-orange bushes from far-off America that Jack's mother had caused to be planted here. Perhaps she would lift the heavy blooms of the Provence and Bourbon roses to sniff in the full sweet scent of them and she caught the heady night-scent of honeysuckle on the still air without any need to find it among the leafy abundance and wondered why this place had been planted so thickly with shrubs that gave up their scent most pungently in darkness.

She felt a fool as the inevitable answer came to her—that it had been designed for lovers to wander through; their already heightened senses overladen with the night-time sweetness of it all as they barely managed to spare even a thought for anything but each other. The handy benches and intimate alcoves, placed in the exact spot for them to best appreciate the night and each other more fully, spelt out just why the late Duke and Duchess of Dettingham had taken such an interest in their wilderness walk.

Luckily she was through the artful wildness of the place and out into the park proper before she could wonder if she and Jack might enjoy such heady summer nights there if she weakened and agreed to marry him. Setting unanswerable questions aside, she noted the gate was not quite latched here either and shook her head over his purpose in taking this dark path into his own parkland.

In sunlight Jessica loved the conceit the famous Mr Lancelot 'Capability' Brown had contrived as the gracious landscape below was revealed in one long gasp at the beauty of it all. How clever that he could direct the bold visitor to this enchanted place through his darkly planted wilderness and use them to make a startling contrast from the neat gardens behind and wide parkland ahead. It always came as a shock of delight when she emerged from the dark of the wilderness into the breathtaking vista of wide parkland, stately trees and magnificent views of the surrounding hills that seemed to cradle the vast bowl of this enchanted valley as if they loved it. To Jessica it had always been a magnificent sleight of hand that made questions of artifice and nature irrelevant. This time she frowned as she tried to think how to cross the moonlit arcadia in front of her without being visible to Jack and whomever he was intending to meet there in the middle of the night.

Her ankle was beginning to pain her again and she hesitated, wondering if she was a fool to go on. Even if he was up to his neck in a mystery that very likely involved Richard Seaborne, Jack wouldn't let her get involved, protective idiot that he was, so she must outwit him and find out for herself. So she would follow the edge of the wilderness until it got close to the shadow of a group of chestnut trees that could hide an army. Cursing herself for leaving all the elegant walking canes her brothers delighted in seeking out for her at Winberry Hall, she fervently wished she had one of them now. Gritting her teeth, she went on, driven by urgency she'd stopped trying to reason away.

At last she spotted a heap of pales left when the fence was repaired and found one strong enough to stand her weight. Sighing with relief, she stumped doggedly on, so far behind Jack she might as well turn round and go back to her bed even if she wouldn't sleep for worrying about him. With his long, easy stride he could be in Ashburton Bartram by now, or halfway to the Welsh border, yet she couldn't bring herself to turn about and return to her chamber without knowing who he was meeting, and why.

By now Jessica was locked into a course she knew to be foolish, but somehow couldn't call a halt. She reached the edge of the trees and fumbled her way through by using her stick like a probe, then eyed the circle of oak trees ahead with a weary sigh. If she could get there without falling headlong they would lead her to the rear of the summerhouse by the lake. At least there she could sit quietly until she had recovered from this stupid odyssey before she went back.

Castigating herself over her own stupidity, she made herself move as smoothly and silently as she could manage. She paused under the canopy of the first oak and the silence seemed uncanny, as if even the night creatures were watching and listening for betraying sounds on the still air. She wondered what it would be like to wander about the parkland on the arm of a lover. If only Jack loved her back, every step would be an enchantment, every murmur and kiss a delight almost too heady to endure.

Yet she was alone here like a moon-led fool,

fervently hoping Jack was far enough away to have no idea she was limping about in the dark, chasing shadows. The very idea she could do anything to protect such a notably vigorous and healthy man was ludicrous and all the shadows were really covering was her shame at being such an idiot as to follow him in the first place. So after a rest in the summerhouse, she would go back to the house and her comfortable bed and forget she had ever seen Jack creeping about his own grounds in the middle of the night.

## Chapter Ten

Somehow Jack made himself stop pacing the floor of the deeply shadowed Grecian temple by the lake and sat on one of the *chaises* his aunt had caused to be set here for the comfort of anyone hardy enough to venture so far from the house. He silently cursed whoever had lured him here for their warped amusement and wished they had something better to do. He had had a busy day, avoiding hopeful young ladies and making Jess see sense about marriage ahead of him, and could do with some rest.

It seemed less and less likely anyone would turn up here at the deliberately melodramatic witching hour, but at least he had seen the sheer perfection of a moon-bright summer night and supposed he ought to bless whoever had lured him here, rather than cursing them for falsely raising his hopes that Rich was still alive. Not that it would have been a particularly peaceful rest, he decided with another quickly suppressed curse, just in case someone was out there listening after all.

Courtesy of his future duchess he burned at the very thought of her as he tore himself away from her tonight, warm and sleepy eyed and recklessly ready to abandon good sense and propriety in his arms again, despite her fury with him for stubbornly wanting to marry her. So why hadn't the idea occurred to him until now? Because she'd made sure she was never under his nose to provoke it, he supposed, and slammed up against the unwelcome idea she'd been avoiding him ever since she came out in polite society and felt as if it might choke him. What damage had he done to her when he was still a reckless young fool, to make her stay away from any occasion he was due to attend? Racking his brains to recall it, he clenched his fists and suppressed an urge to lash out wildly at something.

From the advantage of being four years older

and wiser he remembered giving in to Aunt Melissa's urging that he must attend Jess's come-out ball. He'd torn himself away from the sophisticated entertainments he'd told himself he preferred at the time and he allowed himself a faint groan as he pictured his arrogant younger self being insufferably condescending to the poor darling, even before he recalled her looking as if she was about to be driven to the scaffold and clearly hadn't needed his help to make her feel wretched about the whole business, but of course he'd given it all the same.

At two and twenty he'd been a conceited ass, confident his very presence would make her night and launch her into society better than if the rackety Prince of Wales had graced it instead. He'd even drawn attention to her damaged ankle by absently demanding she dance the first dance with him. That memory made him shudder with revulsion now, yet he'd been too puffed up and proud of himself at the time to perceive his own insensitivity and he finally began to see why Jessica was being so difficult about accepting him as a husband.

Jessica must have felt every one of the pitying looks and whispers that this was one daughter Lady Pendle would never get off her hands with any credit to the family name like coals of fire. Jack damned himself anew for lacking maturity to guess how sharply that low opinion of her prospects had grated on her pride back then. He diverted himself from the disasters of the past by replaying his moment of profound shock only days ago when Jessica stepped out of her carriage, looking travel weary and distinctly unimpressed to be here, and his entire world had re-centred itself.

*Found her, at last,* an inner voice a whole lot wiser than the usual Julius Henry Frederick George Destigney Seaborne had informed him and, if she wouldn't wed him, he'd follow her to whatever rural backwater she was planning to retreat to and make a nuisance of himself until she did, or accepted him as her lover if she insisted on making them a scandal.

He was so lost in considering the most pleasurable ways and means of convincing Jessica he wanted only her, without committing himself to anything as sentimental as loving her for the rest of his days, that the tiny sounds that might have warned him someone was coming failed to register. The only warning he wasn't alone any more was a break in the shaft of moonlight coming into the faux-Grecian temple, then a shift in the shadows that said the mysterious letter wasn't a mare's nest after all.

'So glad you could come,' an educated voice murmured mockingly and Jack searched him memory and came up with a surprising answer.

'What the devil are you doing here, Forthin?' he snapped back.

'Looking after my own,' came the reply and Jack wished the confounded rogue would step out of the shadows and confront him like a gentleman—no, like a nobleman. For he recalled now that his old friend had inherited the family titles. Gentlemen had need of far better manners than either of them seemed to possess.

'I don't think I've clapped eyes on you since you returned from India to step into your cousin's shoes,' Jack said. 'Should I congratulate you, my lord?'

'Not if you would like your noble head to remain on your ducal shoulders.'

'Really, Alex, that smacks far too much of passion for a nobleman such as you have become and you'd have to hit me first.'

'You're the one to play the cold fish, not I, Dettingham,' Alexander Forthin, the latest Earl of Calvercombe, said harshly.

There were no memories of a shared past or an old friendship in his voice and Jack thought it hinted at grudges he could only puzzle over instead, since he hadn't seen Alex Forthin in years and couldn't recall ever harming him. He knew the man had been in India with Sir Arthur Wellesley's army and, once he sold out, the new earl was reportedly too busy with his ramshackle estates to trouble with polite society, or indeed any society at all, if his disgruntled neighbours were to be believed.

'On what evidence do you base that assertion, Alex?' he asked mildly.

'Do you recall exactly why you decided to meet me here tonight, Dettingham?' Forthin asked as if Jack was the one intent on making cryptic queries and not him.

'Of course I do, and how the devil you got hold of those articles that accompanied your letter is something I would dearly to know.'

'No doubt,' Alex drawled as if he had no intention of telling him, which made Jack wonder why he'd bothered to lure him out here alone in the first place.

Instinct told him someone far more dangerous and unscrupulous than Alex Forthin could ever be was behind Rich's disappearance, even if the man had become a bitter recluse and cynic since Jack had seen him last.

'Planning to make my cousin Richard a deeply unhappy man, wherever he might be, are you, Alex?' he asked laconically, trying hard not to sound as if he was as completely at sea about his one-time friend's motives for luring him out here as he felt.

'By killing you and landing him with the dukedom? No need for me to go quite that far if you'll only answer a few simple questions, Dettingham.'

'Tell me what you want to know, then we'll

both find out what reply I care to make,' Jack said, rising to his feet as he felt at a distinct dis-advantage on the chaise. 'Then I have one or two puzzles for you to answer in your turn.'

'What could I possibly know that's of interest to the great Duke of Dettingham?' Alex jeered and Jack wondered at this new talent he seemed to have developed for alienating his friends with-out trying.

'If you don't know the answer to that question, then what in Hades are we doing here, Alex?'

'Finding out what each doesn't know, perhaps? Or maybe I'm more interested in what you want so desperately you're prepared to meet an un-known threat out here in the middle of the night to achieve it?'

'We could stand here all night fencing about what one of us knows and the other doesn't, but it would get us nowhere, so I suggest you say whatever it is you came to say and then I'll find out if I can swallow it without retaliating in kind.'

'Are you calling me a liar, Dettingham?'

'That all depends what you have to say.'

Jack heard a barely audible curse and hid his

smile of satisfaction in the shadows. Alex Forthin always had possessed a far more passionate nature than he would have anyone believe, so if he couldn't get the truth about Rich out of him one way, goading him into a fury should prove a good alternative.

'You did as I said and came here alone, I trust?' Alex asked, his voice soft and urgent and more mistrustful than ever.

Jack heard him move and guessed he was peering out at the silvered parkland, so maybe he had caught some faint whisper of sound or seen a hint of movement from the corner of his eye.

'Of course—did you expect me to bring my current guests and my staff with me to hold my hand?'

'Not quite,' Alex said with a hint of laughter in his voice at the very thought of such an unlikely procession. 'It was devilish inconvenient of you to have all of them here in the first place, when I would have been able to come up to the front door and just ask for you under any other circumstances,' he grumbled, as if Jack had decided to have people staying with at this time purely to annoy his one-time friend.

'Which, once again, begs the question of why you didn't do exactly that at a rather more civilised hour and save us both creeping about in the dark?'

'I'm here because I dearly want to know where my cousin is,' Alex snapped back, as if Jack was deliberately provoking him to a fury by even asking him for a reason why he'd come here in such secrecy when no casual observer would be able to stumble across him.

'Snap,' Jack said, doing his best to add fuel to the flame in the hope it might cause his irascible lordship to add to that cryptic statement.

'Your cousin isn't a vulnerable young girl adrift in a world all too eager to take advantage of her.'

'Well, no, but even you would have to admit that he's been gone the devil of a long time,' Jack said seriously enough, for he'd be a fool not to have considered a number of terrifying reasons for Rich's protracted absence, as well as the other less dangerous and therefore more infuriating ones of carelessness and even plain stub-born contrariness.

'So has Annabelle,' Forthin told him between gritted teeth.

'Unfortunate though I can see that must be for you and the rest of her family, whoever she might be, what on earth can her non-appearance have to do with the protracted absence of my cousin Richard?' Jack asked curiously.

'Something I am quite sure you could tell me, if you chose to.'

'Right, that's enough of this idiocy. If I knew where either of them might be I would tell you exactly where this mysterious Annabelle of yours was, before I called you out for implying I could be involved in her disappearance in the first place. What sort of a venal rogue do you think I've become since last we met, Calvercombe?' Jack said hotly.

'The sort who would turn a blind eye whilst your precious Rich seduced, abducted, then aban-doned a seventeen-year-old girl; the kind of man she then wrote to time after time, desperately pleading for information about where her tardy lover had gone and who replied to not a single one of her frenzied appeals for help or information. You're little better than her destroyer, Dettingham, and if I didn't want to know where she is—if she's even still alive—more than I want to flay your miserable hide off your bones, you would have a very good reason to gather a private army about you before you dared meet me here in the dark of night.'

'I never thought you could believe such a lie about Rich without a great deal of evidence to back it up, Forthin. Even then I'd expect you to have asked me the truth of the matter before you took such lies as gospel.'

Jack heard the note of hurt in his own voice and stopped himself saying any more, instead striding about the summerhouse in an attempt to keep his temper, giving his visitor as wide a berth as he could in the restricted space. If he got too near the deluded idiot he might be tempted to indulge in a brawl. Calvercombe must know how close this was to an insult demanding pistols at dawn. He told himself the man storming in here like this pointed at a deep and painful anxiety over his missing cousin Annabelle and he must make some allowance for that, since he felt the same way about Rich.

'I give you my word I have never so much as heard of a female by the name of Annabelle Forthin, or indeed of any other Annabelle you're about to accuse me of wronging if that's not her name. If I'd had any letters from a woman about Rich, don't you think I would have seized on them as manna from heaven, man? I've been desperate to find even the faintest trace of him since the day he rode away from Ashburton shortly after his father's funeral over three years ago. He hasn't been seen on any of the Seaborne estates from that day to this either, before you accuse me of hiding him somewhere you and this Annabelle of yours can't find him and bring him to book, although I'll be damned before you'll convince me he'd seduce, then abandon an innocent young girl as you find it so insultingly easy to believe.'

'You're his cousin and best friend and prejudiced in his favour,' Alex said with enough doubt in his voice to make Jack wonder if he might still recognise the truth when he heard it after all.

'Always, but your accusation lacks logic. Why should I care if you accept my word as truth when you clearly regard all Seabornes as your enemies?'

'We were allies at least, once upon a time, but I have copies of letters written by a girl I've known since the day she was born, so why would I believe you over her? She was my ward, for heaven's sake, my responsibility, and all I have left of her are some rough drafts of letters to you and her diaries, which seem to be written in some sort of code even I can't penetrate. Oh, yes, and the knowledge she needed me so badly and I was thousands of miles and half the world away and failed her utterly.'

'Which is why you're trying so hard to find yourself a scapegoat in Rich, I suppose, so it won't be your fault that she's clearly as wild as a gently bred female can be, or that she had the chance to walk out of your life and not come back and grabbed it with both hands. At least Rich was never my ward, so I can't accuse myself of failing to keep a minor safe now he's disappeared off the face of the earth,' Jack said bitterly.

'He'd have trouble being that, considering he's a twelvemonth younger than you,' Alex said absently, as if assessing Jack's reply while he talked of unimportant things, like Rich, who mattered to Jack as much as any brother.

He felt fury threaten to blind him to all else and damped it down. Alexander Forthin obviously thought nothing of trampling roughshod over the feelings of others in pursuit of his own ends nowadays, but logic told him that to have become this harshly embittered man, his old friend had experienced something even more unendurable than the disappearance of a much-loved relative.

'What happened to you out in India, Alex?' he asked gently and sensed his old friend had frozen on whatever spot he currently occupied.

'None of your business,' he replied and Jack wondered what the brusque coldness in his former friend's voice concealed.

'You made yourself my business when you demanded I meet you here when all respectable noblemen should be abed and deep in dreamland,' Jack said, wondering if he could be justified in exasperating or tricking Alex's dark experiences in India out of him. Only if it helped him find Rich, he decided, and he could see no reason why it should.

'Quiet!' Alex ordered and Jack froze, then recalled he could make as much noise as he wanted to at the heart of his own estate where he was supposed to have dominion over most of what he surveyed.

'Give me one good reason why and I'll think about it,' he murmured in a tone he knew an eavesdropper would find it hard to hear.

'Think about what I sent with my letter, Jack,' Alex whispered balefully, 'and keep your confounded tongue between your teeth, if you really want to know where I obtained it, of course.'

'Why the hell would you doubt that I do?'

'Perhaps because even I heard those rumours about you and your cousin, or more likely because I've already been to hell and it taught me to doubt everything I hear and much of what I see,' Alex told him balefully and turned away to stand aloof again, obviously listening to something outside.

Jack was reminded of a badly beaten dog he'd

once taken in, despite all attempts by his much-tried uncle and aunt to bribe him with promises of a more suitable pet. The animal had exuded the same air of danger held back on a hair trigger that Alex gave off now—ready to attack any threat that offered, or preparing to flee overwhelming odds if there was no chance of winning. Jack hadn't been able to explain that he kept faith with his unlikely and often difficult favourite because poor old Ares had been treated about as badly as a man could treat an animal and not actually kill it, but he'd not been cowed or broken spirited, despite his ordeal. The dog had died two years ago and no other since then had come close to filling the place the irascible old mastiff had won in his heart.

Alexander Forthin was no abused hound and Jack was no longer a needy youth, angry and grieving for his parents and with time on his hands as well as the youthful stubbornness to win the trust of one the rest of the world had dismissed as beyond it. Jack listened intently, but could hear no one else in the still night. He was on the verge of setting off for his abandoned bed, in the hope Alex would come to the point or leave him to it, when the man bounded down the steps to pluck some poor soul out of the shadows.

Jack was only a yard or so behind him, but his blood ran cold as he heard a distinctly feminine shriek and felt his heart pound at the very idea it might be Jessica out there, helpless in the grip of a battle-hardened avenger. It felt as if any blow that fell on Jess would pound into him a hundredfold stronger; any hurt she suffered would fell him like an axe. Panic threatened to paralyse him like some useless invalid as the connection between them suddenly seemed crucial to his very life.

'Let her go,' he demanded as he wrenched himself into action at last and leapt down the steps after his new enemy. He wrestled Alex off his wildly struggling captive. 'Don't you dare hurt her, you damned maniac,' he bellowed, maddened by the idea that Forthin had laid so much as a finger on his Jess.

'Beast!' the female wriggling in Alex's arms accused him and Jack flipped back to sanity at the sound of her voice, then winced in sympathy with his one-time friend at the sight of Persephone clenching her fingers into claws then trying her best to rake them over her captor's face while he hung on to her wrists with grim determination. 'Uncivilized, presumptuous, repellent brute, how dare you attack me?' she added as Alex struggled to hold, yet not hurt her. Which was just as well, Jack decided, or he might have had to knock him down after all.

'Good evening, sweet cousin,' Jack drawled, hoping the sound of his distinctly unimpressed voice would sober both of them, before they did each other real harm.

As it turned out, he saved Alex a severe headache, since this time his Jess really did burst out of the undergrowth and barrel over to use her piece of chestnut paling as an improvised club to beat off Persephone's attacker. Instead of bringing her weapon down on Alex's thick skull, Jessica twisted round at the sound of Jack's voice, then tumbled over some hidden object on the ground. He dashed forwards to try to save her, only to trip on the same obstacle, then land on top of her, despite all his efforts to twist and turn in mid-air and keep his weight off her.

'Jess, my darling, have I hurt you?' he gasped as he tried to examine her and she did her best to slap his hands away. 'Did we damage your ankle?'

'No, but I can't tell you how much it aches now you've landed on it,' she muttered crossly as she struggled to rise to her feet.

He insisted on feeling for sprains or bruises although part of him knew she wouldn't berate him if she was seriously injured, but the rest was beyond logic.

'Let me be, you clumsy idiot,' she demanded as his searching hand closed on her deliciously rounded *derrière* and she slapped it away with a huff of annoyance.

'Never mind your dratted pride for once—can you stand up?' he demanded, quite reasonably in his opinion.

'Of course I can, you stupid man,' she snapped and felt round her for her improvised prop to help her do so.

Kicking it aside as totally inadequate for the

job, Jack held out his hand imperiously and towed her to her feet, wincing in sympathy when she gasped as soon as she tried to put weight on her ankle. He felt guilt give way to fury when she wobbled perilously.

'Stand still, you fool,' he barked as she looked across at Persephone, frozen in Alex's hold as they watched the tableau she and Jack made and not at all happy about her captivity, and seemed ready to launch herself into the fray once more. 'My cousin is quite capable of looking after herself; she landed enough punches on me in our youth for me to know she possesses an impressive right hook when her fists are free. If you feel you must protect someone, I suggest you plump for Alex,' he told Jess and tried his best to probe her injuries once more.

'Stubborn great ox,' Jessica complained mutinously as he explored her body as best he could while she was doing her best to squirm away from him. 'I'm not injured anywhere else, despite your worst efforts,' she insisted as he ignored her, then had to clutch at his shoulders for balance when he knelt to lift her damaged foot. 'Let go, Jack,' she gasped as he explored the fine bones of her ankle and the slight scars left from operations to try to mend her shattered bones he'd not really bothered about at the time. Now it ground at his heart that she'd borne such agony and wondered if she'd refused to admit it hurt then as well.

'What for?' he barked harshly. 'So you can limp back alone? Then, no, I'll be damned if I'll let you go.'

'If you've quite finished?' she said in a distant, queenly tone. 'I don't believe I've been introduced to your latest guest. An unconventional arrival, perhaps, and an even more odd concept of hospitality, but I dare say this gentleman's eccentricities will be excused if he proves as noble or as charmless as his host. If he improves on acquaintance, he will provide a much needed contrast to yourself, my lord Duke.'

'Very good,' Jack said with a slow handclap of mock appreciation, even if he felt as if steam might come out of his ears at any moment, like the excess escaping from a beam engine stoked so high it was in danger of blowing up. 'But I'm still not going to let you limp back to my house alone so you can blithely do yourself even more damage. Anyone would think you'd been intent on a stroll round my rose garden for the good of your health and got lost.'

'Isn't that what happened?' she said, as if he was a slow infant and she needed to spell every word of her story out to him. 'It was a bright moonlit night and neither Persephone nor I could sleep so, chancing on each other on our way to your library for a suitably boring tome to read ourselves into dreamland, we couldn't resist setting out for a walk on such a wonderful moonlit night together, in order to tire ourselves out and soothe us into sleep at last. The highest sticklers might consider it a risky enterprise for two unmarried and youngish ladies, but we were together and kept within your private gardens, so I doubt that any irreparable damage will be done to our reputations if we're found out, so long as we return alone, of course.'

'I don't care about your reputation, I care about you,' Jack informed her ruthlessly, then swung her up in his arms, despite her attempts to bat him about the face and arms in a weary protest against his high-handedness.

'Boor,' she accused a little too seriously for his taste. 'Managing, arrogant, stubborn, intractable mule of a man,' she grumbled even as she subsided in his arms and tacitly consented to hold still while he strode up the steps to the temple with her and laid her on the couch as cautiously as if she still had her weapon about her and might lay about him with it at any moment.

'Virago,' he countered grumpily. 'There's probably a tinder box in the urn over there, along with a few spills and some candles,' he told Persephone and Calvercombe with an absent-minded nod they almost certainly could not see.

His cousin lit a candle and he saw shock flit across her face before she glared balefully again at his one-time friend. Wincing along with his patient, Jack ordered her not to be missish and insisted on rolling down her stockings to see what he and Jessica had done to her ankle between them.

'I'm tired, that's all,' she protested as she sat on the *chaise* with her arms folded across her chest and a mutinous frown on her face. 'The sooner I get back to Ashburton and rest, the better my ankle will be tomorrow.'

'You're not stirring an inch on this foot tonight or tomorrow,' he barked, the very idea of having to watch her hide her pain and stiffness with every step cutting through him like a knife to the gut. 'In fact, I'm calling Barton as soon as it's a remotely civilised hour in the morning and you're going to spend the day in bed, or resting quietly on the sofa in Aunt Melissa's sitting room.'

'No, I'm not. Not even to escape you,' she snapped with a furious frown.

'Then I'll call for your father's carriage and take you home out of harm's way,' he threatened balefully.

'And leave your guests to their own devices? I only have to imagine the scandal that would provoke and it makes me want to hit you even more fervently than I did before, you great stubborn idiot.'

'That's my girl,' he said affectionately, 'and I don't care, they can say what they like. At least it would get me to the right place to obtain your parents' agreement to our marriage, but if you don't let me take care of you for once, you *will* find yourself the centre of all the attention I can throw at you, like it or not.'

'If you truly want to marry Jessica, then why on earth did you let Mama invite that pack of giggling ninnies here under false pretences?' Persephone asked.

'Because I didn't realise until they got here that she's the only female I will ever ask to be my wife,' he replied reasonably enough, in his opinion.

Jessica and Persephone exchanged exasperated glances and shook their heads over his masculine-chopped logic and Jack spared a glance at Alex to see what another male made of what seemed a perfectly reasonable conclusion. Then he took a second look and realised why the other man had skulked about in the dark and why Persephone had insisted on holding his gaze for that long, rather brave, moment before she allowed Alex the luxury of looking away.

It wasn't as if the latest Earl of Calvercombe was hideous, Jack mused as he steadily met Alex's undamaged eye, as clear, sharp and midnight a blue as ever. Whoever had tortured him had done so with a sharp blade and then the wounds had been neatly, even minutely sewn up. One side of his face was as arrogantly handsome as ever, the other a parody of it, as if an artist had grown impatient with perfection and rubbed half his work into a blurred echo of the other.

Jack did his best to hide a shudder at the calculated cruelty of the twisted mind behind such agony. It seemed almost beyond belief anyone could devise such lingering persecution, for Jack guessed the silvered scars had been inflicted one by one, perhaps day by day, a technique designed to reawaken the pain of all the ones that had gone before with every new incision in Alex's suffering flesh.

'I hope whoever did that to you is dead,' he observed flatly.

'Not yet, but only imagine how ill he sleeps at night, waiting for me to come after him and take my revenge. I make it my business to always know where he is and I'll strike when I'm ready and not a moment sooner,' Alex replied dreadfully.

'If you need help, you'll know where to come, then,' Jack said. Whatever Alex had lost during his ordeal, he considered him a friend, whether he liked it or not.

'You think I would draw you and your lady into such a dark business? Best thank God I know otherwise, Jack,' Alex said bleakly and Jack could see he was determined to walk alone and let the topic die, for now.

'Do you doubt her courage then, Alex?' he said lightly.

'I would never be so foolish,' Alex said with a wry smile as he took in Jessica's haughtily raised eyebrows at his method of addressing her, and her steadfast refusal to look away from him as he evidently expected her to.

If nothing else, Alex had discovered tonight that there were at least two stubborn females in the world who refused to flinch from the very sight of him.

'I'm not his lady,' Jessica said crossly, flicking her dark skirts over her ankles as she looked for her stocking and shoe, presumably so she could reclaim her fencing post and limp laboriously back to the house, consigning Jack and all his works to the devil as she went.

Over his dead body, something primitive, infinitely possessive and fiercely protective in Jack argued silently. He smothered an impulse to roar and rage at her and wondered what was retrievable from the farce this assignation with Alex Forthin had become. He'd come here to find whatever crumbs of information about his missing cousin he could gather from a mysterious enemy. So far all he'd discovered was another mystery and a numbed and damaged friend instead of a foe, one who looked as if he'd like to gallop off into the night as fast as he'd come and forget he'd ever been here. The idea of letting Alex go without finding out more about his adventures felt as if something important had been left undone, as well as leaving him not a jot wiser about Rich's disappearance.

'You're not walking back on your own with a ricked ankle and a clutch of bruises caused by my clumsiness, my lady or no,' he informed Jess brusquely, since he was tired and frustrated and seemed to have got no further either with persuading her to marry him or his quest to find his errant cousin tonight.

'Perhaps you expect me to stay here all night then?' she asked mutinously.

'No, Alex and I will carry you back.'

'Oh, no, Jack, you can leave me out of this,' Alex muttered as if he'd been ordered to lead a forlorn hope not even a death-or-glory-boy would take on.

'I never took you for a coward,' Jack taunted him and saw Alex's good eye flash and his lips tighten before he recalled that there were ladies present and put a hard curb on an urge to vent his fury with suitable curses.

'Not for you, then, but for your…' Alex caught Jessica's glare at him for even beginning to repeat his former description of her and he sent her an appealing, mock-helpless look instead, 'What am I to call you then, ma'am, since we haven't even been introduced yet?' he said with such a strong echo of his old, careless charm that Jack felt his fist clench at his side before he could control the primitive reflex.

'I am Miss Pendle—Jessica Pendle, as you obviously heard Jack address me thus earlier,' she said with a softening of her regal manner Jack found nearly as infuriating as Alex's unexpected return to charming rake about town.

'I'm very pleased to meet you, Miss Pendle. I am Alexander Forthin, current Earl of Calvercombe, but my friends call me Alex,' he said with such a graceful, unstudied bow that Jack felt his demons snap and struggle against the tight curb he usually kept them on nowadays.

'What about me?' Persephone demanded, obviously keeping her own Seaborne temper under control with considerable difficulty.

'What about you?' Alex intervened before Jack could introduce her. 'I only see one lady present,' he said, looking down his rather bony nose at her.

'And I detect a distinct lack of gentlemen,' she said with a nicely judged sniff.

'Alex, this is my cousin, Miss Persephone Seaborne,' Jack intervened before they could come to blows again.

'Lady Henry has my sympathy,' Alex said with inexcusable rudeness and Jack met Jessica's eyes with a suddenly united speculation that both of them protested their dislike of the other a little too emphatically for it ring true.

'Mama has no need of your compassion on *my* account,' Persephone declared with an un-expected wobble in her voice that gave away how bitterly she missed her scapegrace brother, who really was causing Lady Henry sleepless nights.

'I'd send my respects instead, if this happened to be a social call instead of a business meeting between Dettingham and myself, even if nobody would believe it so exclusive with such a lively audience as we seem to have gathered,' Alex said.

'When you're not discussing the fate of my elder brother, you can have all the privacy in the world as far as I'm concerned,' Persephone told him haughtily.

'Never mind depressing my pretensions, Goddess, we need to get you two back to Ashburton before anyone realises you're not abed,' Alex Forthin told Persephone with a sad shake of the head at her headlong misadventures and unladylike ways that made her even more furious.

'Which is exactly what I've been saying,' Jack said with exaggerated patience.

'And what if someone sees me being carried home like a naughty child?' Jessica asked acerbically.

'Well, what if they do?' he asked arrogantly, knowing he couldn't watch her struggle against her current state of pain and weariness for ten yards, let alone all the way back to Ashburton. 'We're Seabornes, we go our own way,' he added as if that explained everything.

'Quite,' Persephone agreed with a regal nod at Lord Calvercombe.

'Well, you Seabornes might think it perfectly acceptable to go about the place refusing to explain yourselves and looking down your noses at all and sundry,' Jessica told them crossly, 'but I would fall flat on my face if I tried it.'

'I think you might surprise yourself, Miss Pendle,' Lord Calvercombe said with a rueful smile that neatly made Jessica stop and think, then give a delightful chuckle.

It drove Jack halfway to fury that his friend could draw her down from the boughs when he had only been able to drive her further up them.

'*Touché*, my lord,' she said with a smile that Jack begrudged him wholeheartedly.

'Never mind flirting with him, get your stocking and shoe back on and let's get out of here before anyone else turns up to join our midnight soirée,' he said gruffly as he turned his back on her and glowered at Alex until his so-called friend raised one mocking eyebrow and complied with his implied order to do the same.

'I'll help,' Persephone offered and did, so quickly and efficiently that Jack couldn't even take another sly peek at Jessica's fine legs out of the corner of his eye.

Feeling thoroughly disgruntled, Jack glared into the night and noted the moon was further to the west than he expected. He wondered how long they'd been standing here arguing uselessly about first Rich, then Alex's mysterious ward and then Jessica's injured ankle and hoped all the local poachers had stayed home tonight. If not, then rumours about odd night-time activities and the dubious status of his sanity would be circulating round the estate like wildfire come morning.

'You and Lord Calvercombe can carry Jessica between you through the parkland while there's space to walk side by side, Jack,' Persephone ordered. 'I shall scout ahead, to make sure nobody else is wandering about the place tonight. I dare say it will be impossible for you gentlemen to walk two abreast when we reach the wilderness, but I can't think of everything.'

'Really?' Alex observed in mock wonder. 'You do surprise me.'

'You are the rudest and most infuriating man I've ever had the misfortune to come across,' Persephone informed him before sweeping down the steps into the night before he could think of a pithy comment to help her on her way.

'Managing little firebrand,' Alex announced with some amusement and what sounded almost a note of admiration in his voice, before he turned and meekly offered the use of his crossed hands for Jack to add to his, so that Jessica could take at least the first part of her journey back to the house in style.

## Chapter Eleven

'Imagine allowing myself to be swept off my feet by both an earl and a duke at the same time! Whatever would the tabbies make of such a scandalous occurrence?' Jessica remarked as she finally acquiesced to being carried.

'Probably that you're obviously more sensible than appearances have argued you must be up to now,' Jack ground out impatiently, since he was having so much trouble fighting the urge to seize and hold her possessively all by himself.

He also had an irrational urge to set her down and thump Alex on the nose for enjoying the feel of her curvaceous *derrière* and decidedly feminine curves against their crossed hands even as he did so himself.

'Or that you possess such a luxury of fatal

charm that you're enjoying a debate with your-self over which to accept as your particular duke or earl?' Alex suggested, clearly enjoying him-self at Jack's expense and rediscovering the fa-mous Forthin charm that he'd once possessed in such abundance.

'Oh, yes, I always knew I had it in me to be a *femme fatale*,' Jessica agreed with that hint of a girlish giggle in her voice that annoyed Jack profoundly since it wasn't directed at him. Had it been, no doubt he would have found it charm-ing and a sign that she might like him a little more than she was prepared to admit. Instead, she seemed to find Alex infinitely more charm-ing than her smitten ducal lover.

'Well, there we are, an ambition achieved, Miss Pendle,' Alex told her lightly, as he and Jack had to match steps and grasp hands to hold Jessica, however curmudgeonly and uncooperative Jack was feeling about it.

'It's laudable to realise as many of those as possible in life, I dare say,' she said lightly and seemed to be enjoying her journey a little too much for Jack's taste, especially after all the protests she'd made about taking it in style in the first place.

'Talking of which, are you ever going to satisfy mine to know whatever you do about my cousin, Calvercombe?' Jack carped gruffly.

'Not in front of Miss Pendle,' that gentleman said curtly.

'Jessica has all my confidence,' Jack argued just as shortly.

'And how can you be sure his sister can't hear us? I could be scandalous.'

'At the moment I don't think she'd be interested in any scandal that doesn't reflect badly on you,' Jack lied, glad at least one female in the world wasn't totally taken in by his glib charm.

'Won't you stay at Ashburton for the remainder of the night, then join Jack's guests for the rest of their stay, my lord?' Jessica chipped in with exactly the sort of assumption Jack least wanted her to make.

His household was hers to order about if she wanted to, his title he would gladly bestow on her and she could scoop her slender hands through his moneybags whenever she chose, but why the devil did she have to invite Alex to endure his hospitality as if it was already hers to bestow and he would be her honoured guest and not the Duke of Dettingham's?

'Yes,' he made himself second her with a fair impression of hospitality, 'why don't you join my other guests and agree to thoroughly infuriate my cousin and provoke me for the duration of your visit, Alex? You would certainly be doing the rest of us a favour if this past evening was anything to go by.'

'It wasn't so very bad,' Jessica defended the fair musicians weakly.

'Don't you think it would be too hard on a pack of susceptible females to subject them to the sight of me?' Alex asked with a would-be laugh in his voice that betrayed how deeply he dreaded the scrutiny and gossip his changed appearance would provoke in some quarters.

'Better here than trapped in the heart of Mayfair and unable to get away from the little darlings,' Jack advised quite sincerely now, for he could imagine watching a débutante pack sidle away from his friend *en masse*, then pretend he wasn't even there a little too easily. 'I can offer you my boyhood rooms in the north tower, Alex, and from there you could mix with my guests if you choose or shun them if you don't. I'd value your advice and support in persuading this intractable female to marry me, as well as any information you care to offer me about Rich's possible whereabouts.'

His invitation came more readily than he'd dreamt it could when he first realised who had come to confront him so furtively tonight, and seen how truly changed his old friend had become. Now he had an inkling of the reasons Alex had changed so much, he could sense the man he had once known under a hard shell of protective cynicism, despite the outward changes and his new title.

'No, but I thank you all the same. I'm on my way to my Welsh estate and prefer to be about my business rather than stopping here to mind yours, Jack,' Alex replied and Jack smothered an unworthy sigh of relief, before realising he still hadn't heard whatever it was Alex came here to tell him.

'Then no doubt you will grant me a few moments of your precious time, once we have Miss Pendle and my cousin safely back at Ashburton,' he replied with a hard look at his eccentric visitor by the light of the setting moon.

'Will I, old friend?' Alex queried silkily, but Jack gave him credit for some honour and integrity and eyed the shadowy darkness ahead of them for signs of Persephone's return.

'Or you could always tell me whatever it is you know now,' he said flatly.

'Very well, for I think you'll demand Miss Pendle's full attention once we reach that cunningly wrought lover's walk I explored a couple of nights ago,' Alex taunted him with that incursion under his very nose. So Alex had been his night prowler—that meant the true enemy he sensed behind that ridiculous scandal in town was still in hiding.

'Miss Pendle truly is a family friend, as well as the woman I very sincerely hope to make my wife, Alex. You can speak freely in front of her, but if you don't get on with it you'll have to do so in front of my cousin as well, and, while she would never say a word to harm her brother, myself or Jessica, I'm sure after your supposed molestation of her she would love to find out something discreditable about you and spread it with gusto.'

'Aye, well, I can cope with her tantrums. I've lived with far worse.'

'No doubt, my lord, but could you not tell Jack whatever news you have of his cousin before we are caught here in broad daylight?' Jessica asked wearily.

'How do you know that's why I'm here?' Alex asked.

'Because you asked for this meeting in the first place, my lord,' she said and since Jack knew Alex Forthin would always oblige a lady, particularly a young and beautiful one like Jessica, he kept quiet and let her persuade him to be reasonable for once.

'I know little enough, Miss Pendle,' Alex said after hesitating so long Jack thought he wasn't going to trust them after all. 'I purchased those articles, which Jack found so intriguing he risked a midnight assignation to find out more about them, whilst tracking down my own cousin's movements to the last lodging I could trace her to before she disappeared three years ago. How those items came to be left at such an unsavoury place, where I virtually had to threaten the landlord with a lawsuit to persuade him to confirm either of them had ever been there, I truly have no idea.

'I doubt the man knew anything more than the very little he could tell me,' he went on, almost as if talking to himself. 'I watched him for a week or more after our encounter to be sure he didn't go on any unexpected journeys or send warning to someone outside his household. There's little point asking for the address of the place; suffice it to say I would never have let my ward set a foot within a hundred yards of it if I'd only been here to prevent it. I can't find a single clue as to where she went after that, so I know she left none since I've been trained to sniff out even the faintest of trails during my years in the army. The landlord is the kind of man nowhere near subtle enough to watch and wait for me to truly be gone before he told a greater villain about me, if he knew one was concerned in my ward's disappearance.'

'Why did the fellow keep such worthless keepsakes for so long, then?' Jack demanded.

'According to him, they were the items my ward valued most in the world, for all he couldn't see why anyone would. He reasoned that when she very reluctantly left them behind as a sign of her good faith, she would come back and pay his bill one day, which he then did his best to dun me for instead.'

'Did he succeed?' Jessica asked as if truly interested in a story Jack sensed had more holes in it than a Swiss cheese.

'I paid him for those keepsakes, and also for a favourite shawl of my young cousin's that I sent her from India that has a hundred times more value to it, after I'd prised it away from the landlord's wife, who was understandably reluctant to part with such a treasure.'

'How shocking to find her wearing something you sent your ward like that and how very disappointed you must have been to get no further with your quest, Lord Calvercombe,' she said softly and Jack only just resisted the compulsion to tell her not to fall for Alex's tall tale hook, line and sinker.

'Shocking indeed,' he echoed, with a sharp look at Alex that he sincerely hoped let the glib rogue know he wasn't as gullible as soft-hearted Jessica.

'Either way,' Alex said, 'I'm no further on than I was when I started, so I thought I'd discover whether his Grace here had any clues as to why his cousin seems to have disappeared along with my vulnerable young relative.'

Jack thought he heard genuine frustration at his lack of progress, as well as equally real annoyance at having to seek help from anyone, in Alex's voice this time.

'I now know they seem to have disappeared at the same time, which leaves me much further on than I was before you came,' Jack said coolly, frustrated himself that there was still no clue as to where Rich had been these last three years, even if he wasn't alone.

'Then I'm glad to have been of service,' Alex

drawled and Jack took a deep breath and managed not to react to the implied insult.

'If you're serious about finding two people we both appear to care about, Calvercombe, I suggest you think hard about how you're going about it whilst you're busy hiding yourself away in your Welsh stronghold like a wounded bear. There's no option open to us but co-operation, given how little we've learnt so far separately, even if neither of us have to like it.'

'I always have options,' Alex said dourly and Jack wondered again if the bull-headed idiot had been involved in clandestine operations for his stalwart general whilst in India.

'Yes, and one of them is to behave like a civilised gentleman and help Jack solve an otherwise intractable problem,' Jessica intervened acerbically. 'I can hear Miss Seaborne returning, so I suggest you either stay as Jack invited you to, Lord Calvercombe, or go away. I seem to recall Penbryn Castle is less than half a day's ride away from Ashburton, so if you care to join us on consideration I'm quite sure Jack will welcome you,' she ended once again as if she were already Jack's wife and chatelaine.

Deciding not to mention that, he nodded his silent agreement and bade Alex goodnight. 'At least you'll have even less sleep than the rest of us, Calvercombe, since you have a goodly way to go tonight if you're aiming to be inside your rocky hideaway before the world is properly awake,' he said cheerfully, because he was human after all and Alex had made his distrust of him a little too clear.

'Aye, so I'll be gone before the asp-tongued Miss Seaborne returns and lays about me with her tongue if not her fists. Goodnight to you both; I expect to find you betrothed at the very least upon my return. I might even accept your generous offer to stay in that vast mausoleum of yours if it's in the cause of watching you get yourself wed to a woman of such decided character as Miss Pendle, Jack, since something tells me you richly deserve one another.'

'You'll wait a long time for that particular invitation, my lord, since I have no intention of wedding the Duke of Dettingham,' Jessica said stiffly and demanded irritably that Jack put her down.

'Nonsense,' Jack said as brusquely as he could whilst engaged in receiving the whole of her slight weight as Alex thrust her fully into his arms. 'You'd fall over.'

'I most certainly would not,' she denied heatedly and Jack saw Alex grin at their fractious method of courtship and decided he would smile on the other side of his face one day, when he was trying to enchant some steely-backboned female into agreeing to become *his* wife. He sincerely hoped he was there to see it.

'Your outspoken cousin is getting too close for my comfort, Dettingham, so I'll be on my way before she gets here and starts nagging about something. Be sure to watch his back for him, Miss Jessica Pendle, and I'm sure he will enjoy doing exactly the same for you,' Alex said before he disappeared into the night, although even Jack's acute senses couldn't catch a trace of his going.

Reluctantly impressed, he mused for a moment about old times and a friendship that might be sound after all, before concentrating on the here and now and enjoying the contrary lady in his arms.

'He thinks more of you than he would have you believe, Jack,' Jessica murmured before Persephone was within earshot and he didn't bother to argue.

'Has he gone?' Persephone demanded urgently.

'Aye, over the hills and far away,' Jack replied.

'Just as well—he would be far too restless and uncomfortable to have about the place while we're still entertaining your guests.'

'True,' he admitted even as he realised that he would rather have Alex at his side in his search for Rich than any other man on earth, but kept that fact to himself since Persephone had taken against him. 'But we can't try to find Rich while we have a houseful of guests either. Just as well perhaps that Lord Calvercombe is intent on business at his Welsh estates and can't join us just now.'

'Confoundedly selfish of him to stay there while he could be searching for Rich in our stead, then,' Persephone muttered.

Jack felt Jessica shake with suppressed laughter at his cousin's disgust at his friend and gave her a warning whisper to contain her mirth until they were alone.

'Say nothing to Aunt Melissa, Percy,' he cautioned. 'I don't want her upset about Rich all over again and the news that he appears to have run off with a seventeen-year-old girl before he disappeared is hardly likely to add to her peace of mind.'

'I wouldn't dream of worrying her with rumours and Lord Calvercombe's tall stories,' she said as if he ought to know she had more sense.

'I'm sorry, Percy. Even though you weren't invited to my assignation with Alex, I wish he'd had more to tell us about Rich's whereabouts or well-being. I suppose you both saw me on my way to meet him and joined the procession. How could I ever have been daft enough to think I could keep our meeting secret?'

'Rich is my brother, Jack, I'm involved whether you like it or not and won't be cut out of any attempt to find him,' she warned so quietly he was impressed. 'Just because I'm female, please don't imagine you can exclude me from finding him.'

'Perish the thought that I would underestimate a resolute woman when I'm doing my best to shackle myself for life to a female of such stubborn resolution she could give the Welsh mountains yonder a lesson in stony immovability,' he replied with a grin he hoped neither of them could see in the shadows.

'Then get on with it. Jessica is due to go home in a week, along with all your disappointed duchesses,' his cousin informed him and left them with a brief goodnight and an order not to get caught stealing in with the dawn by the housemaids.

'Traitor,' Jessica muttered darkly.

'Darling,' Jack corrected and left her to work out if he meant that description to apply to her or Persephone.

At last he was alone with Jessica in Ashburton's eclectic gardens, designed as they were for romantic moonlight strolls through their sensuous midsummer glory. It seemed a shame to waste them, he mused.

'Sauntering about in the countryside in the middle of the night could end in all sorts of trouble, you know?' he teased, sensing that for all her intrepid bravery, Jessica was a little afraid of the dark shadows of his wilderness. Lucky then that she wasn't alone in it this time, he reflected with a wolfish smile he was glad she couldn't see.

'Indeed,' Jessica replied. 'Who knows who we might meet in the dark next?'

Jack could tell her mind wasn't on stray earls or traitorous friends, since her fear had clearly flown and she sounded half-drugged with the romance of the night all about them, the heavy scents and still air made all the more potent now the moon had set. He hardly dared point out she had just admitted there would be a next, in case she took it back. Meanwhile this was a night made for lovers and he would be unworthy of the name if he wasted any more of it, he told himself virtuously.

'Another time we'll make sure there are no stray earls or curious cousins drifting about the place before we creep off into the darkness together,' he murmured. 'If we announced our engagement, they might leave us alone anyway.'

'We're not engaged and, even if we were, that would not help. Just the opposite, in fact, since half the gentry and nobility of Great Britain are related to you, and the other half are connected to me through my legion of brothers and sisters and would descend on us *en masse*,' Jessica rebuked as if they were already wed and everything was therefore his fault.

'You seem to have thought about this more deeply than you admit,' he taunted softly.

'Thought about it, then decided it would be a mistake, as you will when this house party is safely over. Don't you dare try to use this ridiculous business to try to persuade me to accept your lunatic scheme to marry me, Jack Seaborne,' she added, sounding more awake now than he altogether wanted her to be.

'As if I would,' he muttered grumpily.

'Once you've decided you want something badly enough, it's my belief you would do virtually anything this side of the law in order to get it.'

'Then you don't know me as well as you think. I've failed to extract maximum effect from to-night's farce, I haven't so much as offered to seduce you into stunned acceptance so far and I certainly wasn't planning to rouse the household and invite them to be scandalised by whatever we've been up to. Now you've reminded me of all the possibilities the night offers me, I might sink to the level you seem determined to set me at, of course. I'll leave you to plan an effective revenge whilst I go and wake your maid as soon as we get to the house and who knows who else I might manage to disturb while I'm at it? At least she can help you back to bed, where you would have been all along if you weren't such a rackety female you forsook it to follow me.'

'Don't you dare wake Martha, she needs her sleep and you haven't met a truly stern female moralist until you've encountered my mother's maid in full flow. Neither of us would survive the night without a promise to wed and I won't marry you because Mama's dresser demands I do so, Jack.'

'Then marry me because I do, Jess, because I

can't imagine the rest of my life without you in it. No, hush,' he cautioned as he even felt her resistance in her stiffly held body, 'I haven't finished yet, and if you're going to be my wife I shall insist on getting a word in edgewise in my own defence now and again for the sake of my own sanity. I love you, Jess,' he admitted with a wry smile he knew she couldn't see. 'You had me so confused I didn't know what I felt for you until you came charging out of the night and tried to set about Alex with your feeble weapon, but I certainly knew it then. I felt as if the world might crack open or stop spinning if I couldn't get to you in time to stop him hurting you. Even if you insist on rushing in where angels fear to tread, love, I recognise a man who's been trained to hunt and kill—how could I know what he might do to a chance attacker almost by reflex?'

He shuddered at the very thought of the danger she'd launched herself into headlong to protect Persephone. Jack didn't know the details of Alexander Forthin's service to his country, but he guessed he'd been an intelligence officer of some sort and probably knew how to kill quickly and silently in a chilling variety of ways.

'You truly thought I was in danger?' she asked with apparent wonder as she felt his shiver of unease and thought a little harder about her impromptu attack on a seasoned warrior.

'I know you would fight without hesitation for someone you cared about, and you care for my cousin for some reason I can't currently fathom, but Alex probably knows more ways of silently disposing of his enemies than you do of refusing to marry dukes who can't live without you, Jessica. Of course you were in danger, if you had sense enough to see it.'

'Considering you think me witless, I'm surprised you want to wed me,' she said with as much dignity as a lady could summon while being carried, slowly and indirectly, to her bed by her lover.

'Don't change the subject,' he chided as they came to the picket gate into the more formal gardens and he paused, reluctant to return to the house where they might be seen or heard.

'I wasn't, and isn't it a little convenient you suddenly decided to love me?'

'There are times when I could learn to dislike you profoundly, let alone love you,' he said half-seriously. 'If I'd risked my life in the service of my country, as Calvercombe must have done all too often, would you listen then if I told you a solemn truth, Jessica? Had I got myself born in any other bed than the Duchess of Dettingham's, would you believe me when I put my heart in words I lack the glib habit to say well? You might even consider then that a gentleman never lies to his lady, but I'm not a gentleman, am I? Just a duke,' he ended bitterly and went to push the gate open so he could carry her inside, then resort to his library and drink himself under the table.

'All I wanted to know was if you truly meant it, Jack,' she said, brusquely batting his hand aside to stop him as he tried to open the gate. 'And you're right, in our world declarations of love are too easily made about this and that friend, or one or another of a lady's pets, or a gentleman's sporting pastimes, but I didn't mean I wouldn't believe you, my love, only that I wanted to hear it again. I'm sorry if I hurt you, Jack,' she ended with such sincerity in her voice that he dared hope after all.

And Jessica struggled to find words to heal the hurt she'd dealt him as she ordered him to set her on her own two feet again, since this was far too important a conversation to be held while she was being hefted aloft like a parcel.

'I could never think less of you than I do of your strange friend Calvercombe, Jack, not even if he was a king and you were a beggar,' she assured him earnestly as soon as they were face to face, or as close to it as they would ever be considering he was nearly a foot the taller.

She was shocked he'd think she could set him at less than the earl because he'd stayed home and done his duty rather than join the army, but far more shocked at herself for hurting him. Now he was silent and more aloof than ever and her heart hammered with panic at the thought of all she'd put at risk by believing herself so unlovable he couldn't possibly mean it when he said he loved her.

'How could you jaunt off to prove to the world

what a splendid warrior you could be, when you had so many responsibilities resting on your shoulders, Jack?' she asked him. 'I dare say his lordship had his reasons for joining the army in India, although it sounds as if he had responsibilities at home he should have thought about a little harder before he did so.'

'He was the second son of a second son—nobody expected him to inherit,' Jack defended his friend.

'Lucky man, but you were born to be a duke, Jack, and for so long I couldn't bring myself to hope you would ever want me as I wanted you, let alone come to love me. I wanted to love you for so long, Jack, yet you're a rich and powerful duke and would marry a lovely and suitable lady who didn't limp or rebel or rant at you like a fishwife and want all the things she could never have. So I refused to let myself fall all the way into love with you until that day in the herb garden when I suddenly knew I'd loved you all along and refused to let myself see it for what it was. But how can you love a poor apology for a duchess like me, especially when I've hurt you?'

'I've told you how I feel about your habit of traducing yourself before, Jessica,' he warned and she still couldn't tell if she'd won him back.

'So you have, but would you repeat that bit about loving me again instead, Jack? Or have I destroyed it before it could hardly spring to life?'

'How you can believe love so feeble it would die at the first frosty word you throw at me is totally beyond me,' he said impatiently and that alone gave her hope. 'Heaven knows, my love will need to be a far sturdier oak than that if it's to stand a lifetime of being battered by your blistering tongue and hasty temper,' he added almost grumpily and Jessica felt better than she would have done if he'd prostrated himself at her feet and promised to adore her all the rest of their days.

'Perhaps I should flounce off and neglect it a little more, then? My father's head forester always say it doesn't do to pamper a sapling, or it won't grow strong roots,' she teased and felt as if she might dance for joy, if her foot didn't hurt quite so badly and she could see what she was treading on.

'Our roots are strong enough and I don't need you to grow even more obstinate, my love,' he added softly and lowered his head so she could feel his breath on her cheek and shivered with anticipation.

'I love you, Jack,' she promised huskily.

'And I love you, my Jessica. Every headstrong inch of you, from top to toe,' he said solemnly.

'How can you?' she whispered, thinking about her lameness and the twists and eccentricities of her damaged foot that she had flinched from him knowing so much about earlier tonight.

'Because every one of those scars you fret about is a part of you and if I made a contract to love you all my days, which I believe I just did, Miss Pendle, I have to love your damaged foot a great deal more than you do yourself, along with all the rest of you. It kept you aloof and sceptical about my sex for long enough for me to see you as you really are,' he told her as if he meant every word.

'A shrew?' she offered half-seriously.

'No, a beautiful and sensual woman I need as

much as my next breath, Jessica, now and always,' he replied very seriously indeed.

'Then could you perhaps need me a little more right now, Jack, for I think I might not be as aloof and sceptical as I ought to be any more,' she invited shamelessly, her words so soft he had to bend his head even lower to hear her.

'You can be both towards the rest of my sex with my blessing and fervent encouragement, lover, but not to me,' he urged, his mouth coming ever closer until he murmured them against her eager mouth.

'No, never again with you, my love,' she promised and proved it by closing that last quarter-inch of space between them and kissing him, at first a little clumsily as the novelty and boldness of taking the lead held her back, then she felt him respond, felt the fire and storm that always woke in her at his touch flame. 'Love me, Jack?' she asked rather breathlessly.

'What, out here?' he demanded, obviously not quite sure his ears were working properly.

'Do you think there might be earwigs, then?' she teased with faux-innocence and, oh, the glory of being able to tease this man she loved so much, knowing how delicious his retribution would be.

'I know there could be thorns,' he said with heartfelt distrust of exactly where those thorns might end up.

'Faint heart,' she murmured, 'I know of a place where there are very few of them and where nobody else will dare to come at this scandalous hour of the night.'

'Then I would have to remind you that my herb garden is almost next to Givage's cottage.'

'I didn't mean your herb garden, but surely you don't mean he could have heard us that morning and you still went ahead and made love to me, Julius Henry Seaborne?' she demanded indignantly, unable to recall the rest of his ducal oversupply of names with him so close and the promise of mutual satisfaction heady in the scented air once more.

'I knew he was out about the estate upon my business, along with his son, since I had sent them on it,' Jack replied and Jessica wondered if he was looking as sheepish as he sounded.

'Then you planned it from the moment you found me alone there?'

'No, I wanted to kiss you again almost until it became an obsession with me, but I didn't plan to seduce you then and there. That was the inevitable side-effect of you kissing me back so ardently I couldn't stop myself and even then I didn't have the sense to realise I loved you. I knew you were a virgin as well as a lady of impeccable reputation and I could have got you with child, yet even that didn't persuade me to walk away before it became possible. And you're about to find out even more about the nigh-insatiable need a man has for his one and only love if you don't stop that,' he cautioned as he removed her wandering hands from his neat buttocks and gripped them gently to stop her finding some other way to drive him wild instead.

'It seems to me you find it all too easy to control them,' she said sulkily—wasn't it wonderful to be able to behave badly with him like this? 'I would have gone to my grave not knowing how lovers truly are if not for you, Jack,' she told him, suddenly very serious again. 'But I promise you our love doesn't have to exclude our children or wider family from their share of it. With us for parents they cannot help but be good and virtuous and kind, so of course we will love them as immoderately as we love each other,' she added, unable to stay serious with such joy coursing through her that it felt endless and unstoppable.

'They will be a pack of devils incarnate,' he said with a pretend shudder. 'And I can't wait for us to make them and then meet every single one of them,' he added with a wicked smile she could see even in the dark. 'It took the abject fear of losing you to make me realise how much I felt for you, Jess, and you're quite right,' he added, 'I'm not my father or my mother and I can love and fight and make up with the love of my life without loving anyone else a whit less for doing it. Maybe I ought to feel sorry for them for believing there was only a finite amount of love in them and they had to invest that miserly amount of it in each other.'

'You might, but I am not as generous as you, Jack. I could hate them for what they did to you, but they're gone and there's no point. We can love

and still be us at the end of it, Jack. For that matter we already do—I haven't noticed you spouting sonnets to my left eyebrow or thinking roses
grow on the ground I walk on.'

'No, it's a fine unromantic love we have between the two of us, my darling,' he told her
with a rumble of laughter in his deep voice as
he leant his forehead against hers and seemed to
be learning her by feel in the darkness. 'I'm so
glad I was persuaded to join this peculiar house
party of my aunt's, Princess, and God bless all
interfering grandmothers and aunts for interfering in the first place,' he added fervently.

'And mothers, for I don't think my attendance
was left to any chance between the three of them,'
she said, realising how cleverly Lady Pendle had
played on her loyalty to her godmother to persuade her to travel on to Ashburton alone.

'An unlikely trio of fairy godmothers, don't you
think?' he asked and she laughed at the idea of
the Dowager Duchess as a benign amanuensis.

'Oh, heavens, she'll become my grandmother-
in-law,' she realised with dawning horror.

'She's been my grandmother all my life and I'm still here.'

'That doesn't help me much,' she grumbled.

'Regretting you agreed to marry me already?' he joked and she shrugged and decided some things just had to be endured.

'No, but I am regretting you're quite so concerned about thorns and insects, my supposedly bold, bad love,' she chided as she struggled to reclaim the use of her hands where he still held them gently so she could use them to good effect.

'You mentioned an alternative where we might celebrate without them?' he countered as he held on to her wrist with a gently leashed determination that almost awed her into behaving herself.

'In my bed, of course,' she whispered as if the night might hear her make so bold and brazen an invitation and she wondered if any of the queens who had slept in it before her had made a similar one, if probably not to their royal husbands.

'A gentleman should never risk his lady's reputation,' Jack objected half-heartedly.

'I'm not a lady, I'm a princess, even you said so,' she told him loftily.

'Then who am I, a mere duke, to argue?' he asked and scooped her into his arms and marched off to her regal lair as fast as his legs could carry them without courting disaster in the deeper darkness before the dawn.

'You're going to have to stop carrying me about like a stray kitten,' she told him when he put her down long enough to unlatch the side door next to the Queen's Room that she had left unlocked ready for her return.

'But not tonight, Princess,' he told her rather breathlessly and she hoped she wasn't as heavy as that seemed to indicate she might be.

'No, not tonight,' she agreed and snuggled back into them while he strode along this minor corridor to the royal suite. 'Definitely not tonight,' she murmured as anticipation and urgency coursed through her.

'Or even tomorrow,' he managed as he finally opened the door and carried her inside, with the door shut and locked behind them before she could imagine who might see them, so far from the main bedchambers as they were.

'It's already tomorrow,' she objected distractedly as he set about undoing the buttons of her habit he had learned the trick of in the castle ruins with laudable haste, his breath rasping with impatient need. How wonderful that this was all for her, his driven, rampant need for her alone.

'Who cares?' he asked, flinging her jacket aside before he set about unveiling the rest of her.

'Do you?'

'Only about you, Princess,' he promised and his eyes lit up at the sight of the thin nightgown underneath her hastily donned habit and it only took a breathless instant before she was naked in his arms although she had only begun to undo his gentlemanly finery.

'I love you, Jack. I'll always love you, even when you're being infuriating and arrogant and you make me want to rage and rant and be totally unreasonable back.'

'As if I could be,' he said with such an air of saintly virtue she giggled and was still smiling when he picked her up, only to send her sprawling on to the soft goosefeather bed so fit for a queen. He joined her, bracing his strong arms either side of her so she felt his power leashed and lost all desire to laugh with him, mainly because she wanted him so much it was driving her demented.

'How did you get to be naked?' she asked distractedly as she ran her hands appreciatively down his muscled torso and on to the tight tension of his lean belly.

'It's a talent we dukes are born with,' he assured her and kissed her with such rampant hunger that all else but him and her in this fine bed left her head for a very long time.

'I think you're a very talented duke indeed,' she murmured as she drifted in a newly centred world a long time later. 'And don't tell me you were born knowing all that, because I won't believe you.'

'Jealous, my love?' he asked, looking inexcusably pleased at the very idea in the faint and pearly light of pre-dawn.

'Envious,' she corrected and found it was true—she did envy his other lovers for knowing shy and inexperienced Jack, increasingly confident Jack and even the downright arrogant

Duke of Dettingham as their lover. Of course he was now her lover for life, so perhaps she ought to pity other women who weren't so lucky, but somehow she just wasn't that noble.

'You have no need to be. I might have learnt about taking and giving pleasure in their arms, but I didn't know how to love until I learned it from you, Jessica. Never would have learned the knack of it either, if it hadn't been you I had the sheer luck to realise I needed as my duchess before it was too late. I appreciated women until I met you, I pleasured and was pleased—I won't lie and pretend otherwise to you, my love. I was even absently fond of one or two other women, and it was only one or two—not the dozens my ridiculous reputation would make you wary of if rumour was to be relied on.

'The pleasure I gave and took with them didn't even come close to the joy and exhilaration I feel when I make love to you,' he went on, as if convincing her he actually did love her passionately and abidingly might take him a lifetime. 'Being your lover, being in love with you, Jessica, it's the difference between a gaudy chandelier in an over-stuffed ballroom and the clear sunlight of a summer day. How the devil I could have made love with you that morning in the herb garden and not realised the astonishing difference between that and every other sexual encounter I ever had was because I loved you makes me marvel at my stupidity now. Your untouched, almost unseen beauty must have turned me into a dazed idiot who couldn't see beyond the end of his own nose, but the idea of you ever giving yourself to another man after us drove me half-mad, until I wonder I didn't just follow you about like an adoring puppy and publically beg you to marry me and make love only to me for the rest of your days.'

'I'm glad you waited until only Godmama and Persephone were by until you did so then, Jack. Lady Freya would have been mortified,' Jessica murmured as she explored the light dusting of curling black hair on his muscular torso and found his tight male nipples far more intriguing than all the failed duchesses in London and all points west.

'Lady Freya needs to be mortified,' he said, retaliating by echoing every move she made on her own body until she no longer cared what Lady Freya would think of their betrothal, or anything much else but him naked in her bed. 'I don't, however,' he declared arrogantly, 'so I suggest we marry inside the month.'

'Everyone will say that's far too quick for a duke to marry his duchess,' she protested absently.

'Much longer and our first little lord or lady will arrive far too early and give us away for the shocking couple we are, love,' he replied lazily, his long, strong fingers busily intent on making her as incapable of resisting him as he apparently was of refusing her blatant invitation to make love to her once again.

'The Shocking Duke of Dettingham and his Scandalous Duchess?' she asked with a laugh that rose into a moan of ardent need as he drove her half-demented with his amorous attentions. 'It could be the title of a book,' she added in a vain attempt to hold on to her sanity in his arms for once.

'No, it could be real life if you don't wed me

out of hand, love, now be quiet and let me love you, before the servants catch me sneaking back to my private lair and give away the fact I've finally caught myself a duchess before we really want the world to know.'

'Very well, my love,' the future Duchess of Dettingham replied meekly and let her duke love her in every way he knew how and he really knew quite a lot about loving duchesses, which was just as well, since she loved him with all her heart and intended he should never make love to another.

\* \* \* \* \*